The Cowboy Lassos a Bride

By Cora Seton

Print Edition
Published by One Acre Press

To my parents, who raised me in a house full of books.

Author's Note

The Cowboy Lassos a Bride is Volume 6 in the **Cowboys of Chance Creek** series, set in the fictional town of Chance Creek, Montana. To find out more about Cab, Rose, Hannah, Mia, Fila, Ethan, Autumn, Jamie, Claire, Rob, Morgan and other Chance Creek inhabitants, look for the rest of the books in the series, including:

The Cowboy Inherits a Bride (Volume 0)
The Cowboy's E-Mail Order Bride (Volume 1)
The Cowboy Wins a Bride (Volume 2)
The Cowboy Imports a Bride (Volume 3)
The Cowgirl Ropes a Billionaire (Volume 4)
The Sheriff Catches a Bride (Volume 5)
The Cowboy Rescues a Bride (Volume 7)
The Cowboy Earns a Bride (Volume 8)
The Cowboy's Christmas Bride (Volume 9)

Look for the **Heroes of Chance Creek** series, too:

The Navy SEAL's E-Mail Order Bride (Volume 1)
The Soldier's E-Mail Order Bride (Volume 2)
The Marine's E-Mail Order Bride (Volume 3)
The Navy SEAL's Christmas Bride (Volume 4)
The Airman's E-Mail Order Bride (Volume 5)

The SEALs of Chance Creek Series:

A SEAL's Oath

A SEAL's Vow

A SEAL's Pledge

A SEAL's Consent

Sign up for my newsletter HERE.

www.coraseton.com/sign-up-for-my-newsletter

Prologue

October

SHE WAS ALONE at a wedding. Again.

Hannah Ashton lifted a hand to her hair to make sure her elaborate updo hadn't come tumbling down. Her white-blond waves had a tendency to defy hairpins, but as Bella Chatham's maid of honor, she had corralled it mercilessly into a sophisticated style. Her empire-waisted, China-blue gown was flattering, at least. Some of the dresses she and Morgan Matheson—Bella's other bridesmaid—had tried on at Ellie's Bridals had sent them into fits of laughter.

Bella, her boss and one of her best friends, looked pretty as a picture standing next to her dream man—Evan Mortimer, billionaire investor and all around great guy. Hannah had engineered the circumstances under which Bella and Evan met on the set of *Can You Beat a Billionaire*, after Bella's tender heart had nearly bankrupted the Chance Creek Pet Clinic and Shelter where Hannah worked. Bella didn't need to worry about money anymore, and practical Evan would balance out her tendency to want to save any and every animal around. They made a great couple.

Hannah wished she had a man like that. He didn't have to be a billionaire. He just needed to care about her the way Evan obviously cared about Bella. As the two exchanged their vows in the small chapel presided over by the minister, Joe Halpern, they couldn't look away from each other. They were so much in love.

Hannah wanted to be in love.

She wasn't. Not anymore. Today's desertion by Cody was the final nail in the coffin of their relationship—a relationship she now had to admit had been over for some time. He was never there when she needed him. He liked her well enough when she was at home cooking him dinner or listening to another of his endless diatribes against his employees or customers or family, but when she asked him to take on a chore, he refused. When it was her turn to talk, he became suddenly busy. When there were parties or picnics or weddings to attend, he couldn't be found. He disliked her friends, disliked her job, and certainly couldn't be bothered to attend the nuptials of her boss. So here she was by herself, for everyone to see. She'd have an empty seat beside her during dinner at the bridal table since she'd responded to her invitation saying the two of them would come. She'd have no one to dance with once the music started, except for pity invitations from her friends' husbands. And by the time she got home, Cody would be stretched out on the couch in his boxers, too wrapped up in some late night Hollywood western to even care that she was there.

Once she'd fancied herself in love with the man, but that was a long time ago, before he'd let her down in a hundred and one ways. Before she realized they had little in common except for a desire to be with someone. She'd been all set to dump him when Bella and Evan's wedding invitation arrived in the mail. In a moment of weakness, she'd asked Cody to accompany her, placing the fate of their relationship in his answer. If he said yes, she'd give it one more shot. If he said no, she'd leave right away. He must have intuited her intentions—he'd said yes, and she'd stuck with him for several more weeks.

She shouldn't have wasted her time. She'd gone to get her nails done this morning and when she returned home, Cody was gone, his cryptic note stating he'd been called in to work. Since he was self-employed, the excuse bordered on insulting. She had her answer. Their relationship was over.

Hannah sighed. She was sick of being alone. She wanted to find her life partner like Bella had done. She wanted a wedding and a happily ever after. She wanted to be swept off her feet. She was thrilled that things had gone so well for Bella, but she couldn't help feeling a little resentful, too. Just a little. If she hadn't coerced her boss to go on the hit reality television show, Bella would still be broke and lonely. Just like her. Instead, her friend was the happiest woman for miles around. She had everything—a handsome, funny, loving husband, a career she adored, all the money she could ever want…

And Hannah had nothing. She blinked back sudden

tears of self-pity, aware that she was on display up here for all her friends to see. Hopefully they'd think she was overcome with happiness for Bella. Which she was. Hannah dug her nails into the palms of her hands to get control of her emotions. She had promised herself all this wallowing in self-pity was over. Bella was her friend. Nothing would change that. And she'd find a man sooner or later.

It just wasn't Cody.

Taking a deep breath, she made a vow right then and there. She would split up with Cody, and she would manage to do it without having a fight. It was hunting season right now—a perfect time to end the relationship. If she was smart, she'd wait until just before he left on one of his hunting trips to let him know, and then she could remove all her things from his house while he was gone. A cowardly trick, but one that would make things easier for both of them.

She knew the perfect time, too. In a couple of weeks, bison season opened up. Cody had been blathering for days about a bison on some big game ranch out in the western part of the state he intended to go shoot. It sounded silly to her, but it would keep him busy, at least overnight. That was all the time she needed.

With the decision made and her course set, she felt somewhat better, as if she'd gone through a long winter and just seen the first signs of spring. It would be a relief to end this relationship that was heading nowhere. She would have done it sooner if living together hadn't made things so complicated. But she wasn't going to let that stop her now. She would *un*-complicate things, leave Cody, and then she would be free in a few short weeks. Hannah straightened her shoulders and focused on the ceremony again.

Two hours later, she fiddled with her glass of champagne and watched the couples on the dance floor, her resentment creeping back to depress her mood again. It killed her not to feel joyful when this was Bella's wedding, but the fact that her best friend was leaving her behind kept tears pricking at her eyelids. She hadn't expected the wedding to be so emotional in this way and she refused to let Bella know how she felt. Once again she pasted a bright smile on her face and surveyed the room. The night hadn't been all bad. Ethan Cruz had danced with her once as a gesture of friendship. Married to her friend, Autumn, the tall cowboy had always been kind and considerate like that. Several other married men in her group of friends had taken her for a turn around the dance floor, too. That was nice of them, but she didn't want pity-dances. She wanted something else—something more.

It was probably for the best there wasn't anything more to have, she thought, since she hadn't broken up officially with Cody yet. Still, in her mind it was over—and had been for a long time. She and Cody hadn't acted like a couple in ages. She was lonely. She wanted a man's arms around her. She wanted to be kissed.

She wanted to be loved.

"Care to dance?"

She glanced up with a start to find Jake Matheson,

Morgan's brother-in-law, standing beside her table. "Um… sure." Too surprised to say more, she stood up and took his hand. As he led her to the dance floor, she allowed her gaze to trail over him in a way she hadn't looked at any man in a long, long time. Jake was one of the handsomest cowboys she knew and she was shocked he'd deigned to issue her this invitation. Like all the Matheson men, he was tall, broad-shouldered, with blond hair and blue eyes. He was the oldest of four, and everyone knew he'd run the Double-Bar-K when his father stepped down from that job. Any woman who married Jake would enter one of the oldest, proudest ranching families in the county. But Jake seemed to have no notion of settling down.

At thirty-three, he was seven years older than her, so he'd graduated before she'd even entered high school. Their crowds hadn't ever converged until this past summer when she began to work at the Cruz ranch from time to time, helping Autumn with her guest ranch business. Ethan was good friends with Rob Matheson, Jake's youngest brother and Morgan's husband, and she'd gotten to know the rest of the Mathesons in the intervening months, especially at Ethan and Autumn's weekly poker nights.

Still, it was strange to feel Jake's large hand curve around her own as he led her through the crowded tables, and when he pulled her close on the dance floor and put his hands on her waist to sway next to her to the slow dance now playing over the speakers, her breath caught. She'd never been so near to Jake. His dress shirt was smooth under her cheek as she rested her head against his chest. His hands were warm through the thin fabric of her dress. He smelled of soap and man and outdoors, a scent that filled her with an unnamed longing. She hoped he couldn't hear her heart racing in her chest. Jake was so masculine, so utterly out of her league, she'd never even pictured a moment like this.

As her body came alive under his touch, Hannah realized just how bad things between her and Cody had become. He never made her feel like this—her heart thrumming, her pulse racing, her breath caught in her throat. Jake, on the other hand, made her senses reel. She tingled all over from his proximity.

"Enjoying the wedding?" he murmured. If he wanted, she knew he could easily rest his chin on top of her head. He held her carefully but firmly, and she felt safe in his arms. Protected. Valued in a way she wanted to be valued. She could tell by the way he moved with her that he was very aware of her too. Knowing his thoughts were on her—not just his hands—was as intoxicating as any glass of champagne. The play of his muscles under his shirt delighted her. She wished she could touch him. Run a hand over his chest. She tilted her head down so he wouldn't be able to read her thoughts in her face. This was a man who could warm her through any long, cold Montana night.

She bit her lip to keep from laughing out loud. The testosterone leaking out of this handsome cowboy must be playing havoc with her hormones. Jake wasn't interested in her that way. He was dancing with her out of pity, just like the rest of them.

"It's nice," she managed to say finally.

"Where's Cody tonight?"

Hannah leaned back to peer up at him. She was surprised he even remembered Cody. Had the two men even crossed paths? She wasn't sure. "He didn't feel like coming. He's not much for weddings." She suppressed a sigh.

"He ought to know better than to leave a pretty girl like you alone in a situation like this."

"Why? What could possibly happen to me?" She smiled up at him as he smiled down. Flirting with Jake was the last thing she'd expected to happen when she arrived here tonight, but it felt as comfortable to do so as if she'd had years of practice. If only this dance could last more than a few minutes. She wanted it to go on forever.

"Who knows what kind of unsavory elements might get a hold of you."

His fingers pressed into her skin and she leaned into his embrace, realized what she was doing and tried to pull back. He didn't let her. His hands settled more tightly at her waist and kept her pressed up against the length of him. Suddenly Hannah could hardly breathe.

"I'm impervious to unsavory elements," she made herself say, but her voice sounded weak. Unsure.

He stopped dancing for a moment. Started again. "Impervious?" He dipped his head lower so that his lips were near her ear. "Are you sure?"

Not when his breath tickled her neck like that. "Absolutely."

One of his hands slipped down just a fraction of an inch on her waist, but it was enough to make its position almost indecorous. His other arm wrapped around her to make it entirely clear who was in charge here. Hannah was aware of every inch of his body that pressed against hers. Her heart was beating strong and fast. She clung to him, so off-balance as to be dizzy.

Jake swayed with her to the music and Hannah wondered if everyone could see the way desire was setting her nerves alight. She now knew just how intimate a simple dance could become when one partner was determined to seduce the other.

Because that's what Jake was doing. Seducing her. Reeling her in until he was the only thing she could think about. It was working, too.

"Let's test that theory, shall we?" Suddenly he was pulling her back through the tables, across the reception hall and out into a corridor. He traced its length, trying the handles of the doors they passed to storage rooms, smaller meeting rooms and the like. Hannah stumbled after him, not caring who saw them or what they thought. She just wanted to be with Jake. Anywhere he wanted to be.

Finally one opened. Hardly bigger than a closet, it appeared to be a break room for the staff. Jake spun her back into his arms, backed her up against a counter and kissed the daylights out of her.

Hannah only had a fleeting thought of Cody at home on his rundown couch, in his boxers and a T-shirt, a six-pack and a bag of chips on the coffee table, television remote in his hand. Then she could think of nothing else but Jake. The man's mouth on hers, devouring her, kissing her until she had to gasp for breath, his hands smoothing over her waist, almost dipping down over her ass, but hesitating, not crossing that threshold.

Not yet.

Hannah knew this could go as far as she wanted to take it. Knew too that Jake was too much a gentleman to push for more than she was willing to give. How much was she willing to give? She wasn't sure. Except with each passing moment she felt closer to wanting to give him everything. The champagne she had drunk lent a warm glow to the workaday room. Jake's arms around her, his mouth on hers made her forget everything else.

She wondered briefly who this wanton woman was. It couldn't be her—safe, quiet Hannah who'd supported herself since she was barely eighteen. She'd never done something so reckless, so out of character. But she couldn't stop. She didn't want to.

As she twined her arms around Jake's neck, he lifted her suddenly and placed her on the counter. Never breaking off the kiss that was searing her straight down to her soul, he pulled her tight against him and she reflexively wrapped her legs around his waist, her gown riding up over her thighs.

"Hannah," he groaned as he trailed kisses down her neck. "Hannah, you drive me wild."

Hannah blinked, but surrendered to his ongoing sensual attacks. This was news to her. She would have bet he'd never noticed her in his life.

Sure, they'd been thrown together last week at one of Ethan and Autumn's poker nights. She'd asked him some questions about an article she'd read—something about sustainable ranching. Apparently she'd hit on one of his favorite topics and they'd discussed it at length—as acquaintances at a get-together. Then the poker game had started and that had been that. She hadn't given it another thought. Having a crush on Jake would be like lusting after your older brother's best friend—completely safe because its outcome was completely predictable.

Except now Jake was kissing her. As if he couldn't get enough. And she was kissing him back just as passionately because she'd never liked kissing a man this much. Was it the champagne? Or the unexpectedness of it? Whatever the reason, the more they made out, the more she wanted him.

Jake kept one hand at her waist to hold her firmly against him. He slid the other one higher until he almost cupped her breast, but hesitated. Hannah knew he was asking for permission. She didn't think about the consequences. She leaned forward until her breast pressed into his hand. She caught her breath as he ran his thumb over her sensitive nipple. Heat throbbed between her legs. Jake groaned and pulled her even closer. She could feel his hardness through their clothes.

How far would they take this? Would she stop him? Could she?

A sudden tumult in the distance had them both stiffening. There was a clamor of voices. "The bride and groom are leaving," someone called to someone else.

Hannah looked at Jake. Saw regret in his eyes. Knew he'd see the same in hers. "I have to go—I'm the maid of honor!"

Jake backed away. She hopped off the counter and straightened her dress.

"Do I look okay?" she asked as they approached the door.

"You look… amazing." Jake bent down and kissed her again. "Hannah…"

"We'd better hurry."

"All right."

Jake went first. She waited a minute, then followed, joining the crowd that had erupted from the main reception hall to escort the bride and groom to the waiting limousine. She joined her voice to the ones wishing Bella and Evan well. Got a quick hug from both bride and groom. Waved until the limo was out of sight. Then she turned to search the crowd.

And saw Jake bending down to talk to Tracey Richards, a waitress at Linda's Diner who helped Autumn with her guest ranch business from time to time, too. As she watched, Jake tugged a lock of Tracey's hair. Tracey blushed and laughed.

Hannah flushed hot, then cold as realization overtook her. No miracle had taken place here tonight. The hottest, sexiest cowboy around hadn't fallen head over heels for her. He hadn't acted on a long-standing desire. She had no future with him, either. They'd probably never even kiss again. Jake was drunk, horny and out for a good time. That was all. The fact that she'd nearly lost her head with him told her she had drunk too much herself. She wasn't even single. Which Jake knew all too well.

He obviously wanted a one night stand tonight. He'd picked her because he'd counted on her running back to Cody as soon as their tryst was over. One hand pressed to her mouth, Hannah hurried to the ladies' room where she locked herself into a stall and blinked back tears. The night was ruined. She'd never be able to look Jake in the eye again.

Thank God they'd been interrupted before things had gone too far. Thank God she was about to make huge changes in her life, anyway. She wouldn't have time to have a serious boyfriend.

But damn it, why did he have to play with her like that? He'd been so far off her radar she'd never wasted time mooning over Jake before. Now she knew his mouth on hers would haunt her for months. No one had ever kissed her like that. No man had ever made her want to tear off her clothes and present her body to him on a platter.

If Jake walked in this bathroom right now she'd do the same damn thing again. He was like crack cocaine, like heroin, like…

Hannah gave herself a mental shake. She was at a wedding—her best friend's wedding. She was lonely and overwrought. She'd go home, go to bed and forget Jake. Tomorrow she would get on with her life and those big changes she planned to make.

But Hannah knew she was lying to herself. This night would stick in her memory for a long, long time.

Chapter One

Late November, six weeks later

IT WAS NEVER easy to get out of bed several hours before sunup on a cold November morning, but Jake Matheson didn't mind that. Born and raised on the Double-Bar-K ranch in Chance Creek, Montana, he'd known since he could walk that one day this spread would be his and he loved every inch of it. He especially loved these early morning moments when he was alone with his thoughts—before he caught up with his father and brothers and got to the real work of the day. For now he could pretend he was his own man; that the place was all his. Soon enough the others would intrude.

As usual, his thoughts were on Hannah Ashton. Their interlude at Bella and Evan Mortimer's wedding was never far from his mind these days. He'd taken a chance that night, dancing with her when Cody was a no-show, and an even bigger chance pulling her into the break room at the reception hall and kissing her as if he had a right to. But he'd wanted Hannah for months and Cody was an ass who didn't deserve her. He was afraid if he didn't do something she'd marry the idiot and he'd lose his chance forever.

As things turned out, he nearly had lost his chance. When they'd split up to leave the break room and see Bella and Evan off, Tracey Richards had accosted him. They'd known each other a long time, since he often ate at Linda's Diner, where Tracey had worked for years. Their friendship, such as it was, was overly flirtatious. It didn't mean anything, which Tracey knew. But Hannah didn't.

He'd looked up too late and seen Hannah's eyes widen as she watched him tug Tracey's hair in fun. A minute later she'd dashed away. He hadn't been able to push through the crowd fast enough after her, and he'd never found her again that night. Since he didn't want to expose her to talk—she was still with Cody—he couldn't ask around or enlist anyone else's help. When she didn't reappear, he left the wedding, furious at himself for blowing it.

She showed up the next week at Ethan and Autumn's poker night with Cody on her arm and he'd struggled not to take the man outside and kick his ass. It turned out he didn't have to. Cody had soon ruined things with Hannah in a way that set Jake up as a hero in her eyes. He'd arranged to hunt a bison and had taken Hannah to view it before the hunt. When it turned out the animal had been hand-raised and was kept in a pen barely large enough for it to turn around, Hannah flipped her lid.

She went back a few nights later, stole the beast, and

tried to hide it in a corral she'd built in Carl Whitfield's woods outside town. That hadn't gone well—in fact, that night would go down in Chance Creek history as disastrous—but the upshot was that the next day Jake helped Hannah round up the bison she'd named Gladys, and now Gladys lived on the Double-Bar-K.

And Hannah came every morning to see her.

They hadn't spoken yet about what happened at the Mortimer's wedding, but Jake planned to, soon. With Cody out of the picture it was time to make his move. He was determined to ask her out on a date today and he hoped she would say yes. Hoped they could work their way back around to picking up where they'd left off in that break room. Once he had her in his arms again, he wouldn't let her go a second time.

Because he figured Hannah was the one.

As he got to work in the hayloft of the largest of the barns on the property, preparing to fix a leak under the eaves before it allowed any dampness to ruin the hay stored within it, he heard the creak of the barn door as it opened far below him, and his father's voice cut across the stillness.

"Why the hell are those cattle still in the far pasture?"

Jake's jaw tightened as he felt along the top edge of the wall to find the location of the leak. So much for peace and quiet. Someday he'd inherit the Double-Bar-K, and even now he was nominally in charge of the herd, but as long as Holt Matheson walked this earth, he'd remain a glorified field hand. As his fingers traced over the rough wood high above his head, he told himself to rein in his temper and stick with the job at hand.

"I told you we were supposed to move the cattle," his brother Ned chimed in.

Jake stifled an urge to bang his head against the wall. Ned's voice often acted like nails across a chalkboard in his mind. This was one of those times. And it was a reminder that while someday Jake would inherit the Double-Bar-K and finally get to take charge of how it was run, he would still have to contend with his brothers—including Ned.

"We'll move them tomorrow. Today we fix the barn," he shouted down to them, as if he actually held the authority to make such decisions. Which he should.

But didn't.

"I told you last night to move the cattle!" Holt's craggy face appeared through the trap-door entrance to the hayloft.

"And I told you there's a leak in this barn and I mean to fix it today."

"Those cattle aren't going to move themselves." Ned's voice drifted up from below.

Jake fought back a familiar urge to chuck something at him. Like a pitchfork. Ned always sided with their father. Always. They were like two peas in a pod: ornery and stubborn as mules.

"You want this hay ruined?" Jake squared off with Holt.

"You want those cattle frozen when the weather turns overnight?"

"The weather won't turn overnight."

"Tell that to my knees." Holt swore the aches in his knees could predict everything from thunderstorms to drought. Jake didn't see how his knees could get any less accurate. He tilted his head down to address them.

"The weather's going to hold."

"Ha, ha. Very funny. Get out there and move that cattle."

Ned's head and shoulders appeared through the trap door as his father paced across the loft to check the leak. "Told you we should move the cattle."

Jake knew the origin of his father's blustery temper. He understood why the man acted as if there were threats to his authority everywhere, why he was quick to challenge anyone who set himself up as an equal. He knew why Ned followed so closely in his father's path when it came to temperament. Knowing what he knew, he should have been able to keep his own emotions in check. Should have been able to keep his mouth shut.

But he couldn't.

Which is why he said, "I know the weather is going to hold. I *read* the forecast."

Which is why his father decided to ruin his life.

IT WAS STILL dark when Hannah Ashton pulled into the dirt lane that led to the Double-Bar-K ranch, but lights blazed at Holt and Lisa Matheson's stately home and at each of the smaller cabins strung out at intervals beyond it where their four grown sons lived. Hannah knew that Holt and his sons would all be hard at work at their various chores around the ranch. Lisa would be in her large kitchen cooking for any of them who felt like stopping in for a hot morning meal, and preparing for a busy day of her own.

Hannah had begun to understand the rhythms of life on the Double-Bar-K. Owned by Mathesons for over a hundred and fifty years, it meant the world to the family, and it was beginning to have meaning for her, too. She loved the way the land spread in every direction, and the far off mountains that gave texture to the valley. She loved how the stars still winked high above her when she arrived in the morning, fading away during her short visit. She loved the air of expectation as the ranch came to life.

She parked next to Holt's pickup and got out into the chilly late November air. The sky toward the east was just beginning to brighten, but sunup was still a ways off. She walked quickly toward the pasture nearest to the house, anticipation building within her. She was excited to see Gladys again—the bison she rescued just weeks ago.

She was excited to see Jake Matheson, too. As foolish as that was.

Rounding a barn, the split rail fence of the pasture came into view, along with the unmistakably large, dark shape of Gladys grazing on grass not far off. Her heart warmed. She wasn't sure why she loved the large, shaggy beast so much. She'd only seen her for the first time a few weeks back. Something about the animal called to her—Gladys was so prehistoric looking, so different from your run-of-the-mill cow. Maybe she was special because she stood for something in Hannah's mind. The need to stand up for herself. The need to be true to herself—to do something more than hitch her wagon to someone else's life. The day she saved Gladys was the day she proclaimed to the world she would do whatever it took to live authentically. Each time she visited Gladys, it reminded her that her dream to be a vet was important. It was worth the trouble to make it happen. It warmed her heart that Jake was just as interested in the bison as she was. More even, since he wanted to start a herd.

Speaking of Jake... Hannah scanned the area as she made her way to the pasture fence, but Jake was nowhere to be seen. She checked her watch. She had a few minutes. Maybe if she lingered for a while, the handsome cowboy would show up.

She knew she shouldn't wait for him. Knew she shouldn't encourage him if he was interested. She'd made some important decisions since dumping Cody. She'd set her life in a whole new direction—one that didn't allow time for a serious relationship. Her acceptance to Montana State University had come. In two months she'd be starting classes, and if all went well she'd head off to veterinary school in Colorado next fall. But in the past few weeks Jake had been very attentive to her, and she'd begun to wonder if she'd misinterpreted his exchange with Tracey at the wedding. In fact, she'd heard the other day Tracey was seeing a cowboy from out near Bozeman, so whatever little flirtation the two of them had must not have worked out.

Would Jake have acted differently if she'd been available when they'd hooked up at Bella's wedding? She thought the answer might be yes. Now that her relationship with Cody was over and she'd moved into the Cruz ranch Big House, a sort of charged friendship had arisen between her and Jake. He hadn't tried to kiss her again, but every morning when she came to see Gladys, he was there, waiting for her. Each day they stood at her fence and talked. About Gladys, about the ranch in general, about sustainable ranching, a subject he seemed passionately interested in. Hannah liked that he asked her opinion about things, as if she had any knowledge of the subject. She didn't. She could ride a horse, but that was it. She'd grown up in a little house in town.

While she enjoyed this budding friendship with Jake, she longed for more. She still felt his mouth on hers and his arms around her when she closed her eyes at night. No man she'd ever met could compete with him as far as her body was concerned.

She wanted Jake. No matter if it was stupid, or the wrong time, or impossible.

If only he wanted her the same way.

HOLT SQUARED OFF against Jake in the loft, his face like thunder. "You think you're so smart? I'm sick of your guff and I'm tired of your inability to follow orders."

"I'm tired of you giving me them!"

"Are you saying you're ready to leave?"

"No."

"I'm not sure I want you to stay."

"Dad—"

"Don't Dad me." Holt put his hands on his hips and shook his head. "I've had it. It's time for you to grow up."

"I am grown up."

"Prove it. You turn thirty-four one month from today. I'm going to give you one last chance—get married before your birthday or get out."

"What?" Jake cocked his hat back. His father had to be joking.

But the old man looked dead serious. "Do you need me to write it down so you can *read* it?"

Jake wanted to kick himself. Teasing his father and Ned about their dyslexia was a low blow at the best of times. Today he'd stirred up a hornet's nest. "Are you insane? I can't get married in the next month."

"If you're man enough to give me lip, then you're man enough to settle down and start your family, and I expect you to do just that. You've dillydallied enough time away acting like an alley cat. I put you in charge of the herd because I thought you had what it took to the do the job. But you can't even move the damn cattle when I tell you to do it."

"If I'm in charge of the herd, then I'm in charge of when to move them."

"You won't be in charge of nothing if you don't marry by your thirty-fourth birthday. I had four sons by the time I was your age!"

"You can't tell me when to marry!"

Holt turned to Ned. "You ready to take on some

more responsibility?"

"Damn straight." It was obvious Ned was loving this turn of events. Jake, however, felt like the ground had tilted beneath his feet. He'd begun to think of marriage in the last few weeks—in an abstract way as something he and Hannah would do in the future. In the far, far future. Now Holt wanted him to marry within the month?

"I'm the one in charge of the herd." Jake knew he was losing ground fast. Why the hell did he have to throw his father's dyslexia in his face today of all days? Most of the time he was on board with the family's campaign to keep that information private. Holt had quit school young over it. Ned, suffering the same problem, barely lasted longer. Mentioning their affliction was like setting flame to a powder keg.

"For now." Holt brushed past him. "You've got until December twenty-first to bring your wife to the altar—a proper wedding, too. None of this justice of the peace crap. If you're still single on the twenty-second, Ned takes over." He clambered back down the ladder and disappeared from sight.

Ned clapped him on the back. "Don't worry, when I'm in charge I won't boss you around. Much." He followed Holt down the ladder, laughing.

Jake stood motionless, the leak forgotten. Thirty days to get married? Or leave the ranch?

Well, why the hell not. Maybe his father was right. Maybe it was high time to get married. If Hannah was the one, then she was the one. A smile curved one corner of his mouth. He bet Holt hadn't figured on him already picking a bride. Now he just needed to fast-forward his timeline to snare her for his wife.

Hannah Ashton had better watch out.

HANNAH WAS JUST about to give up when she spotted Jake exiting the big barn. He stood for a moment in the dim light and scanned the yard as if he was looking for something. When he spotted her, he immediately strode over.

"Morning, Jake," she said when he was close enough to hear. She hoped her voice didn't betray how glad she was to see him. If she was honest she came almost as much for the chance to chat with him as to see Gladys these days.

More, maybe.

"Morning," he said. He leaned on the fence. Something was different about him today. Usually Jake could be depended on for a smile and a laugh, but now his mouth was set in a hard line. She wondered what had happened. "I think she likes it here." He nodded at Gladys.

"I know she likes it here. What's not to like?" Hannah smiled at Jake, then bit her lip, hoping that hadn't sounded too flirtatious. "I wish your father wasn't so set against her."

"Don't worry about him." Jake shifted closer, the sleeve of his rugged winter work coat brushing hers. She wished he would put his arm around her shoulder and kiss her again like he had at the wedding.

He tapped his fingers on the top rail a few times, still gazing out toward Gladys. Then he nodded once like he'd come to a decision. He touched her gloved hand and her breath hitched. He'd never done that before. He turned to face her. "I like these morning visits."

Hannah fought for composure as her pulse kicked up a notch. What did his touch mean? Was it just a friendly gesture or an intimation that he was still interested in her?

"I like them, too." Did she sound as nervous as a teenager? She sure felt that way.

He leaned closer. "Maybe we could…"

"Jake! What's the holdup? I said to move those cattle!"

Jake muttered a curse before raising his voice to call, "I'll be right there."

"Time's a wasting!" Holt trudged toward them. Jake sighed and turned back to her.

"Are you going to be at Ethan's tonight?" His low voice sent shivers down her spine. Jake was so masculine. So much sexier than Cody had ever been.

"Yes."

"Good. We'll talk there." Jake went to meet his father. Not for the first time, Hannah felt like strangling the old man. Why couldn't he have waited another five minutes? Jake might have asked her out.

The two men conferred a moment and Jake headed off toward the barn. Holt turned her way, and Hannah turned back to the pasture quickly for a final look at Gladys before heading on to work. The bison did seem happy here, although perhaps a little lonely.

"I'd like a word with you."

Hannah jumped when Holt spoke up right behind her. Would she get another lecture about the uselessness of bison? Or would he attack her from a different angle today? Holt had never liked her.

"Isn't she pretty?" She jutted her chin at Gladys.

"She looks pretty tasty." Holt pushed his hat to a better position on his forehead. "I've always loved bison meat." He had the slow drawl of a Montana rancher which only increased her irritation at his words.

"She's not for eating; she's a pet. She was raised by hand."

"I don't see how that figures into it."

"Holt…"

"Now don't get your feathers all in a ruffle, hear me out." Holt still stood as straight as he ever had. Only a stiffness in the way he walked betrayed the fact that his years were beginning to wear on him. All the days he'd spent working outside in the sun had tanned his skin and deepened the wrinkles around his eyes and mouth, but he was still a handsome man in a tough, no-nonsense way. She knew Jake, Ned and Luke did most of the physical labor around here, but Holt still thought of himself as the ruler of this roost, and when he said jump, everyone around him asked, "How high?"

She was not one of those people. She'd be polite because she was polite to everyone, but she wouldn't allow Holt to boss her around.

"Go ahead," she said coolly.

"I have something you want. A long-term pasture for that beast of yours."

Hannah raised an eyebrow. He was right; she did want that, but she knew Holt never did a favor when he could extract a payment. She wondered where this was going.

"I'll let you keep your bison on this ranch for the rest of its natural life if you'll do one thing for me."

He had Hannah's full attention. A place for Gladys forever? She'd been searching far and wide for a suitable home for the animal, but no one within a hundred miles had a place for her. There were a few ranches far to the west who might take her, but the cost was high and she'd rarely get to see the bison, and… well… she'd gotten a bit attached to her.

Okay, a lot attached.

"What would I have to do?" Holt's weathered face was angular, his eyes bright with intelligence and cunning. She wasn't sure she could trust him, but his offer intrigued her.

"Sleep with my son for two weeks."

Hannah's jaw dropped open. Her cheeks flushed to what she was sure was a brilliant red. Had Holt lost his mind? Had she? He couldn't have said that out loud.

Could he?

"You heard me right, but you can get your mind out of the gutter." Holt's laconic tone was shaded with a hint of laughter at her expense. "I said sleep with him, not screw him. What you two get up to is on your conscience. All I ask is that you share a bed."

"I… what…?" She glanced around wildly, wondering if anyone else had overheard him. Surely this had to be a joke. Would Holt's youngest son, Rob, come rushing out with a video camera? He was always playing practical jokes.

"Sleep with my son for fourteen consecutive nights. All night. That's it. Your bison gets a pasture, food, and shelter for the rest of her life. What do you say?"

She sputtered, searching for something to say that encompassed the depth of her anger that he'd even speak to her this way. She settled on sarcasm. "Two weeks? I'll have to check my calendar. Some other guy's father might have extorted me to sleep with him one of those nights."

Holt chuckled. "Just how many bison do you have stashed around the ranches in these parts?"

"I don't need to listen to this."

"By the way, the son in question is Jake." He eyed her sharply and Hannah felt the heat creep up her cheeks all over again.

Jake?

An image of them together in bed—naked, disheveled—flashed into her mind and her body tingled with the idea of it. She and Jake could have a lot of fun between the sheets.

She forced the thought out of her head. "Not interested."

"Then I guess I'll get my pasture back sooner than I thought. And I'll have to find some other woman to get my son's mind on marriage."

"Damn it, Holt—that's not fair."

"Which part isn't? The part where I eat your bison or the part where another woman sleeps with my son?"

Hannah fought mightily against the urge to slug him. "Even if I did this—which I won't," she assured him, "how would you know? Are you going to bug his bedroom?"

"Nah," Holt said. "You'll report to me every morning, look me in the eye and tell me if you slept with him or not." Her eyes widened and Holt guffawed. "No way a girl with your color hair can tell a lie. Your face gives you away every time."

He was right, damn it. The pale, pale complexion that went with her white-blond hair meant that every flush showed like her face had been slapped. She made it a point not to lie because like Holt said, she couldn't get away with it. If she faced this man after a night with his son she'd be scarlet.

Like she was right now.

"How would I even get him to agree to it?" she asked, even though the question was ludicrous. She was not sleeping with Jake, no matter what the reward. Not on his father's say-so. She turned back to Gladys, mostly to get away from Holt's sardonic grin.

"Reckon that's your problem. You're a clever girl, you'll think of something."

"What do you get out of it?" Why was she even having this conversation? Because she was as crazy as Holt? Because she was worried about Gladys?

Because she wanted to sleep with Jake?

Did she ever. How many times in the last few weeks had she dreamed of unbuttoning one of Jake's work shirts and smoothing her hands over his hard chest? How many times had she dreamed of unbuttoning her own shirt and pressing up against him, feeling her skin on his? Ever since the wedding, Jake had been on her mind. More than she cared to admit.

"I get to remind my son he's a man," Holt said. "Seems like he's forgotten that. No sense passing on control of the ranch to him if he doesn't intend to get an heir."

"He's not getting an heir with me," Hannah snapped, stepping away from him. "I don't plan to have children anytime soon."

"No one asked you to. You just need to prime the pump, so to speak."

"I'm not having sex with him, either."

"Like I said, what you get up to is your call. No man can spend two weeks in bed with a pretty woman without getting a notion or two. I suspect that's all it'll take to get him thinking about the benefits of settling down."

Hannah shook her head, the wooden railing under her hand splintery and cold in the November morning. "I didn't say I'd do it."

Holt smiled. "You didn't walk away, either."

"YOU FIX THAT leak yet?" Holt asked.

When his father walked into the living room, Jake set his beer down carefully on the small end table and leaned back on the comfortable couch before the fire. He generally stayed for a drink after eating dinner at the main house with his parents and his brothers, Ned and Luke. His third brother, Rob, and Rob's wife, Morgan, had just moved back onto the ranch until they built a permanent home, but they tended to eat in their own cabin, so he didn't see them as much. When the meal was over, in good weather he'd sit out on the front porch and let his gaze wander over the land his family owned. In the winter he found a place in front of the fire in their formal living room. His brothers had already returned to their cabins, but Jake lingered. In a short time he'd head over to Ethan and Autumn's poker night. Meanwhile he wanted to plan his strategy to convince Hannah to marry him in the next thirty days.

"Yes."

"You sure you got it at the source? The water will find another way in if..."

"Dad, I got it," Jake cut him off.

Holt eased himself onto the other end of the couch. "Don't you forget who made this ranch what it is today."

Jake knew exactly who had made this ranch what it was. His father, and his grandfather, and his great-grandfather, stretching back up the line of Mathesons for over a hundred and fifty years. That made him prouder than he could say about taking his place on the ranch. But along with being excellent cattlemen, Mathesons were also known for being hardheaded. Holt certainly was. "I'm supposed to be managing the herd. That's my responsibility. I've got to be able to do things my way."

"I've got a sight more experience with cattle than you do."

"Dad, I can't second-guess myself out there. You must know what it's like—you took over from Grandpa."

Holt snorted. "Your grandpa called the shots until he was in his grave. And then some. The day after we buried him I found a schedule he'd written out for the next two months. I followed it, too. I was afraid if I didn't he'd claw himself back out of the ground and give me a whupping!"

Jake chuckled despite himself. "You didn't mind that he kept bossing you around?"

"Of course I minded. My father was a stubborn son-of-a-bitch. It's different for you."

"Different how?"

"I'm as sweet as maple syrup compared to him."

"Sure thing, Dad. Sweet enough to kick me off the ranch if I don't marry in thirty days."

Holt shot him a look. "I'm helping you get something you actually want. You just don't know it yet. Now what about that bison? You found somewhere for it to go?"

Jake heaved a sigh and decided to ignore the first part of that statement. He took a swig of his beer and gazed out through the windows. "I want to start a herd."

"Start a herd of what?" Holt leaned forward and held out his hands toward the fire.

"A herd of bison."

Holt straightened up. "Now that's the dumbest thing

I've heard in a long time."

Figured. Holt wasn't one to jump on new ideas, which was one reason Jake was feeling so fed up these days. "Dumb how?"

"The Double-Bar-K trades in cattle, not bison. Always has, always will."

Jake sighed as a familiar restlessness overtook him. Would he ever be able to introduce a single innovation on the ranch while his father was alive? Some days he wondered if he was stupid for staying here. But he couldn't leave. He just couldn't. The very dirt of this place made the framework of his soul. None of those Mathesons before him had taken off when times got tough. He didn't mean to be the first. "We can do both. Bison meat is becoming popular. It's good for you. You can charge twice as much for it, too."

"That's because it's twice as much work." Holt eyed him. "What's really behind this? A pretty girl with white-blond hair?"

"No. You're dead wrong there," Jake lied. He fixed his father with a hard look. "And just for the record, they're half as much work, not twice as much. They don't need all the extra tending in winter our herd does."

"Stick to what you know, boy." Holt stared into the fire. "If you're smart you'll shoot that bison yourself, eat it and be done with it."

"You done lecturing me for tonight? Haven't you made my life miserable enough for one day?"

"You think getting a wife will make you miserable? Getting married was the best thing I ever did. A man can't run this place by himself. He needs a woman by his side. Someone like your mother—hardworking, level-headed, tough as nails. I've waited a long time for you to get to the matter on your own. I didn't think I needed to play the kind of games I did with Rob."

"I would have loved to play that game. Where's my two hundred acres?" A couple of months back Holt had made the announcement that the first son to get married would get a parcel of land for his very own. Then he'd turned right around and told Jake, Ned and Luke they weren't eligible to win the contest. He'd known Rob was on the verge of flying the coop, so he used the ruse to trap him at home. It had pretty much worked. Rob proposed right away to Morgan Tate and brought her from Victoria to Chance Creek. Now he owned property on both the Cruz and Matheson ranches, but while he was building his home on the Cruz side of the property line, he still helped out on the Matheson side, too, and he lived here in the meantime. Not across town or in another county. Holt was satisfied.

Holt dipped his chin. "You don't need two hundred acres. You'll share the whole damn ranch with Ned and Luke."

"If I marry within a month. Otherwise, you'll kick me out and the whole place will go to ruin. You know damn well Ned can't manage his way out of a paper bag. No way can he run the herd."

"You'd be surprised what Ned can do. A good manager knows the strengths and weaknesses of his workers. You're so blind you can't even see your own brother."

"I see Ned. I see that he's a hothead who's as liable to burn the barn down as fix its leak."

"Ned's quick with his anger, but he's quick with his wits, too."

"Yeah. That's why he didn't make it past eighth grade."

Holt was silent a long moment. "I didn't make it past eighth grade, either, and I've done a sight more with my life than you have. Get a wife, Jake. Or get out."

Holt rose to his feet and walked stiffly away, leaving Jake to wish again he'd kept his mouth shut. Both Holt and Ned had a way of pushing his buttons until the basest part of him took control. His father treated him like he was still fifteen years old, and he inevitably ended up acting that way. Something had to change. His whole family needed a new way of doing things.

Jake chuckled to himself grimly. That wasn't likely to happen. A few minutes later he let himself out into the dark and strode the quarter mile to his own cabin. His parents had built a small two bedroom structure for each of their sons when they turned twenty, hoping that would encourage them to stay on the ranch and eventually settle there. He had always appreciated the measure of independence it gave him, while still keeping him close to his work. Now he recognized it for the trap it was.

For years Holt had paid him and his brothers a tiny allowance and gave them room and board in exchange for their work on the ranch. Since they each expected to inherit a share in the spread, and had enough for their trucks and nights out on the town, they hadn't felt poor. They'd been raised to value ranching and family above all else. To an outsider it probably looked like they were at each other's throats all the time, but although they fought like wolves, they were as clannish as a wolf pack, too. Faced with any outside threat, they formed ranks and presented a united front.

It was Rob who finally shook things up enough for them to come to their senses and demand real wages for the work they did. That was a recent development, however. Jake still didn't have much cash. If he struck out on his own it would take him years to save up enough to buy a new spread, and even then it wouldn't replace the Double-Bar-K in his heart. No, he'd stay and figure this out.

If it killed him.

He stood in his small, sterile kitchen and listened to the ticking of the clock on the wall. If he didn't get married—fast—he might lose the life he loved so much. And damn it, he wanted a wife. He wanted Hannah. He wanted a family, too.

But he also wanted more than that. Unlike his father or brothers, Jake believed whole-heartedly in innovation and he wanted to be a part of it. Scientists all around the world were talking about the earth's climate changing and Jake knew that every facet of modern life played into that—including the ranching practices he and his family employed. He wanted to be a part of that discussion. He wanted to experiment with his own herd and ranch. He read all he could, hung out on online forums, and watched the latest talks and movies on YouTube about the subject. But until Holt backed off and let him run things the way he wanted to, he'd remain a bystander in the shift to brand-new ranching practices.

Holt actively resisted all changes to the way things were done on the Double-Bar-K. He distrusted innovation and his dyslexia and bad experience with school had turned him against most forms of education, too. When Jake had talked of going to college after graduating from high school, Holt put an end to that idea by threatening to disown him if he did.

Well, it was his own fault for not sticking up to the man. Holt hadn't kept him here at gunpoint, after all. He could see now that if he'd demanded to go there would have been all kinds of fuss and bother, but it would have blown over in time. He wished he'd stood up to his father back then. It was too late now. Jake picked up his pace. Time to quit feeling sorry for himself and get a move on. He'd see Hannah at the Cruz ranch tonight for Thursday night poker and pool.

Holt was right about one thing; he had wasted a lot of time. If getting a wife would bring him one step closer to taking over the Double-Bar-K, he'd ask Hannah out before the night was over, just as he'd already planned.

And marry her before the month was up.

Chapter Two

HANNAH TRIED TO slip in through the front door of the Cruz guest ranch Big House without being noticed, but just like every other time she failed utterly. The Big House was an imposing structure with large windows that overlooked a sweeping view of the ranch and the mountains far in the distance. Originally designed as a private home, Autumn and Ethan Cruz had transformed it into a guest lodge earlier in the year. Their business had done fairly well so far, but as fall turned into winter, the guests had dropped off and they had no bookings at all for the coming weeks.

That was bad for the Cruzes, but good for Hannah, who'd needed a place to stay when she'd broken up with Cody. Ethan and Autumn charged her a very reasonable rent for one of the pretty guest rooms upstairs. At first she'd wondered if it would be strange living with the Cruzes, but she'd found it comfortable so far. Though Ethan and Autumn were in and out of the main floor all the time during the day, they slept down at the converted bunkhouse at night. The bedrooms at the Big House were meant for guests, not family. Hannah knew they intended to build an addition onto the main floor that would make up their personal quarters just as soon as they could afford it, but that hadn't happened yet. For now they used the fantastic Big House kitchen and living room during the day and retired to the bunkhouse at bedtime.

Hannah wasn't left alone, though, in the large residence. Two other young women—Mia Start and Fila Sahar—had moved in, too, for the time being. Each of them needed a cheap place to stay and Autumn had jumped on the chance to make even a small profit off of three of the empty guest rooms. Come spring when things picked up again they'd all have to move, but Hannah was confident she'd have things figured out long before then.

Although confident might be too strong a word.

The truth was, she wasn't exactly sure how she'd handle her upcoming expenses. She was still paying off her student loans from her undergraduate years. She had a lot of those. Her parents would have loved to put her through school, but with her father's medical expenses they were hard pressed to pay their own way. She'd been ten when her father was first diagnosed with cancer, and twelve when she began to babysit every weekend night for spending money. As her parents' savings slipped away on ever-increasingly expensive treatments, she bought her own clothes and paid for her school supplies. As soon as she was legal, she picked up a part-time job and took over the family's car insurance payments. When she graduated, her parents downsized and moved in with her uncle in Billings to cut costs and be nearer to her Dad's specialists and a hospital. She wished she could help them more, but at the very least she wouldn't burden them with her own expenses.

"Hannah! Good, you're home. Dinner's just about ready," Autumn called. A small woman with lovely brown hair and delicate features, she was moving around the kitchen area of the open-plan main floor. Hannah cursed that open plan every day for just this reason.

"Hi, Autumn." She hung up her coat, kicked off her boots and made her way over to the counter that separated the kitchen from the living room. Autumn bent over the open oven door and awkwardly pulled out a roast. Six months pregnant, her belly was beginning to counteract some of her natural gracefulness. She refused to take it easy, though. In fact, she seemed invigorated by it all.

"It'll just be a minute while I mash the potatoes," she said. "Fila and Mia will be down shortly, too."

"I keep telling you not to cook for me. You're not my housekeeper, Autumn. If anything, I should cook and clean for you since you're putting me up here."

"You're paying rent," Autumn said. "Dinner and clean sheets comes with the room. That's just the way it works around here."

"I'll go wash up. Be back in a minute." Hannah headed upstairs to the room she'd occupied on the second floor.

A familiar feeling of dissatisfaction washed over her

when she thought about her life. She'd started well, but somehow things had gotten off track. When she'd graduated from college with a degree in biology, the recession made it hard to find work, so when Bella Chatham offered her a position as the receptionist at her veterinary practice and animal shelter, Hannah had taken it, thinking it was temporary. Soon work and life swallowed her whole. The job was busier and more interesting than she had imagined, and when she started dating Cody, he took up the rest of her time. She loved working with Bella and she loved the way she got to help with the veterinary tasks. Unfortunately, her limited education held her back from taking a more active role with the animals' health care. Although she enjoyed interacting with Bella's clients all day, she wanted to do more.

She wanted a career. Something challenging. Something that used every shred of her ability. She had already taken the first step toward that career—getting accepted at Montana State.

After she changed her clothes and washed up for supper, she met Fila in the corridor outside her room. Fila was a new arrival in Chance Creek. Born of Afghani parents in the United States, she'd traveled to Afghanistan when she was twelve years old to attend a funeral and ended up staying there against her will for the next decade after her parents were killed. Seized by Taliban relatives, she'd been forced to knuckle under and became a model Afghani woman, but she never forgot her true home in the United States, and she'd managed to escape with help from an organization started by Aria Cruz, Ethan's mother. Once she made it back to the States, Fila had come to the Cruz ranch in the hopes that Aria's daughters would help her learn to raise funds for their mother's organization. She'd ended up moving in.

Hannah found Fila a bit of a mystery. On the one hand she dressed and acted like any other American. She'd quickly lost all trace of the accent her years in Afghanistan lent her, and when she went shopping she gravitated toward the latest styles, although she avoided miniskirts, and the necklines of her blouses and T-shirts remained high. On the other hand, there were gaps in her knowledge of modern life. She'd never used an up-to-date cell phone, iPads and tablets baffled her, and even her skills on desktop computers were hopelessly slim. They all tried to help her acclimate to these most important modern conveniences, but Hannah could see it would be a long haul. Soon after her arrival, some Taliban men had tracked Fila down and come to get her back. The resulting shootout was one of the deadliest nights in Chance Creek history and affected many of them. Hannah had been at the scene of the shooting with Fila and another friend, Rose. Most of the men from the Cruz ranch and the Double-Bar-K had been there, as well.

Hannah still had nightmares about that night and she knew Fila suffered, too. While Fila told them every day how grateful she was to be here, Hannah sensed the woman also felt a profound loss—not for her old life in Afghanistan, exactly, but for all the years she'd spent there, the years she'd never get back. She said she felt like she didn't exactly belong anywhere. Hannah hoped she set down some roots, fast.

"Looking forward to tonight?" Hannah asked her. About an hour after dinner people would begin to show up for Poker and Pool night. Hannah enjoyed these get-togethers, but she wasn't sure if Fila did.

"Yes." Fila's face told a different story.

"If it gets too much for you, it's okay to head up to your room." Fila had done so on previous occasions, and Hannah wanted her to know no one held it against her.

"This time I intend to stay. I'm getting used to it."

Hannah took her hand and squeezed it. "I'm glad. I'm glad you're here."

"Me, too," Fila said, but she sounded wistful.

Mia met them by the stairs.

"Long day?" she asked Hannah.

"It always is. The clinic is overrun. Chance Creek needs another veterinarian." That wasn't why she felt so drained tonight, though. The thought of losing Gladys weighed heavy on her mind. So did Holt's words. As if she could just climb into bed with Jake for fourteen nights and then climb out again. What if she propositioned him and he refused? She'd never be able to face him again.

On the other hand, if she slept with Jake for fourteen nights she'd be hard pressed to give up the habit. How could she possibly handle work and school and a new boyfriend?

As tempting as the idea was.

Mia nodded. She looked tired, too. Hannah knew the reason for that, although she wasn't sure if anybody else did. Mia was pregnant. Hannah didn't know who the father was. From the little Mia had told her, she knew he was married and not pleased about the child. Mia refused to go after him for support, and she knew her parents would be devastated when they found out about her pregnancy, so she'd made arrangements to move out of their home and into the Cruz ranch for the winter. Hannah assumed she'd tell Autumn and everyone else about her pregnancy soon, but she understood Mia's reluctance to broadcast the news. She earned minimum wage at the hardware store. People would have things to say about her ability to raise a child alone. They wouldn't be supportive in the same way they were of Autumn, for example. Autumn's rounded belly brought coos and congratulations wherever she went. Hannah had to admit that sometimes when she caught sight of Autumn she felt a tug of desire to start a family herself, but she quickly brushed that feeling aside. She had plans, and settling down played no part in them.

But maybe a fling with Jake could. She allowed herself to picture what that might be like—two consecutive weeks tangled up in the covers with a sexy cowboy. Fourteen nights of unbridled lust and pleasure.

She could use some unbridled lust and pleasure. In fact, she could use it a lot.

A smile twitched her lips as she descended the stairs with Fila and Mia, her stomach growling as the aroma of another of Autumn's amazing dinners caught her nose.

She was a big girl—she could have a fling with a sexy cowboy whenever she wanted.

Holt's preposterous deal simply gave her a good excuse to do the very thing she'd dreamed about: tumble into bed with Jake long enough to get him out of her system before she settled down to classes.

WHEN JAKE ARRIVED at the Cruz Big House, a fire danced in the hearth, tables were set up for cards, and an enormous Christmas tree stood near the large floor-to-ceiling windows. Just like at his parents' house, the entire space was decorated with figurines, fir boughs and glittering lights. Autumn, setting appetizers out on the counter that separated the kitchen area from the rest of the great room, looked in her element. Ethan was one lucky man to have found her.

Jake frowned and his shoulders tightened at the thought of his earlier conversation with his father. Marry within the month—as if it was that simple. It was ludicrous.

It was just like Holt.

Sometimes he wished he could escape the ranch—to get a taste of the wider world and the knowledge it had to offer. He knew he would have done well at college and if he had gone he would have liked to study modern ranching techniques in a wider context along with land management and environmental studies. The world was changing fast. People were far more aware of how their food reached the table and the impact ranching and farming could have on the state of their environment.

His father dismissed all of that as liberal nonsense, but Jake felt otherwise. He felt like a steward of the ranch. Everything from the soil to the cattle to the people who lived on his family's land was affected by the decisions he made. Shouldn't he know everything there was to know about it?

It galled him his father and brothers didn't support his interests. What kind of family went out of its way to clip the intellectual wings of its own members?

The Matheson kind, apparently.

When he spotted Hannah across the room deep in conversation with Ethan and Jamie, looking up at the two tall cowboys and laughing at something Jamie said, Jake's heart rate increased. Her white-blond hair lay in angelic waves about her shoulders. Dressed casually in jeans and a soft sweater, she looked feminine and sweet, and his fingers suddenly itched to touch her. Maybe do a whole lot more than that.

He wouldn't lie—Hannah was gorgeous, which is why he'd taken her to that break room at Bella and Evan's wedding. But she was smart as a whip in addition to being beautiful. She was curious, too—the sexiest trait there ever was in a woman, to his way of thinking. She'd caught his attention at Ethan and Autumn's poker nights, first because of her angelic looks, but afterward because of her ability to converse with him. Unlike most people, she enjoyed talking about the future of ranching, and about a hundred other topics, as well. So far they'd only chatted for a few minutes here and there, mostly when she came to see Gladys. Still, they could leap from bison to the history of Montana to the strangest thing they'd each ever eaten, to whether or not there was other intelligent life in the Universe in the course of only a short conversation. He looked forward to each meeting, knowing her insatiable thirst for knowledge would have led her to find some new and interesting fact she could share with him. He'd never had anyone in his life quite like Hannah. He was blessed with good friends and a solid family—he couldn't complain. But he'd lacked this meeting of the minds.

He'd been ready to ask her out this morning until his father appeared to ruin the moment. He'd been pretty sure she would say yes, too, judging by the fact she didn't move her hand away when he touched it. That touch had fired him up more than he wanted to admit. For the first time, he'd wanted to take things slowly with a woman, because Hannah was so special. If he blew things with her, he wouldn't just lose a pretty companion—he'd lose a true friend. He didn't think he could stand that.

Now his father was forcing his hand, and he hoped that wouldn't ruin everything. With only thirty days to marry her, he barely had time for wooing. How could he speed things up when they hadn't even gone on a date?

While he wanted to go straight to Hannah, he made his way to the kitchen first, grabbed a couple of Autumn's appetizers and found a beer in the fridge. There he met Rob, whose shoulder was still bandaged from the gunshot wound he'd taken a few weeks back. That had been one hell of a night—a real shootout with would-be terrorists in the woods down the road from here. Luckily

Rob's wound was the worst of them. Jamie's hip had already healed, as had Fila's arm. The bad guys had been rounded up and taken away by the Feds. Peace had been restored to Chance Creek, for which he was grateful.

He worked through the room from guest to guest, exchanging greetings and news. He finally got to Hannah just as Ethan and Jamie headed back to the kitchen for another beer.

He smiled at her. "Hey, Hannah. Sorry I had to take off in such a rush this morning."

"It wasn't your fault. Work never ends on a ranch, right? I talked to your dad after you left, though."

Uh oh. "What did he say?"

Hannah shrugged, but her cheeks grew pink. Jake's heart sunk. His father was capable of all kinds of breaches of etiquette. At least she was still speaking to him.

"I get the feeling he'd rather not keep Gladys around much longer."

"Don't mind him." Jake was worried, though. If Holt kicked him out, he'd probably demand they remove Gladys from the ranch. It figured the old man would urge him to get married, then screw up his chances with the one woman he wanted to spend his life with.

"Holt's more bark than bite," he said, then clenched his jaw at the lie. Holt barked like a pit bull and attacked like one, too, if he felt provoked.

"I don't know. I'm taking what he said pretty seriously."

"I'll work on him," he promised her. "Meanwhile, there's something I've wanted to ask you. Would you…"

"Hey, everybody. Pick a table and sit down. We're about ready to get started," Ethan called.

Morgan, passing by, smiled at them and gestured toward the card tables. "Come on, guys. You heard the man."

"We'll be right there." Hannah turned back to him. "What were you saying, Jake?"

But with Morgan watching he couldn't ask her out. "Nothing. We'll talk later."

Chapter Three

JAKE HAD BEEN seconds from asking her on a date. She was sure of it. So why wouldn't everyone back off and give him the chance?

Not that she'd say yes.

Or maybe she would but she wouldn't get serious with him.

Unless you called a fourteen night stand serious.

Which she had no doubt it would be.

Hannah moved quickly to a table to cover her confusion and sat next to Morgan. The rest of the players took their places at the tables with much jostling and joking. When Jake slipped into the chair on the other side of her, she figured she hadn't been hallucinating about his attentions. *Interesting.*

Interesting in a fling way, she reminded herself. That's all she could afford right now—no heartfelt romances, not even with Jake. Especially with Jake, who could wrap her around his little finger without even trying. She looked at him out of the corner of her eye as he joked with Ethan. He was muscular, confident, his legs taking up way too much space under the table. His thigh brushed against hers from time to time, igniting the longing she'd felt ever since their time in the break room. She would not fall in love with Jake. But couldn't she have a little fun with him before school started at the end of January?

Ethan dealt the first hand of Hold'em and she forced her concentration onto her cards. She was a lousy player and lost money every week at these tables, but the stakes weren't that high and by tradition the winner donated half the proceeds to the kitty for the next weeks' drinks and munchies. Since she'd spend more by far at the local bar if she went out for a night of drinking and dancing, she figured it was a small price to pay for the good food and company.

Jake surveyed his opponents around the table. He must have already looked at his cards, figured his odds and moved on to size up the competition. She'd seen him take the pot many times. Hannah sighed. She'd even gone online to learn more about winning this game, but the truth was the odds and calculations didn't interest her. She came for the chatter and friendship.

Still, she'd better do her best or she'd find herself out of the game, off the table and over with the other losers playing pool.

All the way across the room from Jake.

As he placed his bet, Hannah finally admitted the truth to herself; she'd give anything to get a whole lot closer to him. Two weeks in bed with Jake?

She was there.

JAKE PLACED HIS cards on the table and waited for the groans of the other players to subside before he raked in the pot. Again.

He was on fire tonight, and not just because he was lucky with cards. When he'd spoken to Hannah earlier, he'd seen the interest flare in her wide, blue eyes. He felt confident that given enough time he could win her, just like he was winning this game. Too bad he didn't have much time.

He let his thigh brush hers under the table and was rewarded when she gave a little jump. When he looked her way a blush was creeping up her cheeks. Poor Hannah. Didn't she know she'd never win a poker game with that tell-tale face? What was she thinking about? Getting closer to him? Touching more than his thigh under the table? He'd sure like to touch a lot more of her. Hannah filled out her casual jeans and sweater in all the right places, curvy as a movie star with a mouth made for kissing. As he knew too well. He'd thought a lot about kissing Hannah again since the Mortimers' wedding. Time to get this show on the road. As soon as he managed to ask her out.

Ethan was just dealing out the cards for the next round of play when the house phone rang and Autumn excused herself from the other table to answer it.

Jake studied the new hand he'd been dealt. He could work with this, he mused. The real question was whether he could work with the cards life had dealt him. An interested woman. An ultimatum from his father. Could he take the two and create a winning hand out of them?

A lifetime with the woman who'd tormented his dreams for weeks now?

The timing was short but you only got so many chances in life to hitch your yoke to another person who not only attracted you physically but also stimulated your mind. He felt confident he wouldn't regret marrying Hannah, if he could get her.

Could he get her? That was the real question.

"I see," Autumn said into the phone. "Um… yes, of course. Yes, we have openings for that time period." She had moved to the small desk and computer off her kitchen space where she took bookings for the guest ranch and kept her accounts. She pulled up the booking software.

"Looks like someone's coming to stay," Jake said to Ethan.

"Good thing. It's been pretty thin this past month. Can't blame people for not wanting to visit a ranch in November, but we need the income from the guests or we'll have to tighten our belts."

"Yes. Yes, I think we can accommodate you. What time will you arrive?" As Autumn went on speaking into the phone, asking questions and answering them, they continued to play, but Jake could tell Ethan's mind was on Autumn's conversation. He could believe that bookings were important to him. They'd been able to have Thursday night get-togethers here every week for the past month. That meant no paying guests, which meant business wasn't as good as it needed to be. Everyone knew Ethan's mother had spent much of the ranch's earnings on travel and, as it turned out, funding programs to help women in Afghanistan. When Ethan inherited the ranch it was deeply in debt. Over the last six months he'd banded together with Autumn, Jamie, Claire, Rob, and Morgan to pay down the mortgage and solidify its earnings. With all the businesses they were starting together, they should soon have plenty of cash. Jake envied them their togetherness and the variety of their income sources. He and his brothers and parents worked the Double-Bar-K together, but it was strictly a cattle ranch, and if Holt had his way, that's what it would stay.

Autumn hung up and turned to Ethan. "You're not going to believe it!"

"Tell me." Ethan set his cards face down on the table and rose to go to her.

"A huge family get-together. They want to rent the entire house for four weeks!" Her face alight with happiness, Autumn crossed the room and hugged her husband.

"When are they coming?" He kissed her, but Jake could see he wanted to know the details.

"Next Saturday. We're going to have to work like crazy. They'll stay through New Year's. Apparently they had another lodge booked but a pipe broke there and flooded the place. They won't be back in business for months. I feel awful being so happy when someone else is in such trouble, but I can't help it. Twenty people here for a month! We'll be able to pay our bills for the rest of the winter, easy!"

As people congratulated Ethan and Autumn on their good luck, Jake glanced at Hannah and took in her still, worried expression. Mia was frowning too, and Fila was just as tense.

"What's wrong?" he asked Hannah, bending closer to her. The fresh floral scent of her shampoo teased his senses. He had to hold back from touching her arm.

"Twenty people staying here? Hannah, Fila and I will have to move. I guess we could stay in the bunkhouse, but…"

"You could come stay with me. I have a spare room." He had surprised himself as much as he surprised her. The words just popped out, but the moment they did he wanted her to say yes. He braced himself for the stinging answer he was sure she'd fling his way. The offer was obviously self-serving.

Hannah swallowed, her gaze never leaving his face. "That would be great. Can I move in tonight?"

Chapter Four

"YOU SURE YOU don't want me to stick around and carry your things to the car?" Jake asked. They were alone by the front door, the other guests having already left, but with the open-floor plan of the Big House, Hannah was all too aware of Autumn, Ethan, Mia and Fila all working to clean up the dishes from the get-together.

"No. I want to help clean up first and then I'll need some time to pack. You go on home. I'll be there as soon as I can."

"I'm looking forward to it." For a moment she thought Jake would lean down and kiss her, but then he glanced over her head toward the kitchen area and pulled back. "Don't be too long."

"I won't," she promised him and hurried back to help the others, her body alight with the knowledge that she'd sleep with him tonight.

Sleep with him, not make love to him. Just like Holt said.

Of course, she could be flexible on that point.

As Mia loaded the dishwasher and Fila fetched a broom, Hannah knew each of them was worried about their living situations, but she wasn't sure how to speak up and tell them she was moving out.

"You know we'll make room in the bunkhouse for all of you," Autumn said to them, returning to the kitchen with a tray of glasses. "It'll be a little tight, but it's just for one month."

More than a little tight. The bunkhouse only had two bedrooms. Ethan and Autumn stayed in one. She suspected neither Fila nor Mia relished sharing the other one, certainly not with two other women.

"Maybe I should find my own place," Fila began in her soft voice. Her shoulders looked tight and Hannah could tell the entire evening had placed a strain on the young woman. From what she gathered, it had never been a good thing for Fila to be noticed during her years in Afghanistan. She still seemed to want to escape attention as much as possible. Trouble was, everyone here wanted to make her feel at home and went out of their way to notice and talk to her. On most occasions, Fila slipped off to her room before the poker nights were half over.

Autumn and Claire had helped Fila find a lawyer who could track down information about her parents' estate. Since more than a decade had passed since they died, it was unclear whether there would be anything for Fila to inherit. Sooner or later she'd have to find a job, but everyone agreed she wasn't ready for that yet. Her offer to move wasn't practical.

"No." Autumn moved to her side. "Your place is here with us. Trust me, Fila. We'll work this out and it will be no bother to anyone."

"That's right," Hannah said. Fila needed Autumn's caring presence right now. As much as she'd adapted to life here, she had a long way to go. While Fila had told them much of her story, Hannah knew there was more she hadn't told. She could only imagine the abuse she'd witnessed and maybe experienced herself during her years in captivity. Then, when she'd stepped forward to tell the American authorities her story, she'd been grilled by law enforcement and FBI agents to find out everything she knew and to verify that she herself wasn't a terrorist. Sometimes Hannah thought those interrogations did more to hurt Fila than her time in Afghanistan. She'd expected to find safety in Chance Creek. Instead she'd been treated like a potential criminal. She didn't know who to trust anymore. Didn't know if anyone trusted her. Fila had folded in on herself. She needed gentle company, warmth and safety. The last thing she needed was to rent an apartment somewhere in town and live alone. Not to mention she couldn't afford it. "I'm moving out anyway, so there will be plenty of room in the bunkhouse for you, Fila."

"You're moving? Where?" Autumn turned to her, disappointment in her eyes.

Hannah loved her for it. Autumn was the consummate hostess. She seemed to thrive on feeding and housing people. Still, she'd have plenty of people to house and feed a week or so from now. "Jake has a spare room." She hoped her offhand tone would fool Autumn, but she felt her cheeks warm and Autumn's mouth quirked.

"That sounds... cozy."

Fila said nothing, but when Hannah met her gaze she saw right away the relief in the young woman's eyes.

Mia stared at the floor. "Maybe I should look for another place, too."

"No, you shouldn't," Autumn said firmly. "You two can share the spare room in the bunkhouse for now. Then you'll both move back into your separate rooms in the Big House until spring. Once Cab and Rose get their house built, their cabin will be available, too. I had already planned on the two of you taking it over this spring. You can stay there as long as you want. I know it might be a little awkward at times until then, but we'll make it work. I promise."

Hannah was glad Autumn insisted the other two stay. Both Fila and Mia were young and in circumstances that would make it difficult to make their own way in the world. They needed someone like Autumn to look after them. She'd be fine at Jake's for the time being. After her fourteen days she'd find an apartment in town.

"Jake's pretty handsome. I always thought he was the best-looking of the Mathesons," Autumn said to her.

"Don't let Ethan hear you talking like that," Hannah said. Even if it was true.

"Well, anyway, I'll miss having you here, Hannah."

"Thanks." As soon as she could, she retreated to her room to pack. And plan. Fourteen nights with Jake.

Maybe more.

You're jumping the gun, she told herself. *There's no guarantee Jake wants to sleep with you.* But she wasn't naïve enough to believe he'd offered her his spare room out of the goodness of his heart. She had no doubt she could climb into his bed tonight.

But would she be able to leave it when her two weeks were up?

"STILL SINGLE?" Holt queried when Jake stopped at his parents' house on the way home. He, Ned, Luke and Rob had cell phones and used them frequently to stay up-to-date with each other and ranch matters, but Holt refused to get with the twenty-first century, which meant a nightly check-in was in order, or his father would be banging on his door at four in the morning with a list of the day's chores.

"Yep. But not for long. Hannah Ashton is moving in tonight."

"Hannah Ashton? Weren't there any other single women at that shindig you went to?"

"Yes, there were." But why did Holt want to know? Didn't he like Hannah? Did his prejudice against her bison extend to the woman herself?

"Who?"

"You want a list?"

"Yep." Holt waited, ramrod straight in the door that separated the kitchen from the living room.

Jake sighed. He knew his father well enough to understand that the sooner he answered the question, the sooner this conversation could be over.

"Mia Start and Fila Sahar."

"Humph. And you couldn't land either of them." It wasn't a question; it was a statement of Holt's disdain.

"I didn't want to. Good-night." Jake left before Holt could incite him into an argument. He got back into his truck and drove the rest of the way to his cabin seething with anger. Couldn't his father approve of anything he did? For once he'd like Holt to react with pride rather than his usual snide remarks, but that would be hoping for too much, wouldn't it?

Jake knew his father hadn't had it easy when he was growing up. For all their joking around about Holt's father earlier in the night, the truth was the old man had been quicker to criticize or raise a fist than Holt had ever been. Jake knew his father loved all his children and doted on his wife, but he often had a strange way of showing it. Praise from his father was as rare as a two-headed snake, and often just as disturbing.

Well, it didn't matter what Holt thought. He hadn't specified which woman he needed to marry as long as he married someone, and Hannah Ashton was the only woman who interested him. As soon as they were hitched she'd take that curiosity of hers and apply it to the ranch in general. No telling what she'd come up with. He hoped she'd be a little like Autumn or his mother—a whiz in the kitchen. He, unfortunately, was not. He could picture them sitting across the breakfast table from each other, eating a real ranch meal instead of the cold cereal he shoveled into his mouth these days, and talking about the day ahead. Some chores they'd do together, like riding fences or helping with the hay harvest. Other chores they'd do on their own, him in the barn and her in the house. Their children, when they had them, would have both parents close by on the ranch—not like those city kids who didn't see their folks from early morning to late at night. When Holt finally relinquished control over everything, Hannah would support his experiments with new ranching techniques. She'd help him research and plan and carry out trials. Maybe they could even publish their findings. He hoped Bella would be able to find a replacement receptionist without too much trouble.

Within the month.

He wondered if he should give Bella some kind of heads' up, but decided against it after a little thought.

Time enough for that after his ring was on Hannah's finger.

Chapter Five

IT WAS WELL past midnight when Hannah turned in the lane to the Double-Bar-K. She passed the main house first, where Holt and Lisa lived and the boys had grown up, then drove another quarter mile to the cabins the Mathesons had built when their sons reached maturity. Jake's came first, tucked off beside the lane flanked by two tall pine trees. With its wide front porch and generous proportions it didn't seem diminutive to her, but she knew the Mathesons regarded the cabins as such and had heard from Morgan that they were built with an eye to adding on in the future.

She pulled up and parked in front of Jake's place, but once she switched off the engine she found she couldn't open the door.

What was she doing here? Did she really think she could sleep with Jake for two weeks and then just leave? She'd never entered a relationship before without the hope that it could turn into a permanent one. Now she was starting something with a definite expiration date. She wasn't even sure that was possible.

It would be over a month until she could move back to the Cruz ranch, so she needed a plan for what to do when her fourteen days with Jake were up. She'd better start hunting for a cheap apartment tomorrow. Maybe she could handle a fourteen day romp under the covers with Jake. Maybe they'd spin it out over the holidays and into January, but then it would have to stop. Not only was she taking on a full-time course load next semester, she also planned to work. The commute to and from Billings would eat up more time, and to top it off she'd have to move to Colorado this fall. There were no closer vet programs.

Besides, she knew herself too well. She was already half stuck on Jake. If she got all tangled up with him, how could she concentrate on the years of school that loomed in front of her? All in all, this was a very bad idea.

Maybe the nights with Jake should remain chaste, after all. But how? Could she claim she had nightmares so bad she needed company to stave them off? Would Jake buy that?

"Hannah? You coming in?"

Hannah jumped at Jake's sudden appearance at her window. His voice was muffled by the glass between them, but his words were clear enough.

And so was the stab of pure lust she felt at the sight of him so close by.

Was she coming in? She thought of Gladys safe and sound for the rest of her shaggy life. She thought of sharing a cramped bedroom in the bunkhouse with Mia and Fila for a month.

She thought of fourteen nights with Jake.

Hell, yes. She was coming in.

WHEN JAKE HELD the front door open and let Hannah pass through it he felt a shiver of anticipation run the length of his spine. When she stopped inside the doorway to take in the small living room, dining room and kitchen that formed the main floor, her proximity made his groin tighten.

She wanted him. So badly she'd jumped at the chance to move right in. They were hours—or maybe minutes—from their first sexual encounter and his blood was running hot. He'd waited a hell of a long time for this moment. Hannah was lithe and pretty and smart to boot. She shared his love for animals and she worked hard. She'd be a hell of a lover and would make one heck of a wife. The thought of carrying her in her wedding dress over this threshold one day soon filled him with anticipation and a sense of rightness. This was the woman he was meant to share his life with.

"The kitchen is straight ahead," he said, coming into the living room behind her. "The bedrooms are upstairs." He pointed to the flight of stairs that led to a balcony. "There's a bathroom down that hall. Let me show you around."

The tour of the main floor took a matter of moments. He saw her take in the rough kitchen, the sparsely stocked shelves and lack of a dishwasher. He closed the bathroom door almost as soon as he opened it. He'd forgotten he'd left it a mess this morning.

"Your room is up here," he said, leading her up the stairs a few moments later, hoping the condition of the place so far hadn't put her off. At least the spare room was in decent shape. He'd had the presence of mind to check that. It contained a queen-sized bed, a plain wooden dresser and a desk under the single window.

Hannah stood in the doorway, as if reluctant to come any farther inside. "It's nice, I guess."

Uh oh. Was she having second thoughts? Time to turn on the Matheson charm. "Come on in, take a better look." He entered the room fully and held out his hand.

To his surprise, she took it. Hers was warm and small in his, and he squashed an urge to caress it.

Barely.

Instead, he showed her the closet and opened a drawer in the dresser. "There's a desk here for you, too."

"Terrific."

Her voice was small and thin. Glancing down at her, he caught her glancing up, and suddenly he knew she was feeling the same way he was. Nervous. Interested. A little excited.

He tried to dampen that excited feeling, or at least get it under control, but he was all too aware of her standing next to him in this private place. There was a bed right there, after all—a comfortable, beckoning bed.

"Hannah, look," he began.

"Jake, I…"

They stopped. Laughed a little.

"You first." Jake thought she'd protest, but she took

a breath and began to speak.

"Ever since that night... when the men came for Fila—I haven't been able to sleep very well."

He nodded slowly. It wasn't what he'd expected her to say. He'd expected her to mention Bella and Evan's wedding—what happened in the break room. They still hadn't spoken of it despite the many conversations they'd had since. He thought about it all the time. He figured she must have thought about it, too. Instead of asking him why he'd done what he'd done, however, she was talking about the night they'd reconnected. The night terrorists had come to Chance Creek hunting for Fila. The night he'd been part of a shootout—his first and hopefully last—and Hannah had been there, too. In harm's way. It made sense she had trouble sleeping since then. Less understandable was the blush creeping over her milky skin. He'd been around Hannah long enough to know that she blushed easily, but what had set her off now? Worry that he'd find her nightmares childish? Or something else?

"Sometimes I'm up for hours," she went on. "I usually end up in Autumn's kitchen, drinking warm milk. I read or turn on the television."

She looked at him expectantly but he wasn't sure what she was trying to tell him. "That won't bother me," he hazarded.

Hannah bit her lip. "I guess what I'm saying... what I'm asking," she corrected herself, "is—could I sleep with you tonight?" Her words came out in a rush and her flush deepened.

Well, he'd be damned. She really did want him. A certain part of his anatomy stirred to life and a quick series of images flashed through his mind. Hannah undressed, reaching for him. Ready for him. "Uh… sure. You bet. No problem." Hell. He sounded as eager as a schoolboy. Time to get a grip.

Time to act like a man. If Hannah was woman enough to ask that favor, he wasn't going to leave her in any doubt of his willingness to comply. He tightened his hold on her fingers, tugged her closer, slid a hand under her hair to cup her head, bent down and kissed her.

Her mouth was as soft and sweet as it had been at the Mortimer wedding, and he thought he could spend hours just like this—kissing her like he had that night in the break room. She hesitated only a second before sighing and melting against him. He wrapped his other arm around her waist and pulled her in closer, his whole body set alight when her breasts touched his chest, her thighs pressed against his. He nibbled her lips, then searched with his tongue until she parted them with a sigh and allowed him in. The taste of her turned him on until he thought his blood would boil with wanting her.

He waited for her to pull back, but she didn't. In fact, she answered his kiss with a hunger of her own. She wrapped her arms around his neck, and stood on tiptoes to lean into him. Jake didn't realize that he'd been edging them toward the bed until his shins grazed the mattress, and then laying her down seemed like a brilliant idea.

He worried for a moment Hannah might not agree with him, but when she sighed again, all rational thought flew out of his head. Sliding his hands down to cup her bottom, he squeezed gently and she moaned in answer. On fire with wanting her, Jake lifted her up and set her onto the bed, quickly joining her. He laid her back against the pillows, and still kissing her, began to unbutton his shirt. Her fingers joined his in a race to get it off. Soon it was loose, and Jake chucked it over his shoulder, then turned to the business of unbuttoning her blouse.

With him starting at the top and her starting at the bottom, it was only a moment before he could spread the panels wide and dip his mouth down to trace the edge of her bra. Trailing kisses over her smooth skin, he longed to see the rest of her.

He couldn't believe this was happening so fast—*at all*—but he wasn't one to squander an opportunity. Maybe Hannah had wanted him all this time, like he'd wanted her. Now they were finally together. He slid his hands under her back and fumbled with the clasp as she arched to allow him access. When it came free, and he slipped the lacy garment from her shoulders, she moved to accommodate him, then stretched beneath him.

The movement of her breasts entranced him and he dipped his mouth to take one rosy nipple into it. Heaven. He'd died and gone to heaven, and the angel in his arms, her white-blonde hair spread over the pillows, was his proof.

Hannah gasped as he sucked on her nipple and swished his tongue over it. He moved upward to kiss her again, then over to her other breast, worshipping it in turn. Jake took his time over teasing her with his mouth and tongue until he ached with too much longing for her to wait another minute. When he pulled back, Hannah forestalled his questions by reaching down, unsnapping her jeans, and wriggling out of them.

"Are you sure?" he breathed against her neck as he swooped in for another kiss. Her breasts blazed against his chest as skin touched skin and he gathered her up in his arms, held her tight and trailed more kisses under her chin, down her jaw, under her ear, and down her neck on the other side.

Hannah nodded, and he pushed himself up to his knees, undid his own belt buckle and shucked off his jeans. He watched her all the while, taking in every inch of her body, bare to his gaze except the tiny silky panties she still wore.

He groaned when she hooked a finger under their thin strap and pulled them off, too. If he'd had any doubts of her willingness to take things further, he was under no illusions now.

She wanted him as much as he wanted her.

"JAKE. PROTECTION," Hannah whispered in his ear as he covered her.

She wanted to throw protection to the wind. Wanted to throw everything to the wind and pull Jake inside her. When she'd said yes to moving to the Double-Bar-K, this was exactly what she'd hoped for, no matter all the practical things she told herself about not getting involved with a man just before starting school.

She wanted to be right here. In Jake's arms. Him inside of her, moving with her. Why on earth had she stayed with Cody so long? Why on earth had she ever dated anyone else than Jake?

He pushed back. "You're not on the Pill?"

"No. Not now. And even if..."

"Got it." He thought a second. "Hold on."

Bereft of his presence, she moved to draw the coverlet and blankets over her. She'd barely accomplished the maneuver when he was back. He tossed the blankets aside, climbed back on top of her and fiddled for a moment with a box and wrapper before throwing them aside, too. He gave her his full attention.

"All set," he said, and she wasn't sure if he was making an announcement or asking her a question. She lay back and searched the face of the man poised above her. She'd always remember this moment, she thought; the moment just before she and Jake became truly intimate. Heat pulsed between her legs and she could stand the distance between them no longer.

"All set," she agreed and wrapped her arms around his neck. She pulled him down to her, met his mouth with her own, and felt the weight of him settle on top of her, his hardness pressed against the juncture of her thighs.

Heat flooded through her. She wanted this—wanted him—more than anything she'd ever wanted before. As Jake shifted above her, settled between her legs and then nudged her core, she thought she would explode with longing right then and there.

"Tell me," he grunted by her ear as he pressed into

her. Just enough to tease her; not nearly enough to satisfy her need for him.

"Please," she said, holding onto him tighter, pressing her hips to his, trying to draw him inside. "Please, Jake…"

"Hannah," he said and plunged farther inside her. She ached for more; wanted all of him.

"More," she said through gritted teeth, tipping her hips, sliding her hands down his back to his ass. "More, Jake. I want more!"

He stroked into her hard and she cried out in pleasure. Picking up his pace, he pulled out and stroked in again. Hannah held him tightly, his every movement bringing a rush of sensation that threatened to overwhelm her. She dug her fingers into his flesh, urged him on with kisses and the press of her hips. He stroked faster, harder, until all she could do was hang on and ride the wave of sensation with him. She never wanted this to end, she wanted to feel this close to Jake, this turned on by him, this overwhelmed with ecstasy for as long as she lived.

She went over the edge with a rush of feeling, and cried out as Jake bucked against her in his own release. Arching against him, she rode the sensation until she collapsed against the pillows, numb to her fingertips from the power of her release. Jake fell on top of her and she welcomed the weight of him.

"These next two weeks are going to be so much fun," she said, luxuriating in the feel of him. Tracing a lazy finger down Jake's back, she felt him stiffen.

“Next two weeks? I thought Autumn’s guests were staying for a month.” He pushed himself up on his elbows and gazed down at her.

“Right. I meant month.” Whoops—she’d nearly blown it. Jake thought she meant to stay here at least until Autumn’s guests went home in the new year. Well, that was fine with her. She’d stay here as long as she possibly could.

The intent, infatuated look in his eyes from just moments ago faded into something else, something deeper. “I want more than a month,” Jake said. She blinked up at him, suddenly cold. Something serious was coming. Something more than she was ready to hear. A chill rushed down her spine, perking her nipples into hard peaks.

“Hannah Ashton,” Jake said. “Will you marry me?”

Chapter Six

HANNAH'S EYES WENT wide and she tried to pull back, but trapped as she was beneath him, she had nowhere to go.

"Jake, I…"

"Hold on, let me finish," he rushed to say, knowing he had moments to fix things before he lost her completely. They were still joined together, something that made this moment transcend simple intimacy. He knew he had just risked everything. Whatever he said next would make or break them. "I want you, Hannah. I know it's too soon. I know I should wait, but I can't wait to tell you how I feel." He bent to kiss her. "I want to wake up to you. I want to go to sleep with you, and I want to spend as many moments in between with you as I can. I think we can build a life together here that will beat just about anything else the world has to offer. You're a pretty woman, Hannah, and I thank God for that, but what really turns me on is your mind." He tapped her temple. "I can talk to you like no one else. Do you know how sexy that is?" He slid out of her an inch or two and slid back in, just enough to remind her how suited for each other they were in that department, too. "Say yes to me, Hannah. Let's do this together. Let me make your dreams come true. What do you say?"

"I… I… Jake, we just…"

They'd been with each other less than an hour. The enormity of what he'd done crashed down on him like a bucket of ice water. "Oh, man," he groaned, closing his eyes and resting his forehead against her chin. "Oh, hell, I just blew it, didn't I?"

"No, but… we've only…" She still wasn't able to say a complete sentence and Jake couldn't blame her. Talk about rushing things.

"Okay, hold up." His mind raced. "You know how I feel now, and I know," he kissed her nose, "that at the very least you're attracted to me. That's something. We'll just pretend I didn't propose to you and give it a little time before I try it again. Okay?" He disengaged himself from her and rolled to his side to give her space.

"It's just… I have plans." Hannah scrambled up to a seated position. She scooted back against the headboard and pulled a sheet up to cover herself. Jake instantly missed the view. Still, he figured he'd better take a moment to dispose of the condom and set himself to rights.

"Wait a second, would you?" His trip to the en suite bathroom in his bedroom down the hall took less than a minute. When he returned, he took her hand. "Tell me about your plans." He rubbed circles against her palm then traced up her wrist with his finger. Her skin was soft and smooth and he longed to kiss it, but he wanted to hear her more.

"I'm going back to school."

He stilled. "Really? I thought you already had a degree."

"I do. I need to upgrade a few classes and then I'll go to veterinary school."

He dropped her hand. "Veterinary school. You want to become a vet?"

She nodded her head vigorously. "I've wanted to for years."

Jake quickly tried to revise his vision. He'd work on the ranch. She'd work in town. She'd be gone from morning to night. Disquiet filled him at the idea. That wasn't exactly what he'd hoped for. He'd wanted an ally at the ranch, someone to be just as involved as he was. He'd pictured them doing chores together and poring over books and computers at night figuring out what to try next. If she was a vet she'd have a different life outside of his—a separate life. She'd have her own issues and plans to work on. He wasn't sure how he felt about that.

Would she change her mind if she got to know the ranch—and him—better? Could her interest in animals be funneled into the cattle and other critters they decided to raise?

Maybe. It was worth a shot.

"How about this. We give it two weeks to see if your plans and mine go together. Then I'll ask you again."

THIS WAS ALL going way too fast. She'd come here planning to share a bed but nothing more. Now they'd made love once and he wanted to marry her?

"That's not very long."

"It's long enough," he assured her. "We'll either know we're compatible or we'll know we aren't. Trust me."

He was so sexy sitting among the tousled covers, his muscular chest right there for the touching and the rest of him beckoning to her, too. Could she marry this man? She instantly pushed the idea away as ridiculous. What about school? What about her new career? She wouldn't derail that because they'd had sex.

The best sex of her entire life.

On the other hand, the thought of climbing out of this bed and leaving Jake's house forever left her cold with dread. She liked Jake a lot. She might be able to love him. She doubted she'd figure that out in the next fourteen days, however.

She'd heard his hesitation when she told him her career plans. He'd dropped her hand like a hot coal. For all his insistence afterward that their plans might go together, she figured his first reaction told the truth—they didn't fit at all.

And she refused to sacrifice her plans for his. She'd have to leave him when the two weeks were up, and if she was smart she'd leave him right now.

But there was Gladys to think of.

And herself. If she couldn't spend a lifetime with Jake, at least she could spend thirteen more nights with him.

"Okay," she said. "We spend two weeks together and we don't mention marriage until the time is up."

"Then I get to ask you again?"

She nodded, not trusting herself to speak. Her answer would still be no.

JAKE SHIFTED TO join Hannah where she leaned against the headboard and drew the covers up around them. He hadn't gotten the answer he wanted, but then he hadn't meant to propose quite so soon. Waiting two weeks was a hell of a chance; he wouldn't have time to find another woman to marry. But he wouldn't find another woman he wanted to marry no matter how much time elapsed. It was Hannah or no one. In fact, he couldn't think too deeply about what would happen if he didn't eventually convince her to marry him. It was one thing if they missed the deadline and he got kicked off the ranch. It was another thing altogether if she refused to ever become his wife. There wasn't another woman in Chance Creek he wanted the way he wanted Hannah.

She leaned against him and he relaxed a little. Hannah liked him, that was obvious. Making love to her was better than anything he'd ever experienced before and he already wanted more, but a silence stretched between them and he figured he'd better fill it.

"I've been making some plans of my own."

"Really? What kind of plans?"

"Changes to make around the ranch."

She was so beautiful he wished he could pull her into

his arms and go back to making love to her, but he figured if he tried she'd get mad and leave. Women liked to talk at the strangest times and this was one of them. He couldn't put a ring on her finger, but she was still in his bed, still naked, still interested in what he had to say.

"I want to add a bison herd, for one thing. I've done some reading about them. Did you know they're far more hardy than our cattle? They're built for our winters; you barely have to help them through. Their meat is better for us. Since it's a specialty meat you can charge more for it. I don't see why we shouldn't have a herd."

"Gladys would like that." She turned to him with a smile and her breast grazed his arm, sending heat straight through him.

Jake couldn't help himself. He tilted her chin up and kissed her softly on the mouth. "We could set up relationships with restaurants and distributors." Her hand slid up his arm to his shoulder and she kissed him back. Jake lost his train of thought. "I want to talk to you, slow things down a bit, but the truth is…"

"What?" She leaned into him, arching her neck as he trailed kisses down it and gasping when he bent down to cover one nipple with his mouth. "Jake."

Her arms slid over his shoulders and she allowed him to tilt her back until she lay on the bed. "Jake, we should really…" But her hands caressed his back and shoulders, and she moved with him as he began to nuzzle her breasts.

"We will," he said. "In a minute." It was plain she welcomed this distraction as much as he did. He had no idea what they'd do tomorrow, but it was too late to sort anything out tonight. They were in bed together. Naked.

He traced kisses around her breasts, down to her stomach and lower still. Hannah moaned when he found her core and tasted her. She was so sexy leaning against the pillows, her back arched in pleasure, her thighs spread to grant him access. She trusted him, that was clear, so on some level she knew he wouldn't hurt her. Knew, in fact, he'd do whatever it took to bring her happiness.

He let all thoughts of the future slide away and concentrated fully on the woman before him who had given him her body, if not her heart quite yet. He had to make her understand how fully he wanted her. They were meant to be together. He had to make her feel the same way.

He teased her with his mouth and tongue, stroking her until she began to move beneath him, uttering small, sexy moans. He slid his hands under her to cup her ass, lift her closer, spread her legs farther apart. Hannah gripped the sheets and tilted her head back, her eyes closed. Taking his time, building her desire, he waited until he could see she couldn't take much more, quickly pulled on protection and lifted himself into position.

With his hardness pressed against her, he asked, "Is this all right?"

"Yes." She gripped him urgently.

"I can take you all the way there the other way."

"No, I want this." She pulled him close.

He loved that she wanted him like this. Loved that

she let him cover her, let him stroke into her from this position of power. He loved that she trusted him fully to bring her to the edge. Loved that she was content to ride over it with him.

He began slowly with powerful, deep strokes that left Hannah panting and gripping his back with insistent fingers.

"Jake." She lifted her hips to meet him. He knew what she wanted and gave it to her. Faster strokes, harder, pulling out and pushing in until the friction built within her and she couldn't hold back anymore. "Jake!" she cried and arched against him. His own release close, he bucked harder against her, slammed his hips down to meet hers. He felt something give, something not quite right, but went over the edge, lost in his release, lost in the waves of ecstasy that pulsed through him, pounding into Hannah again and again.

When he collapsed against her, she wrapped her arms around him and kissed the side of his head. "You make me feel so good."

"I always want to make you feel good." He pressed his mouth against her neck. "Let me always make you feel this good."

She wriggled under him without giving him an answer and he followed her lead, pulling the covers with him until they spooned together under the blankets. He didn't press her. Instead he watched her eyelids drift closed and her breath even out. She trusted him enough to fall asleep beside him. That had to mean something.

As quietly as he could, he slipped from beneath the

covers and moved to the bathroom off his own bedroom to clean up.

Only then did he find the tear in the condom, a gaping hole too wide for any doubt that it might have done its job. Jake dropped it in the trashcan as an irrational hope flared within him. If Hannah became pregnant she wouldn't hesitate to marry him.

Should he wake her up and tell her what happened? Urge her to think over his proposal again?

No, she'd feel pressured, he decided. She might become so upset she refused to think about it at all. Would she know the condom broke? She hadn't said anything, but then she hadn't gotten up and moved around after their lovemaking. She might not discover any evidence until morning.

And then what would she want to do. Rush off to a doctor? Take care of it?

Jake's hands balled into fists. Accident or not, practical or not, if she made that kind of decision it would end their relationship before it even started. And what if she thought he'd tampered with the condom to force her hand? She'd hate his guts.

Gripped with indecision, he returned to the guest room and watched Hannah sleep peacefully in a tangle of covers. If he woke her now neither of them would get any rest tonight and that wouldn't help anything. Best to sleep on it and decide what to do in the morning.

Chapter Seven

HANNAH WOKE TO find Jake gone and one look out the window told her why. The sun was almost up, which meant he must have been busy with chores for ages. She could never keep rancher's hours.

Rancher's hours.

The events of the previous night came back with a rush, and she lay back against the pillows taking in the luxurious ache between her legs with a rush of pleasure, desire and shock. They'd made love twice, and it had been great. Jake was the perfect lover. Affectionate, generous… insatiable. Too bad he had to get up so early in the morning. They could have gone for another round.

And he'd asked her to marry him. For a split second she felt like saying yes. What would it be like to wake up with him every morning, and come home to him every night? When she'd mentioned her career plans, he'd seemed somewhat disappointed, and she figured he'd wanted a stay-at-home wife. But surely they could work that out.

Maybe.

She'd better get up if she didn't want to be late. She slipped out of bed reluctantly and stopped cold. Something wasn't right. Something… down there. Whirling around, she threw on the first thing that came to hand—Jake's shirt from the previous night—and ran down the stairs to the bathroom on the first floor. Was it the only one in the house? She didn't know, since they hadn't completed their tour last night. She didn't care, either. What she cared about was the slipperiness between her legs. Evidence that their protected sex hadn't been that protected after all.

A few moments later she was sure. Hadn't Jake put on a condom the second time around? She thought back. He had. So why…?

Could it have torn?

What a time to be off the Pill. She'd only gone off a couple of months ago because she'd had a series of bad headaches this summer. She'd meant to give her body a break then try a new brand. She even had the doctor's appointment lined up next month. That didn't help her now, however, and she suspected those headaches had more to do with being with Cody than the stupid Pill, anyhow. Her body knew she needed to leave him before she did. But how would her body respond to a broken condom?

By getting pregnant?

She yanked open the cupboard door under the sink but saw no sign of a condom in the small wicker trash can. Racing back upstairs she saw only two doors leading off from the balcony—her own bedroom and presumably Jake's. His door was closed. She knocked hesitantly and when she received no answer, turned the handle and barged in.

A masculine room lay before her. The bed unmade. Clothes tossed here and there. A desk piled with paperwork. Like in her room there was a generous closet, but a second door lay beyond it.

Bingo. A small en suite bathroom with a shower. She pushed inside it, ignored the mess and looked in the cupboard under the sink.

This bathroom, too, had a tan wicker trash can.

It was empty.

JAKE LET CHESTER put his muzzle down and drink from Chance Creek. The small river formed the border between the Matheson and Cruz ranches. As kids he and his brothers swam the creek often and forded it when they wanted to visit the other ranch rather than going the long way by road.

What a night. The last twenty-four hours had blindsided him. Not only had he slept with Hannah—twice—he may have accidentally gotten her pregnant. If she was excited about marrying him and settling down with him here, he wouldn't have minded the torn condom one bit. Given the current circumstances, though, he was beginning to feel mighty guilty.

Did she know what had happened? He'd better assume so, which meant she'd be hopping mad the next time she saw him. What would she say? It was no accident he was as far from his cabin as his chores could take him. He'd gotten up this morning prepared to bring her breakfast in bed with an apology and explanation, but no sooner had he walked downstairs than Ned knocked on his door with an emergency with one of the horses. He might have raced back when they were done and caught her before she left for work, but he decided not to give her the chance to throw his proposal back in his face and storm away. Maybe if she had some time to cool off they'd be able to discuss it rationally tonight.

He sure hoped so.

In the back of his mind was the truth of the matter—that he hoped if she took a few hours to consider the ramifications of a pregnancy, she'd want to stay with him and have the baby. If there was a baby. Not telling her straightaway was the most ass-backward thing he'd ever done, but here he was doing it, nonetheless.

He hoped he hadn't messed up everything.

The sound of hoofbeats caught his attention. Ned and his father.

"Taking the rest of the morning off?" Ned said laconically. Holt chuckled.

Jake shrugged. "Just doing some thinking."

"I saw your company drive in last night," Holt said.

"Yeah? So?"

"Did you propose?" Ned drawled.

Jake didn't like the satisfied look in Ned's eye. His brother had been jealous of him all their lives. He couldn't wait to steal Jake's position out from under him. Time to let Ned know he didn't plan to surrender any time soon. "Yes, I did." He was rewarded when Ned's grin disappeared.

"But let me guess," Holt said. "She declined."

"You don't know that."

"The hell I don't. If you and Hannah were engaged we'd all be toasting you around my dining room table. You wouldn't be out here in the middle of nowhere hiding from your chores."

Jake swallowed the angry words he wanted to say. His father was right. What was the use in arguing? "She just needs some convincing. She wants a career. She's afraid marrying me will tie her down too much, but you wait. She'll say yes before long."

He hoped.

"What do you want with a career woman?"

"I like a woman with a brain."

"Brains are fine, but there's too much work around here for your wife to be fluttering off to town every day."

"That's my problem."

Holt shook his head. "It's everyone's problem if you're too busy keeping house and raising kids to do your chores. Ned, you better get ready to run this place. This one wants his wife to wear the pants."

"For God's sake," Jake began, but Ned spoke over him.

"I am ready. I've been ready."

"Whether or not my wife works, the agreement still stands," Jake said to his father. "If I'm married by the twenty-first, I stay in charge."

"Fine," Holt agreed. "We'll change her mind about that career nonsense soon enough." He wheeled his horse around. "So quit your moping and get back to work." He cantered away, followed quickly by Ned. Jake watched them go, a sinking feeling in his gut. Ned couldn't wait to replace him and if he didn't look out, he'd find some way to scare Hannah off. If his father didn't scare her off first. He couldn't do much about Holt, but he should be able to stop Ned from making trouble. He thought fast, scanning the horizon without seeing it. He needed to distract Ned, but how? A thought occurred to him and he smiled. How else? A woman.

He checked his watch. Hannah wouldn't get home from work until dinner time. He might as well distract himself until he could talk with her and sort this mess out. He turned Chester around and headed back to the barn.

Time for a trip to town.

HANNAH SHOWERED SLOWLY, trying to warm up but failing miserably. She couldn't stop trembling no matter how hot she made the water. She didn't have the torn condom as evidence, but she knew beyond a shadow of a doubt that something had happened.

What if she was pregnant? What about all her dreams?

Sadness rippled through her. She wanted children and maybe she even wanted them with Jake. But not now—not right as she was headed out into the next stage of her life. How could she possibly do nearly five years of college in a field as challenging as veterinary medicine and raise a child at the same time, especially with a husband consumed with ranch work?

She could read between the lines of what Jake had said last night. While she hadn't grown up on a ranch, she knew all about what it took to run them. Rancher's wives did ranch chores, too. Plus they kept a large house, ran interference for the hired hands, who tended to get into trouble in their spare time, raised their families, and participated fully in community activities as well. She simply didn't have time for all that.

She wasn't going to give up her dream for Jake's, either. She was one hundred percent sure of that. There was no way this could work, but… if she was pregnant, she wouldn't give up the child.

So what would she do?

And why had Jake run away and stolen the evidence?

She turned off the shower and wrapped herself in a towel. Back in her bedroom, she searched her suitcases for a suitable work outfit and hurriedly got dressed. As she clattered down the stairs to the main floor, however, another thought struck her and stopped her cold. One hand on the banister, the other gripping her purse, she teetered on a step.

Had Jake sabotaged the condom deliberately? Was he trying to make her pregnant so she had no choice but to stay?

She scanned the area below her, focusing on the dirty dishes still in the sink in the kitchen and the haphazard way Jake's belongings filled the living room. She recalled the messy bathrooms and the disaster of Jake's bedroom. Maybe Jake wasn't the man she thought he was. Maybe Jake cut corners whatever he did.

Fury filled her as she stormed down the rest of the stairs. She was going to find Jake right now and tell him exactly what she thought of him, and then she'd pack her bags and get the hell out.

Her anger propelled her all the way to Gladys's pasture where she guiltily realized she'd forgotten all about the beast. She'd forgotten to pick up more corn on the cob, the bison's favorite food, too. As she neared the fence she spotted Gladys right next to the spot where Hannah normally stood each morning to talk to her and leave her a treat.

Hannah's heart squeezed as she realized Gladys must look forward to those morning treats. Usually the bison stayed away from the fence, not coming to retrieve the corn until Hannah left for work. Now she was close enough to touch. Not that Hannah would do something so foolish. When she got close, Gladys raised her head a fraction and huffed out a breath. Was that a greeting?

"I'm sorry. I forgot your corn." Hannah wondered if she could get some on her lunch break. Gladys huffed again and moved an inch closer. Hannah held her breath. Did the creature want to be touched? Had she made a connection with this giant animal?

As she bent down to look Gladys in the eye, the bison suddenly snorted and wheeled away. Surprised, Hannah nearly fell back, but an iron grip on her bicep prevented her from doing so.

"Came to talk to my lunch, did you?" Holt said.

"She's nobody's lunch." Hannah regained her footing and yanked free of him.

"Oh, someone will be happy to eat her, I'm sure. Just as soon as I sell her to the local butcher."

"You promised…"

"Did you sleep with my son last night?"

Hannah flushed hot and only just resisted clapping her hands to her cheeks to hide their color.

Holt looked amused. "I guess you did after all. I thought Jake was telling tales." He bent forward to peer at her. "I'd say more than sleeping went on, too."

"Oh, for heaven's sake." Hannah turned to leave.

"Not so fast. Your bison's won another day on the ranch, but you've got thirteen more nights to go. Jake's no slouch at one night stands. What I'm trying to teach him is the benefit of a sure thing for a lifetime. The wife and I are getting older. I thought our grandkids would have learned to ride by now."

For one split second Hannah saw a trace of sorrow flit over the older man's face. She blinked and it was gone, but it shifted her perception of the situation. A little.

"Grandkids?" she repeated.

"I thought the ranch would be crawling with them, given I have four sons myself." Holt surveyed the pasture in front of them.

"Do you have brothers and sisters?" She wasn't sure why she was prolonging the conversation. This was the first time she'd seen a softer side to the old man, though.

She was curious to know more.

"No, ma'am," Holt said. "I was the only youngster on the place when I grew up."

Hannah bit her lip. There was no way the rancher standing beside her would admit to any weakness, but he'd exposed one nonetheless. Holt wasn't known for his wide circle of friends. Maybe he didn't know how to get close to people and make those friends, so he thought he'd build a circle for himself through his family. He wouldn't be the first person to do that. Now his boys were dragging their feet on creating the next generation. All except Rob, anyway.

And maybe Jake.

Her hand went unconsciously to her stomach and she wondered again if the torn condom could possibly lead to a pregnancy. She glanced up to find Holt staring down at her. His eyebrows lifted but before he could speak she shook her head.

"Don't look at me. I already told you I'm not having children any time soon."

Holt put his hands up in a placating gesture. "I know, I know. But you also told me you wouldn't sleep with my son."

"That's…"

"The truth," Holt said. "And I'll tell you another truth. You're a slob."

Hannah stiffened at this new attack. "I am not!"

"I just stopped by Jake's cabin looking for you and I beg to differ."

Outrage straightened her spine. "That's your son's

mess, not mine."

"As of right now, my son's mess is your mess." Holt leaned in to make his point. "And it's her mess, too." He waved at Gladys. "And I don't like messy critters on my farm."

"What the hell are you saying?" Hannah couldn't believe this. A second ago Holt had almost seemed human. She'd been mistaken, obviously.

"I'm saying clean it up by the time my wife and I come to dinner tonight or the next meal I eat will be bison burgers." He turned to go, but Hannah dashed around and stopped him with a hand on his chest.

"You said if I slept with Jake for fourteen days Gladys would be safe. You promised!"

"Well, now I'm saying that cabin better be clean for fourteen days, too, and you'd better have one hell of a dinner on the table each night for my son. And for me and my wife tonight at six o'clock. I have a full day of chores ahead of me and I'm bound to be hungry." He pushed past her toward the barn. "By the way, Lisa has a sweet tooth, so serve something good for dessert. She prefers a formal table setting, too."

Hannah gaped at him as he strode stiffly across the frozen ground away from her. Dinner? Clean the cabin? She worked until five-thirty. How on earth could she pull that off?

And did she even want to? What kind of sick, twisted game was Holt was playing? What new demand would he make tomorrow if she went along with these ones today? She looked at her wrist. She was already late for work.

Bella depended on her. So did their clients.

She still hadn't found Jake to give him a piece of her mind and figure out what to do about the ripped condom. Should she call into work and go see a doctor instead? Get a pill to take so she could stop worrying?

She should, but she wouldn't. As much as it made sense to do so, she just wasn't wired that way. Whatever happened next, she'd deal with it, even if it overturned all her carefully made plans.

She placed her hands on her abdomen trying to channel information out of it. Was she pregnant? Could she possibly be?

Wouldn't she know?

"Did my brother knock you up already?"

She spun around with a gasp to find Ned watching her, his head cocked to one side. "Why the hell would you say that?"

He mimicked her, leaning back and cupping his abdomen with his hands as if he were pregnant. "Doesn't take a genius to decipher that gesture. So was it Jake who knocked you up, or Cody?"

Her mouth dropped open. "It sure as hell wasn't Cody!" Too late she realized how that sounded. "It wasn't your brother, either. I'm not pregnant."

"If you say so."

"Ned! I mean it—I'm not. Don't you dare say anything—to anyone!"

"Why not? You're going to marry Jake, aren't you? Did you have a little condom trouble? Or just forget to use one altogether?"

Was he for real? "Who said anything about marriage?" Her voice slipped into a higher register.

"Jake did. Said we should expect a wedding by Christmas—just as soon as he talked you out of your crazy career plans. He prefers his women where he can keep an eye on them. It's kind of a Matheson thing." He turned to leave. "Ginger tea is supposed to help with morning sickness, by the way. You look a little pale."

"Damn it! I don't have morning sickness."

"Yet." He strode away.

"I am not pregnant!" But he was gone.

Giving up, she turned on her heel and stalked off to her truck to head into town. She'd call every ranch around these parts during slow times this morning to find a home for Gladys. And if that didn't work, she'd take the afternoon off. She wouldn't let Holt boss her around anymore and she wouldn't give Jake another chance to trap her in a marriage she wasn't ready for. Career nonsense? Had Jake really said that? She'd had enough of the Mathesons.

Especially Ned.

JUST AS JAKE had hoped, Mia Start was working the till at Dundy's Hardware store. He rounded up a couple of items, brought them to her register and smiled when she began to ring them up.

"Hi, Jake. How's it going?" As usual, Mia had pulled her long, dark hair up into a ponytail near the top of her head. It made her look younger than her twenty-one years. It made Jake feel old.

"I'm good. Ran into Fila earlier, though. She wasn't looking so hot." Now that he was here executing his plan, he wasn't so sure it was a good idea. He'd told himself that with a houseful of guests descending on Ethan and Autumn, Mia might like to move out just like Hannah had. He figured Autumn was stashing the two women somewhere on the ranch, but that couldn't be as comfortable for Mia as having her own room. He was just doing her a favor. Now that he was faced with her, he had to admit that the only person he was helping was himself.

Mia's hands stilled. "Fila? What's wrong with her?"

In for a penny, in for a pound. He braced himself to tell the lie as convincingly as he could. "She seemed upset. Something about moving somewhere temporary? Not having a place for herself? She was crying too hard for me to understand her."

"Crying?" Mia's eyes widened. "I knew she wasn't really comfortable with the idea, but…"

"Sounds like she had a real hard time back in Afghanistan." Jake cringed. Normally he prided himself on being honest. It was true Fila had a lot to get over from the time she'd spent as a captive abroad, but he had no idea if she was upset about her upcoming move out of the Big House.

"She did seem down this morning. I thought it was because Hannah left the ranch. How's that going by the way? The two of you living together?"

"It's going great. The cabins my brothers and I have each have two bedrooms and two bathrooms. They're perfect for sharing." He didn't think it wise to mention that he and Hannah had only used one bedroom the night before.

"I wish I could afford something like that. I feel like I've sponged off of Autumn and Ethan long enough." Mia slowly began to ring up the rest of his things.

"Ned's looking for a subletter," Jake said quickly, seeing his chance. "He'd be happy to have you take his guest bedroom. He'd like some extra cash to save up to buy a new truck."

"Really?" She brightened, then quickly frowned. "But Ned… he's kind of got a temper."

"That's all for show. He never acts like that at home." God would surely strike him dead for that whopper.

"I don't know…"

"He's hardly ever in the house, anyway," Jake blustered when it looked like Mia would decide against it. "He works all day and most nights he's tinkering in the shop he's got out in one of the barns. Have you ever seen the stuff he builds?"

She shook her head.

"He can do anything mechanical. Fix anything." It was the first time Jake could ever remember bragging about his younger brother, but it was true; Ned was a whiz with gadgets and gears. He kept all the equipment on the ranch running. Jake didn't know what they'd do without him—it would cost a fortune to hire a mechanic every time something broke down. "What kind of rent are you paying at Ethan's place?"

"Five hundred dollars a month."

Jake made a sympathetic face. "Heck, Ned would

take three hundred."

"The five hundred includes food, too."

"Ned will provide the food. And sometimes you can eat with Hannah and me. It'll be fun. In fact, why don't you come by tonight for dinner? I'll make sure Ned's there, too. Afterward, he can take you to his place so you can look it over and make up your mind. Six o'clock okay?"

"Okay." Mia nodded, beginning to smile. "Yeah. That sounds great!"

Chapter Eight

HANNAH ADMITTED DEFEAT at lunchtime. She'd combed through the ranches in southern Montana once before and this time she had no better luck finding a place to board Gladys. Bison ranches had gained in popularity but there were none close by, and the rest of the ranches weren't interested in introducing a whole new kind of critter to their herds. A few places far to the west might take her, but the cost of the proposition was outlandish. Keeping her at the Double-Bar-K was her best bet. Hannah closed the browser on her computer and glanced at the calendar on the wall. She could take thirteen days of Holt's abuse, she decided, and the thirteen nights of Jake's company would be… bearable. As long as he didn't discuss marriage and his outdated ideas about wives.

She had to stay on top of her emotions, though. Jake was the best lover she'd ever had, but she didn't know if the torn condom was a fluke or if he'd done something on purpose. She couldn't be with a man who would try to force her hand like that. And even if it was an accident—which she suspected it was—it pointed out all the reasons she shouldn't get caught up with Jake. She didn't intend to stay with him. Not when they were at such different places in their lives.

Her phone buzzed with an incoming message. A text from Jake.

Speak of the devil, she thought, reading it. "Plan on two extras for dinner." A jolt of anger spiked through her at the reminder that Holt was forcing her to cook dinner for him and Lisa, and that Jake probably thought it was a fine idea. Two extras—*duh*. She rolled her eyes, but figured it was a good thing Holt had let Jake know he and Lisa were coming to eat with them tonight. Now he'd get home on time and maybe he could help her with the last-minute details.

And afterward they'd have a serious talk. About the condom, about the next two weeks, and about how they'd handle a pregnancy if there was one.

Hannah fought the urge to cry. How had she gotten into this mess? Twenty-four hours ago the prospect of living with Jake had sounded fun. Now she was so confused she didn't know where to turn.

It was all Holt's fault.

And now she was supposed to clean up Jake's cabin and cook for the man?

Plus the man's wife. Hannah wondered if Lisa knew about any of Holt's schemes. She had always wondered why such a smart, lovely woman would marry such a pain-in-the-ass. What would Lisa say tonight at dinner? Would anyone tell her what was really going on?

Hannah decided she'd make the upcoming ordeal palatable to herself by pretending she had voluntarily invited Lisa to dinner. Forget Jake and forget Holt. Lisa had always been sweet when they'd met up. She had no problem cooking a meal for a woman like that. The rest of the Mathesons could go hang themselves, though.

Bella ushered a client out of the examining room—Patty Akins and her schnauzer, Prince. Once Patty had paid her bill and said her good-byes, Hannah asked Bella to stay and talk a moment. "I hate to even ask, but is there any way I can take the afternoon off?" She gave her boss and friend a sanitized version of the events of the past day. "I told Holt I'd have him and Lisa to dinner since they've been so great about letting Gladys stay." She nearly choked on the lie, but it was better than admitting the truth. Bella would think she was an idiot to allow Holt to blackmail her.

"You really like Jake, don't you?" Bella asked.

Hannah figured she was referring to the blush she could feel heating her cheeks. She hesitated. "Yes," she conceded, "but it's not as easy as that."

"Somehow love never is, but you'll figure it out."

"I hope so." She hoped she'd figure out how to last through dinner.

"Why don't you head out right now? Just leave me the rest of the files for this afternoon."

"Thanks! I'll come in early tomorrow to get back on top of it all. I promise."

"Oh, please. You've been working like mad, we both have!" Bella said. "I, for one, am looking forward to

Christmas vacation." She disappeared into the back and Hannah began to gather her things.

By Christmas vacation she'd know whether or not she was having a baby. If Jake had his way, she'd be married, too. Reeling under those thoughts, she headed out the door.

An hour later she set three bags of groceries on the kitchen table in Jake's cabin and went out for her next load. She'd picked up everything she needed for a roast chicken dinner. With chicken, mashed potatoes, gravy, biscuits and a salad, she figured she'd please the pickiest rancher, and all of those dishes were easy as pie to make, as long as she got to it right away.

Thank goodness she'd thought to stop at Autumn's house and borrow some pots and pans, she thought half an hour later. Jake's house was stocked with the barest of cooking essentials and she'd have been up a creek without a paddle otherwise. With the chicken in the oven, she turned her attention to cleaning house. She'd start with the most visible areas—the kitchen, living room and downstairs bathroom—and work her way up, leaving Jake's room for last. The thought of cleaning up his personal things made her cringe. She wasn't some sort of maid, after all. She didn't want him to get used to this treatment.

As anger grew within her once more, however, Hannah took a couple of deep breaths. Why was she letting Holt and Jake stir her up like this? Right now she was reacting to Holt's machinations. She was being his victim. That wasn't the kind of woman she wanted to be.

She had taken the afternoon off to throw a dinner party, and she was going to revel in it. No more moping or simmering with anger. She wasn't doing this for Jake or Holt. She was doing this for Lisa—and herself. She deserved a beautiful, clean home to live in for the next thirteen days and she deserved a wonderful home-cooked meal to eat tonight. Her mood somewhat restored, she got to work.

Along with the groceries, she'd bought a number of different cleaning supplies, a bucket, mop and scrubbing sponges. She set her iPod to her most upbeat playlist, snapped on a pair of gloves and got to work. Just as she'd suspected, Jake already owned a broom and vacuum cleaner. She piled everything that didn't belong on the first floor on the stairs and cleaned like a mad-woman, telling herself the faster she went, the better workout she'd get. The mindless tasks weren't as bad as she expected. Some places needed a better scrubbing than she had time for—such as the refrigerator, the bathroom tiles and inside the oven—but when the rooms sparkled, she picked up the load of Jake's belongings and hauled them up to his room.

Back downstairs, she whipped up a pan of brownies, prepped the biscuit dough, made the salad, and peeled the potatoes. With her busy schedule she never took time to make a fancy supper—certainly not since she'd been staying at the Cruz ranch where Autumn seemed to cook from morning to night. It was kind of fun as a change of pace. As the afternoon progressed, she realized that Holt could try to boss her around and Jake could try to force her hand, but in the end she was the one who decided whether or not to let them. She'd made a choice to secure a place for Gladys and she could stand two weeks of Holt's craziness. She'd made a choice to sleep with Jake and she'd accept the consequences of that action. If she was pregnant, she'd add a baby to the mix and go to school anyway. Why not? Other women did and survived.

The thought made her feel powerful after feeling so controlled by Holt and Jake, and she sang along to her tunes as she cooked. While the brownies baked, she whipped back upstairs and unpacked her things in the spare room. She estimated she had fifteen minutes of cleaning time left when she was done. After that she'd need to put all her attention on preparing the evening meal for her guests.

Guest.

She only cared about Lisa. Holt could go to hell.

Approaching Jake's room with trepidation, she wondered how Holt would even know if she'd cleaned it. She decided she'd straighten up the big things first, and get to the bathroom if there was time. Holt might stick his nose into the room, but she doubted he'd inspect his son's private bathroom.

Of course, this was Holt she was talking about.

Hannah sighed and decided to tackle this last room as if she was running sprints. She made the bed, threw dirty clothes into the laundry basket, picked up papers and miscellaneous items from the floor, lining them up on his desk and dresser in ways she hoped made sense.

She ran the vacuum around as quickly as she could and shut the closet door, before racing into the bathroom and scrubbing and tidying as fast as she could in the few minutes she had left.

Good enough, she decided when the buzzer went off downstairs. Racing back down again, she saved the brownies from overcooking, scuttled around to put all the cleaning supplies away, and popped the biscuits in the oven. She set the brand new tablecloth she'd purchased over Jake's dining room table and carefully set four places. She placed a bottle of wine on the counter top, removed the cover over the roasting chicken to brown the top, and spooned out the broth to start the gravy. A look around told her everything was in place.

A look down at herself told her she looked like hell.

Hannah panicked, then rolled her eyes at herself for caring as she raced for her room and tore off her clothes, reaching for the first thing that came to hand in her closet—a clingy dress of cobalt blue that made her eyes pop and her hair glow. It was far too dressy for the occasion, but there wasn't time to try again. She shimmied into it, did up the zipper, yanked her pony-tail holder out of her hair and fluffed it up, checking her reflection in the mirror.

She was flushed with the heat of the kitchen and all her exertions and her hair was wild, but the effect wasn't awful. In fact… she pursed her lips. She didn't look half bad. Maybe a day out of the clinic now and then wasn't the worst thing in the world, although she'd prefer to do something a little more exciting than clean house.

What would Jake think when he saw her?

She didn't care what he thought, she reminded herself. Jake was out of bounds from here on in. She was in control. She would determine her own future.

A knock sounded at the door and she hurried to the stairs, realizing it must be Holt and Lisa. Where was Jake? He should have been home by now, especially since it was his father who had forced this little dinner on her.

When she reached the door, however, Ned pushed through it. "Jake said dinner's here tonight. Smells good. Got any beer?" He walked straight to the kitchen, pulled open the refrigerator door and grabbed one of the bottles she'd bought just in case Holt disliked wine.

"Um… help yourself." Hannah's mind raced. Jake had invited Ned to dinner, too? Why hadn't he told her?

Maybe Holt never told Jake he and Lisa were coming to dinner, after all. Which meant Jake's cryptic text referred to Ned… and someone else. Who could that be?

"I told Luke I was eating here. He said he'd come, too."

Hannah bit her lip. She'd better set three more places then—for Ned, Luke and the mystery guest. She hoped she'd made enough food for seven. Should she throw some more potatoes in? Setting out three more plates, she jumped when the door banged open again and Jake rushed in.

"Sorry, I'm late," he said as he rushed past. "I got held up with chores. You got my message about Ned and Mia, didn't you? I'll throw a couple of pizzas in the oven in a minute."

"Mia?" She set the last plate down on the table with a thump. Why would Jake invite Mia?

"Yeah. I told you there'd be two more for dinner. Hey, Ned. Got yourself something to drink?"

"Yep." Ned raised his beer to Jake and flopped down on the couch.

Hannah followed Jake into the kitchen. "But your parents are coming, and so is Luke," she said. "And I only cooked for four people." Her voice rose as she calculated how little she had to serve. If she had a microwave she could cook some more potatoes fast, but Jake had no microwave.

"Maybe you better cook that pizza," Ned called out, chuckling at their discomfort.

"No," Hannah said. "Your dad said your mother wanted a formal dinner."

"Wait, what?" Jake stopped midway across the room and looked around him. He took in the tablecloth and candles on the table, seemed to realize how clean everything was. "Wow! It looks fantastic." He sniffed the air. "Smells great, too." A smile broke across his face as he closed the gap between them, pulled her close and gave her a kiss. "You're amazing. When I left the message I didn't think you'd do anything like this. I thought we'd toss something frozen in the oven and have a few beers."

"I… it wasn't…"

Jake pulled away and checked the oven. He laughed,

a low, masculine sound that stirred Hannah's senses even in the midst of chaos. "You're right; that bird's a little light for this clan. We Mathesons like our grub." He straightened up. "We'll need more chairs, too. Ned—go get the ones from your place." He opened the freezer and pulled out a couple of pizzas. "Tell you what—Ned's right; we'll pop these in the oven now and when they're ready we'll cut them up in little squares and call them appetizers. What do you think?"

Despite her annoyance, she was impressed with his creativity and take charge attitude. She doubted she would have thought of that. "It might work."

"I'm on it." Jake whistled as he opened the boxes and placed the pizzas on cookie sheets, then disappeared upstairs to change. Hannah worked on her gravy and got her biscuits out of the oven, replacing them with the trays of pizza. She placed the salad on the table and brought out the salad dressings as well, and by the time Holt and Lisa arrived, she felt like she had the meal under control again.

"You cleaned my bedroom," Jake whispered in her ear when they met again in the kitchen ten minutes later. He'd poured his mother a glass of wine and handed Holt a beer. All three of their guests were seated in the living room. Jake's breath tickled her neck.

"It's no big deal," she said shortly.

"It is to me. No one's ever done something like that before. Except Mom."

That's because you're a grown man, she wanted to say, but she didn't want to start a fight right now. Not with an audience. She pulled away and went to stir the gravy.

Jake followed her. "I think it's the sexiest thing any woman's ever done for me." He slid an arm around her waist and hugged her from behind.

Hannah's body welcomed his touch, but her mind rebelled against his words. "That's got to be the most sexist thing any man's ever said to me," she retorted, and slipped away from him again.

"Hey." He put a hand on her arm to stop her. "Are you mad? I'm just trying to say thank you. It would be sexist if I expected it. It's sexy because I didn't. Not from you."

She squinted at him. "I don't know whether that makes it better or worse."

Jake sighed. "All I'm trying to say is that I appreciate what you did. All of this." He waved a hand to encompass the meal and the table setting. "My work is never done. It's hard to go, go, go all day, then come home and do some more, you know?"

She did know. She knew exactly what he meant, because she went to work at the clinic, skipped her lunch half the time because of the overload of patients, and then had to come home and deal with her own mess. Didn't he know that? She opened her mouth to spell it out for him, caught sight of Mia through the glass panel of the front door and sighed instead.

"Thank you, for everything," Jake said and dropped a kiss on her forehead. Hannah forced a smile to her mouth and went to open the door.

JAKE COULDN'T BELIEVE how much effort Hannah had put into dinner, when all he'd intended was to heat up a couple of pizzas and chat over the meal with Ned and Mia. He wasn't exactly sure what made her extend the invitation to his parents or why Ned decided to bring Luke, but none of that mattered. In fact, it made his plan easier to execute. Ned didn't know that Mia planned to move into his place, and as hard as he'd thought about it Jake hadn't come up with a way to force his hand. Now it would be easy. How could Ned refuse her in front of this crowd?

Once Luke showed up, his hair still damp from a quick shower, they settled down to the meal. Hannah played hostess, serving her guests and making sure everyone had what they needed. Conversation quickly turned to ranch work and the herd, and the menfolk synced up their schedules for the following day.

"It's good to see you," Hannah said to Mia when there was a lull in the conversation. "I already miss hanging out with the gang around Autumn's dinner table."

"Well, I think you'll see a lot more of me, if Ned's agreeable." Mia bent forward to smile down the table at him. "Did you bring the rental paperwork?"

Ned stared back at her, having just taken a bite of mashed potatoes. Luke was staring at her, too. In fact he'd been staring at her throughout the meal so far. Jake hurried to fill the sudden silence.

"I told Mia how you said you were looking for someone to move in with you, just like Hannah has moved in with me," he announced to Ned. "You know—to rent your spare room? Mia says three hundred dollars a month suits her just fine. She'd like to move in as soon as possible."

Ned swallowed hard and took a swig of his beer before he answered. "I… uh…" He met Mia's wide-eyed gaze and choked back the harsh words Jake figured he meant to say. "I guess… that would work," he ended lamely.

"Are you sure?" Mia wrinkled her brow. "You sound a little hesitant."

"No. It's just…" Ned scanned the faces of his family, obviously looking for help. Jake just smiled at him. His parents watched curiously.

Luke leaned forward. "If he says no, I'll…"

"I didn't say no," Ned snapped. "That would work fine for me. We don't need any paperwork, though. We'll just shake on it. I'll make sure the room is empty and ready for you by noon tomorrow."

Mia smiled and her whole face lit up. She wasn't Jake's type, but he could see she could easily be Ned's. Or Luke's. "That would be terrific! Maybe I can cook for you the way Hannah does for Jake. I don't mind—it would be fun!"

Ned sat back. "Well, now. If you'll do the cooking, I'll do the eating." He gave her a considering look and then flicked his gaze to Luke, whose face looked like thunder. Jake realized he might have made a misstep. Did Luke have a thing for Mia? And did Ned, too? Or did he simply relish the prospect of sticking a knife into

Luke's heart and twisting the blade?

"You shouldn't take advantage of her good nature," Luke said.

"You're just jealous no one's trying to move into your cabin," Ned said.

"That's enough," their mother said mildly. "Hannah, you've done a real fine job with this meal. A fancy table cloth and everything! Is this a special occasion?"

"Not really," Jake hastened to say when Hannah didn't answer. Hannah had been quiet most of the meal and he sensed she was angry. He still hadn't had a chance to talk to her about the torn condom. He had a feeling he was going to pay for that, but he couldn't understand why she'd worked so hard to clean and prepare this fancy meal if she was mad at him.

"Now, that's not what I heard." Ned helped himself to another dollop of mashed potatoes and then placing an even bigger dollop on Luke's plate. Jake knew for sure Luke hated mashed potatoes. Ned seemed intent on stirring up trouble tonight.

"Ned." He wasn't sure what his brother meant to say, but he was positive it wouldn't be good.

"I heard," Ned cut right across him, "that this is a very happy occasion indeed!"

Hannah stared at him. Jake was at a loss. His parents waited expectantly. Mia had a smile already forming on her lips.

"What occasion?" Lisa prompted.

"Didn't you know?" Ned threw an arm around Hannah's shoulders and gave her a vigorous squeeze. "Hannah's pregnant!"

Chapter Nine

As chaos erupted all around her, Hannah wished more than anything a hole would open up in the hardwood floor and she could sink out of sight into it. Now six other people knew her secret—or a twisted version of that secret—which meant the whole town would know in seconds flat. So much for any chance to decide on her own which course to take. Should she even be pregnant—the chances of which were slim to none.

"You told him about—" Jake's hands were flat on the table, his expression shocked.

"Is that true?" Lisa's voice cut across the din.

Hannah raised her gaze to the older woman and shook her head slowly. "No. Probably not."

"They had a little trouble." Ned leaned forward. "Jake might need a refresher course on prophylactics." He sounded out each syllable of the long word.

"Ned!" Lisa and Jake spoke at once.

Hannah stood up on shaky legs. "Excuse me." She pushed back from the table and hurried away, catching only a glimpse of Jake's stunned expression and Mia's concerned one. Ned was grinning, the bastard, and Holt seemed amused, too. Lisa's lips had pressed into a thin line.

"Hannah, wait," Lisa said before she made it to the stairs. "My son owes you an apology and I'd like him to make it before I beat him into a coma."

"Mom—Ow!" Hannah glanced back in time to see Lisa take hold of Ned's ear and tweak it, hard. Ned tried to jerk away from her and got a second tweak for his efforts. "Darn it!"

"Apologize!"

"Fine! Sorry, Hannah. I didn't realize it was a big secret; you were talking about kids with Dad in the middle of the ranch for all to hear."

"That's the sorriest excuse for an apology I've ever heard!" Lisa was truly angry. Ned slid a glance her way and straightened up.

"Sorry," he murmured again. "That was uncalled for." He shot a dark glance at Jake and Hannah suddenly understood. Ned hadn't said it to hurt her, he was getting back at Jake... but for what? Well, who cared? She'd never understand this family and she didn't want to.

"If Hannah does turn out to be pregnant, which is unlikely—and nobody's business but ours," Jake said in a steely voice, "we will deal with it as we see fit. I might as well say right now I've asked her to marry me." At his mother's intake of breath he held up a hand. "Hannah hasn't said yes. She's asked for some time to think it over, and I've given it to her."

"I hope not too much time," Holt said caustically.

"Two weeks," Jake shot back. "We'll let you know what we decide."

Lisa let out her breath, but her eyes sparkled. "A winter wedding. How exciting."

"Mom!"

"I won't say another word," Lisa said and pretended to zip her mouth closed, but she couldn't hide her smiles and Hannah warmed just a little to know that as far as her potential mother-in-law was concerned such a marriage would be a happy thing.

She hesitated at the base of the stairs, wanting to escape, but not wanting to offend Lisa. She also didn't want to give Holt an excuse to come up with more unreasonable demands for her to meet during the next thirteen days.

"Come on back, sweetie. I'll keep these boys in line," Lisa said. "Now, Mia—tell me about yourself. Where do you work again?"

It could be worse, Hannah thought as she sat stiffly back down in her seat, holding herself apart from Ned. The Mathesons could all hate her guts. From the reactions of the family around the table, it looked like she'd be welcome here if she did marry Jake. She couldn't imagine belonging to this crazy family, though. Maybe if she could remember that Holt and Ned's disagreements were with each other and Jake, not with her, she might do better at maintaining her equilibrium. Time to get a grip and stop letting them throw her off her game. Mia grinned at her—probably in solidarity—and Hannah tried to smile back. At least as of tomorrow she'd have an ally on the ranch.

MIA THANKED JAKE when they said good-bye on the front porch after dinner.

"You were right about Fila," she confided in him.

Jake felt a guilty pang. "Really?"

"She didn't come right out and say so but I could tell she was really grateful when I told her I was moving out." Mia leaned in to whisper, "She actually cried a little. I gave her a hug and she held onto me so tight."

Jake's heart sank. Was that gratitude or sorrow? Maybe Fila felt like her friends were abandoning her one by one. He hadn't meant for that to happen.

"I'm glad it's all worked out," he said slowly, feeling that nothing had worked out even remotely the way he'd planned. Everyone knew about Hannah's potential pregnancy; he'd somehow insulted her when he tried to thank her for cleaning the house; instead of Mia's presence acting like a brake on Ned's behavior it had spurred him to new heights of tormenting Luke; and now Fila was brokenhearted over being left behind at the Cruz ranch.

Mia slipped off to her car and Luke caught up to him. He looked as anxious as she had been glad. "You don't think Ned and Mia will become a couple, do you?" he said without preamble.

"I don't know and I don't care." Jake had enough problems of his own.

"But he's not right for her. He's not right for anyone!"

Jake had to agree with that. Ned had dated some, but not much. Not many women could deal with his moods or his penchant for trouble. Although…

Jake scratched his chin. When was the last time Ned had gotten into trouble? When they were younger it was just about every week. He couldn't count the times Cab Johnson had driven him home and dumped him on their parents' doorstep. Drunk and disorderly, or sometimes just disorderly, Ned had made a name for himself in town. And it wasn't a good one.

The man could work, though, he had to admit, which was why they put up with as much of his crap as they all did.

"Work it out with Ned. This isn't any business of mine."

"But you're the one who got her living with him," Luke complained.

Jake turned on him. "How was I to know you had a thing for her? You never said."

Luke retreated. "Well I do. So, now what do I do about it?"

The muscles in Jake's neck tightened. As if he didn't have enough to worry about. "I don't know. Get her to move to your cabin, I guess."

"How?"

"Living with Ned will be torture to a girl like that. You heard him earlier. He'll get her to do all the work and he won't give her any thanks, will he? He's bad-tempered and rough. She'll hate it there. Make sure your place is more inviting. Time will do the rest."

"Maybe. Maybe not. I can't just wait around and hope for the best. I have to do something."

"Then… get Fila to move in with you," Jake said, surprised at his own brilliance. He could kill two birds with one stone.

"Fila? How will that help?" Luke leaned against the porch railing.

"She's sad that both her friends have moved away. She wants to move here, too—I'm sure of it," Jake told him. "Get her to your place and she'll do the rest."

"But if she's staying with me, there won't be room for Mia."

Jake thought fast. "There's plenty of ways around that. Put another bed in Fila's room, or move yourself onto the couch, or…" He flashed a wicked grin at Luke. "Seduce Mia and she can stay with you in your room."

Luke smiled. "I like the sound of that last one. I'll do it."

WHEN ALL THE guests left and Jake came back inside, he joined Hannah in the kitchen, picked up a tea towel and dried the dishes as she washed them. As angry as she was at him—at all of the Mathesons—she couldn't help notice the sweetness of the situation. If they were married they might do this every night. She couldn't help but appreciate the tall, handsome cowboy beside her, his strong fingers taking care not to damage the delicate stemware and dishes, the concern on his face when she glanced up at him.

"I'm sorry," he said. "None of this has gone the way I hoped it would."

"I know." She did know. It was as much her fault as his when you got down to it. She should never have tumbled into bed with him. He couldn't help that Holt and Ned seemed determined to drive her crazy, either. When she moved onto the Double-Bar-K, she set herself up for problems.

"Will it help to have Mia nearby?"

"I guess. I didn't expect Ned to ask her to move in with him."

"No, me neither."

She looked up at his wry tone of voice. "What?"

"Nothing."

She let it go, but determined to keep an eye on things when Mia arrived. Something was going on here she didn't understand. There seemed to be bad blood between Jake and Ned. Hannah had already paid a price for it; she didn't want Mia to pay that price, too. They did the rest of the dishes in silence, and Jake took her by the hand to lead her upstairs. She followed him, bracing herself for what would come next.

"I'll understand if you don't want to sleep with me tonight." He hesitated in front of the guest room door and leaned against the frame. He was such a handsome sight, even concerned as he was. He still held her hand and as she fought for words, he caressed it with his thumb. Hannah struggled against the surge of desire deep within her.

He was right. Her mind told her to pull away from

him, crawl into her bed alone and think over this whole debacle, but if she did she wouldn't be able to lie to Holt tomorrow, and the truth was, she'd miss Jake.

"I'd prefer to sleep with you," she said quietly. "But…" She meant to say she wanted to only sleep with him, not make love. There was no way she'd take any more chances with him, not while he was ripping condoms and talking marriage. Maybe, just maybe, they could find a way to be together long term, but they couldn't fall back into bed until they had things on a solid footing.

Before she could finish her sentence, however, Jake pulled her close, tipped her head back and kissed her thoroughly. As usual, all her other thoughts scattered when he was so close. There was just Jake—the strength of his arms, the scent of his soap, the clear intent behind his kisses. To seduce her. To tumble her onto the bed. To make love to her as only he could.

"Thank God," he said when they pulled apart to catch their breath. "I didn't think I'd make it through the night if you hated me for what I've done."

"I don't hate you but I don't trust you either." She fought for clarity. For common sense. "To deliberately rip a condom…"

He flinched back. "Is that what you think? That I did it deliberately?"

"Why hide the evidence if you didn't?"

"I panicked. When I saw the state of it I couldn't believe it. I thought you'd leave…I wanted to keep you around long enough to explain." She searched his face, trying to decide whether or not he was telling the truth. "Hell," he said when she didn't answer. "You really don't trust me."

"Why should I? I barely you know you. The second time we make love the condom breaks. That's never happened to me before."

"It's never happened to me either." Jake touched her. "And I would never do something like that deliberately. If we get serious and decide to have a family, I want to make that decision together. I want us to talk about it." He took her hands. "Hell, I want the fun of trying to make you pregnant on purpose." He pulled her in for a kiss and Hannah blinked, heat surging through her at the idea of how much fun that could be. Someday. Not right now, but... "You don't really think you're pregnant, do you? I mean, I know it's possible, but what are the odds?"

She shrugged.

"I would never hurt you. You have to believe that." Jake gathered her closer. His arms around her made it difficult for her to think. She was still picturing Jake *making her pregnant...*

"I guess." She leaned against him.

"Come on." He scooped her up into his arms and kicked the bedroom door open. He tumbled her down onto her bed and followed her, rolling her back into his arms as soon as they were both prone. He didn't waste words before sweeping her into another long kiss, one that left her senses reeling. She gave up fighting him and wrapped her arms around his neck, kissing him back, instead. What did it matter if she made love to him again? The die was already cast. She planned to stay with him for thirteen more nights.

Might as well make the most of it.

She let him peel her clothing off of her, and when they were naked his hands left trails of heat up and down her skin. This time he lay back and urged her to climb on top of him. She did, gladly. She bent forward to slide her breasts across his chest and he caught her and pulled her forward to take one nipple into his mouth. Hannah sighed with pleasure as he took his time lavishing his attention on both breasts. Soon she was rocking her hips and enjoying the feel of his hardness between her legs.

She was already slick with need for him. Soon enough she was opening to him, begging him with her body to press inside her and start the climb toward ecstasy. When he paused to put a condom, on he took longer than usual and she realized he was checking it carefully to make sure it wouldn't fail them like the time before.

She didn't care anymore. She was already too far gone.

"Ready?" He gripped her hips, fingers splayed toward her ass. Hannah lifted herself on her knees and positioned herself to give him access. His powerful hands guiding her down onto him made the sensation that much better. When she started to move with him, he kept his hand where it was and used the other to draw her down to a hard kiss. Wild with need she sunk and rose, sliding him far inside of her and out again. Her breath came in pants, her thigh muscles tensing, releasing and tensing again.

"I could watch you forever." Jake's eyes shone up at her. He was clearly taken with the sway of her breasts and her own gaze watching him. She braced her hands to either side of his shoulders when he slid his hands down to grip her ankles.

Now he could plunge deep inside her and although she rode him, he was calling the shots. Hannah didn't care. She was too close to sliding over the edge of her release to think of anything but the sensations of her body. The grip of his fingers, the friction of their joining, the bob of her breasts against his chest. A few minutes later he brought her to a release that shook her to her fingertips and she cried out his name. He grunted, thrusting hard within her, and urged her to even higher heights. Hannah cried out again and again and Jake shuddered within her, gripping her tight. Afterward they didn't talk much, but Jake wrapped a possessive arm around her and held her close as he fell asleep.

How would she be able to give up these nights when her two weeks were over? How could she make any plans that would take her away from this man?

Hannah pushed the uncomfortable questions away, determined to savor every minute she was here.

Chapter Ten

"IF SHE'S PREGNANT, she'll marry you quick enough," Holt pronounced at lunch time the following day. The family was gathered around the table at the main house. Jake helped himself to a slice of ham and put it between two thick slices of bread to form a man-sized sandwich. He wondered what Hannah was eating for lunch at work. She'd been quiet this morning as she hurried to get ready. When she'd stopped to make the bed he helped her, remembering how prickly she'd been when he tried to thank her for cleaning up his mess the day before. Then he trailed behind her as she cruised through the rest of the house straightening the pillows on the couch and making sure all the dishes in the sink were done. She was a lot neater than he was, that was for sure. He kind of liked it.

"I don't know about that."

"Of course she will. What else would she do?"

"Times have changed," Lisa said. "A girl can do whatever she wants to now."

"She's going to Montana State," Jake said.

"When do classes start?" Lisa passed him the platter of ham.

"End of January."

"She won't go to school if she's pregnant," Holt assured him. "No woman would do that."

Lisa gave an exasperated sigh. "This isn't the Middle Ages, Holt. No one cares if women are pregnant. They do what they like. Half of them don't have husbands."

"Damn fools," Holt said.

"If she doesn't marry Jake, her baby won't be a Matheson," Ned put in, stirring things up as usual. Jake shot him a dirty look that Ned ignored.

"You mind your own business," Lisa said to him. "Jake's got trouble enough without you giving him more to worry about."

"Jake's going to be a daddy," Ned said. "An unwed daddy. What'll they say at church?"

"You'll never know since you never attend," Lisa said. "Besides, Hannah wouldn't have cooked such a fabulous dinner for us all last night if she wasn't in love with you, Jake."

Holt snorted.

Lisa eyed him. "What's wrong with you?"

"I'm surprised a woman like Hannah knows how to cook or clean at all. She cut some corners on that dinner, too. Frozen pizza for appetizers? And that refrigerator was a mess."

Jake dropped his fork. It hit his plate with a clang. "She worked all day, Dad. I don't see you cleaning and cooking when you're done out in the barn."

"That's why I have a wife. A damn fine one, too." He lifted his glass to Lisa.

"Now, I've always loved this life and I'm fine with the way we split the chores," Lisa said to him. "But Hannah's a whole other kettle of fish. She'll have her own ways of doing things. She and Jake will have to work them out."

"She and Jake can learn from our example," Holt countered. "Men and women are different and they're naturally called to different things."

"How the hell do you stand him?" Jake asked his mother.

Lisa chuckled. "I don't listen to half of what he says, and I ignore the rest."

"That's good advice." Jake stood up to take his leave. Lisa followed him to the front hall.

"Don't mind your father," she said. "It's Hannah you have to worry about. What do you plan to do?"

"What can I do? It's all up to her now. She knows what I want."

"I don't think leaving everything up to Hannah is a good idea. Do you love this girl?"

"Yes."

"Then you'll have to push your cause. If she's about to start school, she's probably not planning to get married or have children right now. On the other hand, if she is pregnant, she may not have a choice about having a child. Not one she's likely to take, anyway. Am I right?"

He nodded.

"So why don't you take this opportunity to show her how it can all work out."

"How can it all work out?"

"The same way things always work out," Lisa told him. "By working hard, by making accommodations for each other. By asking your family for help."

Jake shoved his hands in his pockets. Asking his family for help. Yeah, right. If he did that, his father would make sure he ruined everything and his brothers would stab him in the back. At least Ned would. When had his family ever come to his aid? For as long as could remember, Holt had bribed him with the promise that he'd one day head the ranch. That day had never come. Now he had Hannah in his sights, Holt seemed determined to drive her away. "I don't see how it's possible."

"You better start seeing how. You don't have much time to change her mind."

AT FIVE-THIRTY, Bella ushered her last client out of the examining room. She lingered while he paid his bill and carried his cat out of the clinic, then shut and locked the front door behind him.

"Okay, spill it," she said to Hannah. She leaned on the counter and watched as Hannah turned her computer off and gathered her things.

"What do you mean?"

"What is going on? You haven't been yourself all day."

Hannah thought about telling a white lie and leaving quickly, but she knew that wouldn't help matters any.

"You won't believe it."

"I bet I will. Come here." Bella gestured toward the waiting room. She took a seat on a plastic chair and leaned back. "Start at the beginning."

Hannah joined her. "There's good news and bad news." She wiped her suddenly damp palms on her slacks. "I applied to Montana State and got in. I start classes in February."

Bella's eyes went wide. "You're going to graduate school? You never said anything!"

"It isn't exactly graduate school. I have to take a few extra classes this semester before I can apply for the grad program I want."

"That's great, Hannah. Don't worry, we'll figure out your hours and everything. I'm so proud of you. What are you going to study?"

Hannah felt a blush creep up her neck. She knew it was silly, but sometimes when she'd pictured telling Bella, she wondered if her friend would think she was copying her. "After I'm done with my preparatory classes, I'd like to go to veterinary school."

Bella leaped from her seat with a whoop and came to hug Hannah. "Oh, my goodness. I'm thrilled. We desperately need more vets! We'll be able to be business partners someday!"

"Really?" Hannah's voice broke. "I didn't know if you'd be mad."

"Mad? You're kidding, right? I can't wait!" Bella hugged her again and tears of relief pressed against Hannah's eyes. She tried to hold them back.

Failed.

"Hannah! Hannah, what's wrong? Is it the money?"

Hannah shook her head vigorously.

"What is it?" Bella crouched down beside her.

"I screwed up. Big time." Hannah's tears fell faster. She dropped her head into her hands. "I slept with Jake."

"Okay, you slept with Jake. That's… kind of nice, isn't it?" Bella asked. "I've seen how he looks at you. He likes you. Did he do something?"

"He proposed!" Hannah wailed. "He wants to get married and have kids…"

Understanding dawned on Bella's face. "His timing wasn't so great. But that's okay, you can be with him and wait on the kids, can't you?"

Hannah shook her head again. "The condom… it broke…"

"Oh, honey," Bella swept her into another hug. "Sweetie, oh, I'm so sorry. But you can't know yet that anything's happened. You won't know for a while. Chances are that everything will be fine. You'll just be more careful in the future, right? Aren't you on the Pill?"

"No. I'd been having issues, so I went off them a few months back. I have a doctor's appointment next month to try another kind…" She dragged her sleeve across her face and shrugged. "I guess it's too little, too late."

"What did Jake say?"

"He wants to marry me—right away."

"Well, that's… good," Bella said. "At least Jake loves you and wants the child, if there is one."

"This is all happening way too fast."

"Okay, first of all, congratulations on your acceptance to Montana State. Whatever happens, you'll do a great job there and you'll be a great veterinarian. Second, until you know whether you're pregnant or not, you don't have to do anything as far as Jake's concerned. Just try to relax and focus on other things for a few weeks. If you do turn out to be pregnant, you still have plenty of time to make decisions, right?"

"I guess so. But Jake wants an answer in two weeks."

"Too bad. He'll just have to wait. This is an important decision, Hannah. You have to think it through." She stood up. "Come on, let's go give the animals in back a little love while we talk."

Hannah nodded and followed her to the shelter at the back of the clinic. Bella stopped at a kennel in which an older mutt lay chewing on a bone. "Where will you go for vet school? To Colorado like I did?"

"I'll go wherever I get in," Hannah said. "You know what the competition for spaces is like."

Bella nodded. "I do know. Can I ask a personal question?"

"Sure." Hannah waggled her fingers through the bars of a cage where a tan puppy lay curled in a fluffy ball. She loved this guy. If she had her own place she'd adopt him in a heartbeat.

"How are you going to pay for school?"

"I have a little savings to get started," she said. "Enough to cover spring semester. I'm going to pick evening and weekend courses and still work as much as possible. Then there's financial aid and scholarships. I've already got a bunch to apply for."

"No." Bella said, petting the mutt's floppy ears. "Forget it."

"What do you mean?"

"I mean, you're not going to work full time, go to school full time and try to fit in all those hours of homework, too."

"I'll manage just fine. Everyone does."

"No, you won't. Because I'm offering you the first Bella Mortimer Full-Ride Scholarship for veterinary students."

Hannah's mouth dropped open and for one second her heart surged with hope. Just for one second, though. Nearly as quickly, reality set in. She shook her head. "No way. I'm not taking your money."

"You know, I'd buy that line in any other situation than this one," Bella said. "I mean, if I was some random friend of yours who offered to pay for school out of the goodness of my heart, you'd be right to turn me down and pay your own way. That's not the case here, though, is it? First of all, I wouldn't have won so much money if you hadn't signed me up for the reality show. I should pay your way for the rest of your life. Second, I wouldn't have married a man who's even richer than me if you hadn't signed me up for that show. So I should doubly pay your way for the rest of your life. In fact," she grew serious, "I've been trying to figure out how to do just that, Hannah." She reached for her hand. "I owe you everything. I can't carry that burden forever. I've been talking to lawyers about how to set up a trust for you. Just let me pay for your schooling. It'll be so much simpler."

"No." Hannah shook her head. "I can't do that. It's wrong. It's weird!"

"Um… we passed weird a long time ago, sweetie. Billionaire." She pointed to herself. "How weird is that? Please don't make this weirder than it needs to be."

Hannah thought a moment. Bella was right, not that she'd signed her up for the show in order to profit off it; she'd only wanted her friend to be able to hold onto the clinic so they'd both have a job. But Bella did win and she did marry Evan, and there was a bit of strain between them now that Bella had so much money and Hannah… didn't. "Okay," she nodded. "You pay for my school and we'll be quits, okay?"

"Sure thing." Bella grinned.

Hannah narrowed her eyes, but let the subject slide.

Chapter Eleven

"IT'S NOT FAIR; you're stealing all of my friends," Autumn said when Jake and Luke came to pick up Fila and her things. The shy young woman showed Luke her bags and he began to haul them outside.

"They won't be far off," Jake assured her. "You and Ethan are welcome to come by any time."

"It won't be the same." Autumn waited until Fila passed by them, carrying a few of her lighter bags. "I'm worried about Fila. Living with Luke? That's crazy for her. She barely talks to men."

"Luke's a pretty steady guy. They'll do fine."

"I'm not so sure. She hardly leaves the house, you know, and she trusts us. Over at the Double-Bar-K..." She met his gaze. "No offense, Jake, but you and your brothers and Holt can get pretty rough."

Jake's jaw tightened. She was telling the truth. None of them pulled any punches when their ire was up. Sometimes things got loud and out of hand.

"She'll have my Mom, Morgan, Hannah and Mia to take care of her. She'll be fine. I promise."

"Well, tell Hannah to stop by soon. I miss her already."

"Will do," Jake said. He went to help load Fila's things and realized she and Luke had already finished the job. Fila hadn't been in Chance Creek long enough to accumulate many possessions. The ride back home was quiet, so he was glad it only took a couple of minutes. He left Luke and Fila to carry her things into Luke's cabin while he went to find Ned.

He met Mia on the front porch of Ned's house, wielding a broom and singing along to a song on her iPod. Again he marveled at how young she looked, although she and Fila were about the same age.

"How's it going?" he asked when he caught her attention. She pulled the earbuds out of her ears and grinned.

"Great! Come and look! Tell me if you think Ned will like what I've done."

Jake followed her inside and stopped dead, blinking at the sight in front of him. All of Ned's things were still here. They were just… different.

"Let me guess. Your favorite color is… pink," Jake said.

"Scrape that look off your face, cowboy. I know people think pink is too girly, but I love pink. You know why?" Mia grabbed his hand and tugged him farther into the house. "It's bright. It's bold. It doesn't hold back. The color pink stands for unconditional love and that's my thing, you know? I don't hold back my feelings or emotions. I'm not cold like so many people are. I don't judge people. Do you judge people?"

"Um… I don't know."

She stopped and he nearly bumped into her before he noticed her scrutinizing him. "You do. I can tell. That's a shortcoming, Jake. You have to let people be people. You have to let them express their true selves and follow their passions—otherwise you'll just make them miserable."

"Okay." Inside the house he got a full view of the changes she'd made. A hot pink tablecloth covered the table and matched the curtains on the main living room windows. Evidently Mia didn't have enough curtains to go around, because the rest of the windows on the first floor were still dressed with the ones his mother had provided. There were candles everywhere. All kinds and sizes, short and tall, fat and thin, some in glass holders, some sitting right on the furniture, which Jake doubted was a good idea in a cabin constructed primarily of wood.

The old comfortable couch had a new pink covering with raised white polka dots. Pink and white striped pillows were plumped in its corners. A bouquet of red and white roses sat in pride of place on the dining room table. Something was cooking, but Jake couldn't place the smell.

"What's in the oven?" he asked. He was afraid to comment on the décor.

"A quinoa casserole. It's got spinach and kale and shallots. It's so good for you! Do you want to stay for supper?"

"Uh… no! I mean… I have plans with Hannah."

"That's so sweet!" Mia tied a frilly apron around her middle and pulled hot pink oven mitts on her hands. She opened the oven and peered in. "Just another half hour. I hope Ned's hungry."

"I hope he is, too," Jake said and made a quick escape.

LUKE MADE AN appearance at nine o'clock that evening, tapping on the front door before he let himself in.

"Is Jake here?" he asked Hannah, hovering just inside the doorway. He looked uneasy.

"I'm here," Jake said before Hannah could respond. He'd been up in his bedroom doing some paperwork while Hannah put her feet up on the couch. Now he clattered down the stairs. "What's wrong?"

"It's Fila. She's crying."

Hannah sat up. "Crying? What did you do to her?"

"I didn't do anything," Luke said. "I just put on a movie for us to watch. It's really awkward sitting there with nothing to say."

"What movie?" Jake asked as Hannah went to get her coat.

"Jarhead."

"A war movie?" Hannah twirled around. "Seriously? You asked her to watch a war movie?"

Luke looked stricken. "I didn't think…"

"No, you didn't." Jake put his hands on his hips.

"We've got nothing in common," Luke was saying as Hannah slammed out the door. Did the Matheson men ever think, she wondered as she stalked toward Luke's cabin. On the way, she passed Ned's place and was startled when he called out, "Anything wrong?"

"Ned?" She peered through the darkness. "What are you doing out there without the lights on?"

"Just thinking." He came down the steps from the porch to join her. He paced beside her as she continued on her way. "Kind of hard on the eyes inside my place just now."

Hannah stifled a giggle. "Jake told me about Mia's decorating spree."

"Think I might have hurt her feelings," he said. "Didn't mean to. That's just a lot of pink to spring on a man. My reaction was a little… abrupt."

"Oh, no."

"What's wrong with Fila?" At her look of surprise he said, "I saw Luke hightailing it toward your house a few minutes ago. Figured something happened to upset her and he couldn't take her tears."

"You're right. He tried to watch *Jarhead* with her."

"Idiot." Ned picked up the pace. "You don't show that kind of thing to a woman—not one like Fila."

"What do you know about it?" The words popped out before she could think them through. Ned stopped short.

"I know more than people give me credit for."

"Okay, okay. Didn't mean to touch a nerve."

"Yeah, well. You did." He didn't explain further. Just resumed walking. Hannah followed him.

When they reached Luke's cabin all was quiet inside.

The lights were on and a fire blazed in the fireplace. Plates had been scraped and left by the sink but there was no evidence that anyone had cooked. Hannah got the feeling they'd eaten frozen dinners. There was no sign of Fila.

"Fila?" Hannah called. "Are you here?"

They moved quickly through the main floor but it was obvious she wasn't downstairs. Hannah climbed to the second story thinking Ned would stay behind, but he followed close on her heels. This cabin was laid out exactly the same way as Jake's, so she approached the guest room door and knocked.

"Fila? It's Hannah. Can I come in?"

After a long moment, she heard something that might have been an invitation to enter. She turned the door handle and opened it slowly. "Fila?" The young woman was huddled on the bed, pressed up against the headboard. "Are you okay?" She quickly moved to Fila's side and pulled her close, instinctively wanting to give her comfort. "It's all right. I'm here. Nothing is going to hurt you."

When Ned entered the room she shooed him away vigorously, but he didn't leave. He came to stand next to the bed, his hands in his jeans pockets. Hannah ignored him. She stroked Fila's hair and let her sob against her shoulder.

"What's wrong?" she asked, thinking if she could get Fila to talk about it, she might settle down.

"I can't do this," Fila cried. "I can't… I just feel… I'm too…" Her sobs deepened until her body was wracked with them. Hannah gathered her closer, wishing she could somehow prevent Fila from ever being hurt or scared again. She didn't know everything that had happened to the woman in her time in Afghanistan, but she could only imagine how scared and alone she must have been. Had all that fear she'd held inside for a decade overwhelmed her now that she was out of danger? Was it a matter of crying it out or did she need more help? Professional help, maybe.

Hannah tugged the comforter up around the two of them to make a kind of nest and rocked Fila in her arms. She wished Ned would go away. He was a reminder to Fila of everything that made the world frightening to her. Didn't he realize that?

After some minutes Hannah began to get frightened herself. Fila's sobs weren't abating at all. She was getting louder, if anything. Verging on hysteria. Hannah held her closer as if her arms could form a protective cage that could somehow bring her back to herself.

Suddenly Ned yanked the comforter away. "Time to stop," he announced.

Fila shrieked and Hannah jumped. "Ned!"

"No. This isn't helping her. Fila—stop!" His voice was like a slap, loud and sharp.

"What the hell?" Hannah scrambled to her knees. She placed herself between Fila and Ned, ready to do battle against him if it was necessary. What was he thinking, being so harsh at a time like this? Fila needed care and comfort, not tough love. "Get out of here. You're scaring her!"

Ned paced around the bed to the other side and crouched to bend over Fila. "Am I scaring you? Really?" He straightened, holding up his hands so she could see them. "I don't have any weapons. You've got a friend with you." He pointed to Hannah. "So am I scaring you?"

Fila gaped at him. She was a mess, her long black hair tangled and plastered with tears to her face, her beautiful eyes red-rimmed from crying.

"You can't live in memories. You can't stay where you've been. You've got to be here!" He slapped a hand down on the mattress and both women jumped. "You think you're helping her, Hannah, but you're not. You're teaching Fila to be a victim. That's not what she needs."

"Ned Matheson, you get the hell out of here!" Hannah yelled and launched herself at him. Of all the times for him to interfere. And of all the ways. He thought yelling at Fila would do her any good? He was a fool. She braced her hands against his chest and pushed him away with all her strength.

"Okay. I'm going." He didn't even look at Hannah as he set her physically aside. Instead he directed all of his words to Fila. "But I'm not going far and I won't let your friends turn you into a weakling. You're a fighter, Fila. Remember that. You beat those sons of bitches with your brain when they outnumbered and outgunned you. You made it here. You got free. Don't lock yourself up again inside these walls. Get back on your feet and get out there."

He turned and stalked from the room. Hannah

rushed back to Fila's side and tried to gather her back into her arms. "I'm so sorry. I'll keep him away from you."

"No," Fila said, her tears gone. She extricated herself from Hannah's embrace, stood up and smoothed the hair back from her eyes with a shaky hand. "He's right." She hugged her arms to her chest. "I can't stop fighting. Not now." She took a deep breath. "I'm going to wash my face. Please tell Luke he can come home."

"DID NED COME over here?" Mia let herself into Jake's cabin without knocking first. Jake didn't mind. He and Luke were sitting uncomfortably in the living room as the minutes ticked past and there was no word from Hannah.

"No. Isn't he with you?"

"No. He went out for minute and then never came back. I got bored waiting for him." She looked from one brother to the other. "Who died?"

"No one. Fila's upset." Luke was looking intently at Mia, Jake saw, the puppy love evident in his eyes.

"Maybe I should go help," Mia said.

"No!" Luke snapped. "I mean, Hannah's already gone to see her. You'll just… overwhelm her."

Jake bit back a chuckle at Luke's tone.

"I guess." Mia trailed over and sat on the couch beside Luke. Jake's mouth quirked as color flooded into his younger brother's cheeks. Luke was acting like a schoolboy with his first crush. His brother didn't have quite the history with the ladies that he had, but he was no slouch.

He should have a better command of his emotions than that.

Still he could see the attraction. Mia was petite, cute, lively, with hair that a man would like to wrap around his wrists and pull to get her a little closer. She was much too young and inexperienced for him, but she might suit Luke just fine.

If Ned didn't want her. Somehow he didn't think Ned did want her, or he wouldn't have disappeared and left her time enough to wander over and get distracted by his younger brother. Ned would fight fiercely to keep hold of any woman he really wanted. He was the kind of man who kept tabs on what he felt was his.

Mia sighed. "What's there to do around here?"

"We could watch a movie," Luke said eagerly. "Do you like *Jarhead*?"

Jake rolled his eyes. "Didn't you leave that at your place? Where Fila's upset?"

Luke deflated. "Yeah. Right."

"Actually, I love military movies. Soldiers are hot." Mia brightened. "I'll go grab my laptop and we can stream it. I'll make some popcorn, too." She popped up off the sofa and was out the door in a minute. Luke trailed after her happily. Jake shook his head. He was only two years older than Luke. How come his brother seemed so young?

Because he wasn't the one trying to head up the ranch, Jake mused. He had always craved the responsibility of that position without considering its downside—the long hours, the stress of having to get everything right, the worry that was digging lines into his face around his mouth and eyes. Someday he'd end up as haggard as his father.

Jake smiled at the thought. If he did, it meant that he'd have a number of solid ranching years behind him and that's all he'd ever asked for.

The door opened again and Hannah came in.

"Everything all right?"

"Yes, actually." She looked bemused.

"What?"

"Ned." She shrugged. "He… surprised me."

"Really?" Jake sat up. "How?"

"I was making everything worse, but Ned knew exactly the right thing to say."

Chapter Twelve

THE DAYS PASSED all too quickly. Hannah and Jake fell into a rhythm of playing house that was more pleasant than she might have imagined. She began to get up much earlier than she ever had before so they could talk over their plans for the day before Jake headed out to do his chores. He liked to follow her around as she spiffed up the place and she liked that too, since he unconsciously helped her, picking clothes up off the floor in the bedroom, drying the dishes in the kitchen and keeping her company, if nothing else. As they worked, they kept up a constant stream of talk. Jake quizzed her about the animals in her and Bella's care, asking about their injuries and illnesses and what they were doing to help. He was surprised to hear how much she assisted Bella with the animals and interested to know she could stitch up an incision and give shots. She questioned him about his duties around the ranch. It fascinated her that Jake, his father and brothers knew what to do each day when so many chores vied for their attention. She learned that Jake knew all kinds of things about tending minor wounds and injuries among his cattle. He promised to fetch her the next time a medical emergency occurred.

Hannah remembered what Jake had said the first night they were together: that her mind was sexy. Now she knew what he meant. Jake's body would always turn her on, but it was this mental connection, this ability to fire up each other's curiosity that would make him hard to leave.

Once he left to do his chores, she showered, dressed and started a load of laundry before Holt appeared at her door. As much as she hated his early morning visits, she appreciated that at least she didn't have to hunt him down. He never asked her outright if she'd slept with Jake the night before, just gave her a hard look as he pushed into the house and nodded his head when a blush crept up her neck.

"You're getting the hang of it now," he said as he swept a look around the first floor one morning. "Neat as a pin. It isn't so difficult, is it?"

Hannah repressed an urge to punch him. It was one thing to appreciate her own labors. It was another thing altogether to deal with his condescending insistence that everything about the house was her job. She didn't tell him that Jake cleaned up right alongside her in case Holt would count it against her. In fact, she didn't answer him at all.

"Evan Mortimer was by last night," he went on, not expecting her to. Nine days into this routine, they had it down pat.

"Really? What did he want?" He'd surprised her into the comment. She tried to maintain an icy silence on these morning visits to demonstrate to Holt how inappropriate they were, but she was rarely successful. Holt was a master at jolting her out of her calm.

"Seems Jake's not the only one interested in a bison herd. Evan is, too. Of course when you're a billionaire you can piss your money away any way you want to."

"Why'd he come to see you?"

"Because I have a bison."

Hannah's eyebrows shot up.

"We have a bison," Holt amended. "Evan is interested in a joint venture."

"With Jake and me?"

"With the Double-Bar-K. Which I own." Holt frowned. "I'm not dead yet."

Too bad. "Of course not. So what do you think about the idea?"

"I think it's a bunch of tomfoolery! But money has always got its uses. If Mortimer wants to invest, I can at least think about it."

"Jake would certainly be pleased."

"What about you?"

"What does it matter?" Hannah said. "I don't come into the equation."

Holt crossed his arms. "When you marry Jake and raise his children you'll be part of this family. Mathesons stick together. That makes you part of the equation."

She crossed her arms and stared back at him. "I haven't agreed to marry Jake or raise his family, but a bison herd would be lovely. Besides offering companionship to Gladys, I believe that bison are a better alternative to cattle—both for us and for the land."

"Humph. Spoken like a liberal."

She knew that was an insult. "Spoken like someone who cares."

"Do you? Care?"

"Of course I care."

"About Jake? About that baby?" He nodded to her belly and she placed a hand protectively over it.

"There probably is no baby," she reminded him. "But yes, I do care… about both of them."

"Enough to put your own wishes behind you and do what's right?"

Anger flared within her. "How come I'm the only one who has to put my wishes behind me? Why are you trying so hard to box me into this corner?"

"Because if I don't you might just make a run for it and my son might follow you." He looked away, swallowed, and Hannah saw the same sadness she'd seen in him before. She reminded herself that as deranged as his methods were, he only wanted what most parents wanted—to see his grown children happily settled down, preferably close by. "You youngsters don't think I pay much attention to what's going on. You underestimate me. I know my son. He loves this ranch more than I do, but he's restless and he's hungry for something he may not be able to find here; a wife and a mission."

"A mission?"

"Every man likes to innovate and Jake is no different. My father was a conservative man. He grew this ranch slowly and carefully. When it was my turn I learned everything I could about maximizing the land and the herd and I doubled the size of it. Now Jake wants a chance at the helm. He wants to look back to our past heritage to find a more natural way to run the ranch. He wants his bison herd. He thinks it will preserve the integrity of the land. Maybe it will. If I try to stop him he'll jump the fence and find a new pasture." He turned his iron gaze on her. "If you jump the fence he'll follow. Maybe not today or tomorrow, but eventually."

"So I just give up, stay home, forget about my career? That's my fate?"

"It's the fate my wife chose. Can't be too dire."

But it felt like a prison to her. She wasn't Lisa or Autumn. She didn't find joy in transforming a house into a home. She wasn't Mia, playing with redecorating and cooking. She wanted something big to do, something hard, something lucrative. She wanted a career.

"You've got that look on your face," Holt said.

"What look?"

"That jump-the-fence look." She saw a flash of desperation in his eyes. Then it was gone. She felt for him, knew he wanted to be surrounded by a loving family, but she couldn't give up her own dreams to make his come true.

"The thing is, Holt, you've made it crystal clear," she said. She gathered her purse and coat and ushered him toward the door. "I can either be with Jake or I can have my career. In that scenario I choose my career."

WHEN JAKE OPENED the barn he found his brothers facing each other, nearly nose to nose.

"Just stay away from her," Luke said.

"Don't tell me what to do."

Jake wanted to turn on his heel and walk straight back out, but he knew his father would show up soon and that would make things worse.

"What's going on?" He tried to pitch his voice with the same fearsome authority Holt mustered at the drop of a hat, but judging by the way his brothers ignored him, he still didn't quite have the knack.

"How do you suggest I stay away from Mia? She lives with me," Ned snarled.

"She's supposed to come live with me," Luke said. "That's why I brought Fila here in the first place."

Jake closed his eyes. Uh oh.

"You what?"

"I thought…" Now Luke looked to him for support but Jake refused to offer it. If his brother was stupid enough to explain this to Ned he deserved what he got.

"You thought what?" Ned said.

"I thought if Fila was staying with me, Mia would want to come stay with me too. Then they could be together."

"You thought you'd use a traumatized kidnap victim to lure another woman to your house?"

Luke sent a pleading look Jake's way. "It wasn't my idea, it was…"

"Shut your trap," Jake intervened quickly. "The way I see it, it isn't up to either of you where those girls choose to live. It's up to them. They're not here for your pleasure."

Both his brothers turned to face him. "That's rich, coming from you," Ned said slowly. "You used your house to lure Hannah in, then got her pregnant so she's stuck here."

Jake's jaw tightened in anger. "That's not how it went at all. And she's not pregnant, so quit saying that like it's a done deal. If you were any kind of gentleman you would have kept your mouth shut the other day. No one else would even know about what happened."

"If you were any kind of gentleman you wouldn't have forced me to take in Mia."

Luke's mouth dropped open. "Forced you? If he forced you to take in Mia, then give her to me, because I actually want her!"

"I ain't giving her to nobody. She's not mine to give."

"You got that right."

Jake pushed between them. "Simmer down. Dad's coming. He'll be here any second and he'd love to see the two of you like this. Nothing makes him happier than the both of you with your fists up."

That silenced them because they knew it was true. For all Holt's talk of family he seemed to get a charge out of seeing them fight.

"Ned, do you care for Mia?" Jake asked. Ned made a face and tried to walk away, but Jake grabbed his shoulder. “Answer the question.”

Finally Ned shook his head. “No.”

“Luke, what about you and Fila; something going on between you two?”

“No,” Luke said quickly. “I don’t understand her at all.”

“Well then, seems simple enough.” When the two of them still looked at him blankly, Jake threw his hands up. “Swap them!”

“But… what do we say to them?” Luke asked.

“Hell, I don’t know.” A light went on. “Actually I do. Luke, you just tell Mia your favorite color is pink.”

HANNAH WAS EYEING the clock and tapping her fingers on the reception counter by the time Bella finally returned from her latest house-hunting trip that afternoon. Four clients and their pets waited impatiently in the small waiting area, and she knew she’d be hard pressed to finish up at work, run to the Cruz ranch to pick up her mail and still meet Jake for dinner on time. He’d invited her to eat out at DelMonacos—said it was the least he could do to repay her for all the delicious meals she’d cooked. Bella had left the office for an hour to visit more housing possibilities, but that hour had stretched to two by the time she walked in the clinic door.

“I’m sorry,” Bella said, rushing in. “After we walked through the house, we ended up going to another one that just came on the market. Neither of them worked. Evan says that in either case we’d have to tear down the house and start from scratch.”

Hannah could see her disappointment. "Were they too old?"

"Too old, too small, the wiring wasn't up to code… it's bad enough we want a comfortable house, but the fact that Evan's going to run his business out of it…"

"You're going to run your business there, too."

"Yes, but we already knew we'd have to build the clinic and shelter. I thought we could just buy the house."

"We'd better get going." Hannah shot a glance toward the waiting room. "Don't forget I have to leave at five."

Bella made a face when she looked at her watch and saw it was already past four. "Shoot. I forgot all about that. I'm sorry, Hannah. You're not going to have a chance to run home and change."

"That's okay—I brought some clothes. I can change in the bathroom." She handed a chart to Bella. "Annette Hill and her puppy, Lucy. Lucy needs some shots."

"Well, that's easy enough. Hey, if you want, you can duck into the trailer in a half-hour or so and use my shower to freshen up. Evan's working at the coffee shop this afternoon."

"Thanks, but with all these people here…"

"Let me get through a couple of appointments, and then I'll hold down the fort. You've done it for me enough times!" Bella called Annette and ushered the gray-haired woman and her lively puppy into examining room one. Hannah glanced at the clock again and down at the canvas tote bag under her desk where she'd stashed a change of clothing this morning in case work ran late. She'd love to make use of that shower.

A half-hour later, she stood up and addressed the remaining clients. "Folks, I have to head out for a bit. I'm going to give each of you your chart. Please wait for Bella to call your name. I'll be back as soon as I can." Feeling like she was skipping class, she handed out the folders, grabbed her bag, darted out of the clinic and across the large yard to Bella's airstream trailer. She knocked on the door even though she knew Evan wasn't there. Prone to claustrophobia, the man spent most his days hunting for their new home and working at a coffee shop or Linda's diner. That was why Bella was so determined to get a new place; she knew sooner or later Evan was going to revolt over their current living conditions.

As she let herself in and approached the tiny shower, she thought over what Bella had said. They wanted a large property fairly close to town. It needed the right zoning for Bella's veterinary clinic and shelter, and the main house needed to be executive quality so Evan could host meetings with his clients and potential investors. Hannah was a little hazy on just what Evan did. She knew he'd inherited his billions, but he bought and sold patents and funded all sorts of research, too.

Her mind kept traveling to Carl Whitfield's mansion. Just up the road from the Cruz ranch, it sported a huge log mansion that was definitely executive quality, and acres and acres of prime Montana ranch land. Cab and Rose were keeping an eye on it over the winter, since

Carl had returned to California. Too bad it wasn't for sale.

Forty-five minutes later, she was ready for her date with Jake. She'd chosen her clothes carefully so no one could accuse her of making too much of the occasion. Tailored pants, a soft, silky blouse, and plain black flats made her feel businesslike, but pretty, too. With her hair freshly washed, it fell in gentle waves over her shoulders. She often saw Jake look at her hair and knew it was one of her better features.

She wished she didn't care what Jake thought of her, but of course she did. They had five more days before she would fulfill her bargain with Holt and earn Gladys a permanent home. Five more days before Jake asked her to marry him again. He seemed more than happy with their current state of affairs. He complimented her on her meals nightly and smiled every time he walked into his fresh, clean house, which always rubbed Hannah the wrong way. He didn't know Holt was forcing her to step up her cleaning routine, nor did he realize that by getting him to help out a bit she was subverting Holt's rule. The first time she folded the laundry and put away a stack of clean clothes in his dresser, Jake had been just about over the moon. He didn't realize all his gratitude felt like a slap in her face.

What would he do if she married him and went straight back to her normal state of affairs—frozen dinners, laundry done on the run at the last possible moment, a monthly cleaning frenzy just before friends came over? He'd probably have a heart attack and then ask for a divorce.

The thought made her frown. It was going to be hard to leave in a few days. Apart from the caveman era chore assignments, she liked being with Jake. She'd never dated such an intelligent, ambitious, not to mention sexy man. When they got to chatting about something he read in the newspaper or something she heard on the radio they were equally curious—and equally apt to run for a computer to research a follow-up question on the Internet.

She loved the way he worshipped her body, too. She'd never experienced anything like it—this easy sexuality, the multiple times they could coax each other to the edge of ecstasy. She trusted him in bed in a way she'd never trusted another man. She wished she could trust him the same way out of it.

An hour later she pulled up at the Cruz ranch and entered the Big House to fetch her mail. Ethan and Autumn's guests would arrive in a day or two and the place was spotless and decorated beautifully for the holidays. Time for her and Jake to think about putting up some decorations, she thought, then stopped. She wouldn't be at Jake's house at Christmas time.

Her sadness at the thought nearly bowled her over.

Where would she be for Christmas? In a hotel? Or some new, tiny rental apartment on the other side of town?

Pressing her lips together she made herself keep walking.

"Hey, stranger, how is it going?" Autumn asked

when she spotted Hannah. "Your mail is on the counter, by the way."

Hannah hesitated when she saw she'd stumbled in on a Cruz ranch meeting. Ethan, Autumn, Jamie, Claire, Rose, Cab, Morgan, and even Rob with his still-bandaged shoulder sat around the dining room table with a laptop and papers in between them. She knew the four couples met at least once a week to go over things. Since all of them owned part of the ranch, they all had a say in how it was run. Hannah had been here long enough to know their disagreements could get heated, but they generally worked them out.

"Um… fine." She headed for the counter.

"Fine?" Rob echoed. "Uh oh, what's my brother done wrong now?" A tall man, with the same blond hair and blue eyes as Jake, he watched her with a smile.

"Not so much your brother," she said, "Your father, on the other hand…"

"My father can drive anyone crazy," Rob said.

"What did he do?" Morgan asked.

Hannah sighed and slowed her pace. "It's just that he… has some strong ideas."

Rob roared with laughter and the others exchanged amused grins. "You don't say," he choked out when he got control of himself.

"Ideas about what?" Autumn's eyes were bright with curiosity.

"Let me guess," Rob said. "Marriage. He's got some scheme to marry you off to Jake and get an heir, right?"

Hannah's mouth dropped open. "How did you…?"

"He's my father," Rob said. "And Jake is my older brother. I'm sure he's in on it, too. You think Jake is going to wait around to marry now that I have? He's never let me win any race. I bet it's killing him I beat him to the altar and I'm the first to have a kid." He put a hand on Morgan's belly and smiled. "Wouldn't surprise me a bit if Jake knocked you up on your first date just to get back at me."

Hannah nearly tripped, but she caught herself with a hand on the edge of the kitchen counter. She picked up the pile of envelopes there and pretended to study them.

"Hannah?" Morgan asked tentatively when the silence Rob's statement brought stretched out too long. "You're being awfully quiet."

"I'm not interested in marriage right now." Hannah hoped her tone was even. "I want a career. I've decided to go back to school."

Another silence greeted this statement, until Autumn got up from her seat and came around the table to join her. "I wondered what was in that fat envelope from Montana State." She pulled it from the bottom of the pile in Hannah's hands and waved it.

"You're going to college? Good for you. Women need to nurture their passions." Claire stood up, too, her sleek black bob swinging. She came to join Hannah and Autumn.

"Well? Open it! See what it says." Autumn pushed the envelope into Hannah's hands.

"It's just some information." But she couldn't help herself. When she opened the envelope she found a course catalog and all sorts of information for incoming students. She had seven weeks to register and prepare. She held the paperwork up. "Time to pick out my classes!"

Autumn ran to fetch glasses and a bottle of juice so they could toast her success; there were too many pregnant women present to use anything stronger. Hannah was ushered to the table where everyone took turns looking through the contents of the packet.

"It says you'll get a separate envelope with financial aid information," Claire said. "You know there are lots of scholarships for adult learners. Do your research. You shouldn't pay a dime more than you have to."

"I will," Hannah assured her. She didn't say that Bella had already offered to help. She still felt shy about that fact. She was accustomed to paying her own way in life.

"What are you studying, anyway?" Jamie said. "You never told us."

All eyes turned her way and Hannah's confidence drained away. "I want to be a veterinarian. Like Bella," she said.

The room fell quiet and she saw Autumn exchange a glance with Claire.

"How many years of school is that?" Morgan said.

"Four and a half for me," Hannah said. She thought she heard the words they didn't say: How would she manage that? Was she smart enough to be a vet? Was she overreaching herself?

"What does Jake think about that?" Rob asked.

"He thinks I should forget it and just marry him. He

wants me to keep to the ranch."

"So he does want to marry you," Autumn said slowly. "Being a rancher's wife is great, but you can be more than one thing. I run a guest house. Claire's an interior decorator. Morgan's going to head up a winery. Why can't you do both?"

Rob spoke up. "Look, one thing about the Mathesons is once we get an idea into our heads it's hard to shift us. Hard, but not impossible. Stick to your guns. In the end Jake will come around."

"You really think so?"

Rob hesitated just long enough to undo all the confidence his words had instilled in her. "I hope so."

Chapter Thirteen

THE DRIVE TO DelMonaco's seemed to take longer than usual, but once she was seated in a booth across from Jake in the noisy restaurant, their menus in front of them, Hannah relaxed a little. As he scanned his menu she found herself watching his hands. The way he held the laminated rectangle of plastic. The way he fiddled with his silverware. He had square palms and long, blunt fingers. And she knew from experience exactly how they could make her feel.

A little shiver coursed through her.

"Are you cold?" Jake asked. She hadn't thought he was paying her any attention.

"No, I'm fine. What are you having?"

"Manicotti." He tossed the menu down. "You?"

"Chicken parmesan." She cast about for something else to say. "Thanks for asking me here. It's a nice change."

"Figured you could use a break." He bent forward. "The way you've worked so hard to keep the cabin straight and the way you've been cooking—it means the world to me."

She couldn't meet his eyes. "You know I won't be able to do that when I go to school, right?"

He set his menu down. "You're still planning to go to school?"

"Of course. Why wouldn't I?"

"Even if you're pregnant?" He lowered his voice, although the din in the restaurant would cover anything they said.

"Especially if I'm pregnant," she said. "Look. I know you want a traditional wife, but you're not getting one in me. Not by a long shot. You either have to give up that notion or you have to give me up."

Sarah-Jane Lafferty, a casual acquaintance of Hannah's, approached the table, notepad in hand. "You two ready to order?" she asked cheerfully. She looked from one to the other of them with frank interest and Hannah decided to move things along before she started asking any embarrassing questions. It was bad enough the Matheson clan seemed to think it their right to discuss her relationship with Jake. She didn't need Sarah-Jane gossiping about it to other patrons of the restaurant.

"Sure thing. I'll have the chicken parmesan, Jake wants the manicotti and we both want the side salad with house dressing." Jake's eyebrows shot up, but he didn't contradict her.

"How about to drink?"

"A beer for Jake, just water for me."

"Perfect. I'll bring you some garlic bread in a minute." Sarah-Jane headed back for the kitchen.

Jake's eyebrows were still raised. "I guess you're right; you're not going to be traditional." He took her hand and tugged on it gently. "You do know the man is supposed to order the meal, don't you?"

"Whatever."

"Look, it's all right with me if you want to be a vet. I've thought about this a lot. I would like it if you joined me in my work on the ranch, but it's not necessary. More than anything I want you to be happy. If being a vet is what makes you happy, then so be it. The only thing I want is for you to commit to me—to commit to us. Let's make a plan for our lives together—a plan we're both happy with."

She sat back, surprised by his change of heart, and for one moment she wanted to leap across the table and hug him. But then she took in all of his words and began to shake her head slowly. She appreciated what he was saying, but it didn't go far enough. "You don't get it. I already have a plan and there isn't anything I can change about it. First I'll go to Montana State, then I'll go to Colorado, and then I'll come back and join Bella's practice."

"Wait. Hold up there. Colorado? Why the hell would you go there?"

She almost pitied the handsome cowboy. This was exactly what she'd feared—he could make adjustments to his life-view, but only small ones. "Jake," she said, her voice softening. "You realize I can't do a veterinary degree at Montana State, right? I'm just doing my preliminary classes there. The nearest veterinary program is in Colorado. I'll be there for four years."

"FOUR YEARS?" Jake couldn't breathe, his chest had gone so tight. He leaned across the table. "You can't go away for four years."

"That's what it takes to be a vet."

He sat back, stunned. All his dreams went up in smoke. Hannah wasn't going to yoke up with him—two partners working side by side toward the same vision. She was so committed to her own dreams she'd leave him high and dry for four entire years. And what about their child?

"You can't leave if you're pregnant."

"Watch me."

"Are you serious?" He stared at her in disbelief. How could she sit there so calmly and tear his heart out of his chest? "That's my kid, too."

"If there is one." She looked exasperated. "I didn't ask to be pregnant—not right now. I've told you the truth since day one. I have plans. I know what I want from life."

"Guess it's not me." He fished in his pocket and pulled out a small velvet box. Thumped it on the table. "I asked you here to give you this. I wanted to make our engagement official." He opened it and held it out to her. The classic diamond ring inside it glittered in the low light of the restaurant.

Sarah-Jane, who'd just approached to place a basket of rolls on the table, veered quickly away.

"PUT THAT BACK in your pocket," Hannah hissed at him. "You're such a hypocrite. Two minutes ago you said you supported my desire to be a veterinarian, but the second you find out it will take some personal sacrifice you change your mind. At the same time you want me to commit to *you* and *your* life plan? I don't think so."

"I didn't know being a vet would mean you had to move away for four years. That's a pretty big deal," Jake protested.

"Exactly my point. We can't be together, Jake. We're totally incompatible."

"That's bullshit. We're compatible every night."

Hannah rolled her eyes. "Sex isn't everything."

"It's a hell of a lot, though." He took her hand again. "Every night you can't get enough of me and every day you're so angry you look like you want to spit. Why does it have to be like that?"

"Why?" Tears of frustration pricked her eyelids. Why did it have to be like that? Because of Holt. Because of the Mathesons' archaic beliefs. "Because none of this is real!"

"What?" Jake scowled. "What are you talking about?"

"This… situation." Hannah waved a hand. "You and me together. We didn't meet and date the normal way—your father forced us together!"

The color drained out of Jake's face. "What do you mean by that?"

Damn—if she blew her cover, she'd lose everything she'd worked for. Gladys would lose her home. But she couldn't stop now that she'd started. She was too angry with Holt. Too angry with herself.

"For one thing, I'm talking about the way your father has been forcing me to cook and clean like some household slave—that's not normal, Jake!"

"Wait... what?"

"He threatened to kill Gladys if I didn't do it. You think I like doing all the housework for you after a full day at the clinic? I have news for you. I hate cleaning. I hate shopping, and I hate, hate, hate laundry."

"My father threatened to—"

"To kill Gladys. To eat her, actually. Because that's the only way he could get me to do for you what your mother does for him—to be the kind of stay-at-home wife you want me to be."

"I just told you I'm okay with you having a career—"

"And that's only half of it." She talked right over him.

"What do you mean?" Jake looked wary.

"He used the same threat to make me sleep with you." She stood up. "There. I've said it. I'm done here. I'm done with all of this. You can tell your father to shove his threats. I'll move Gladys by the end of the week." She turned to go.

Jake gripped her wrist. "Sit down. Now."

The steel in his voice stopped her cold. She'd never seen Jake so angry. For the first time since she'd known him she felt a tendril of fear curl through her gut. His grip was so tight she couldn't budge. If she tried to pull away from him now, she'd make a scene in the crowded restaurant. As it was, several heads had turned their way.

Hannah sat.

"LET ME GET this straight." Jake felt disembodied from his own voice. Surely this couldn't be him in this restaurant, hearing these words from Hannah. He couldn't be the one shaking with anger as he thought about what Holt had done. "My father told you he'd kill Gladys and eat her if you didn't sleep with me?" He shouldn't have been surprised that Holt would play Hannah the same way he'd played him, but he was.

She nodded.

"Just like that. Straight out—no hinting?"

"He said it clear as day."

"He told you to sleep with me," Jake repeated, unable to believe it.

Hannah squirmed. "He said I had to spend fourteen nights with you. In the same bed. What we did there was up to us."

"And you did it. You went along with it." Jake ran his free hand through his hair. The other he kept locked around Hannah's wrist. "Did you hate every minute of it?" His voice was rough.

"Of course not! You don't understand—"

"You're damned right I don't understand. Was that really your only option? Prostitute yourself to save your animal? Really?"

His cruel words stung her and she blinked against the tears that filled her eyes. "Jake—"

He leaned across the table toward her. "You know, I

couldn't figure out why day after day you cleaned my house and cooked for me. It didn't make sense, because it so obviously bothered you. You felt those chores were beneath you but you did them anyway. I thought…" He scraped a hand over his face. "Well, you know what I thought and you set me straight. But I never—*never*—guessed that you would sleep with me because my father forced you to." His jaw tightened. "You don't give a damn about me, do you? That was my father's hand again. Forcing you to live with me. Forcing you to make my house a home. Forcing you to fuck—"

She slapped him. "Don't you dare. Don't you dare say one more word."

The restaurant went quiet, but Hannah only had eyes for him. She was just as furious as he was.

"It's true, isn't it?" The slap stung, but he didn't care.

"No, it's not. Holt pushed me into moving in with you, but I was interested long before that."

"Why should I believe you?"

"Because of how it felt when you fucked me."

SHE HAD PITCHED her voice low but she still heard a startled gasp from the nearby diners. She didn't care. They were finally getting to the heart of the matter, and she wanted to put all her cards on the table. Everything she had said was true; Holt had pushed them together in an unnatural way, but despite all of it she wanted Jake desperately.

Jake sat back. Watched her through eyes that were hard and cold. "I don't know what to say to you. I can't believe my father. I know he wants me to get married, but to do this…?"

"Believe me, I feel exactly like you do. His behavior is so far out of bounds it's unbelievable. I'd be the last one to defend him, but I think I know why he did it. Do you realize what a lonely life your father has had?" She hoped she could bridge the chasm that had opened up between them. She was losing him. Had lost him, maybe. He thought she'd only been with him because she'd been forced, and that wasn't true—it had never been true. A proud man like Jake wouldn't care about nuances, though. If he thought she'd lied to him, he'd turn his back on her.

He scowled. "Lonely? How do you figure that? He's got four kids."

"Now he does. But he was an only child growing up. Sounds to me like he might have had it hard. He wants to be surrounded by family. He wants you all to marry and have children. It's important to him."

"Important enough to threaten you?"

She shook her head, desperate to make him understand. "You know, looking back, I think your Dad was smart enough to know it wouldn't take much to nudge me into your arms… and your bed." Color crept up into her cheeks. "We're good together, but the problem is we're not right for each other. Or it's not the right time for us to be together. I don't know."

Jake straightened. Surveyed her, his fingers still tight around her wrist. She could tell he was thinking it all over. Weighing her words and the truth of them. "If you think we're good together, then we should be able to make this work." His grip tightened. "You should be able to marry me."

He wasn't getting it. "We want different things…"

"There's nothing we can't solve once we're married."

Hannah shook her head. "Really? You'll adapt to the time I need to spend away from you? You'll support my career? Because that's non-negotiable. I am going to veterinary school."

"I won't stop you from going to veterinary school," he said slowly. "I don't have anything against you going."

"Do you have anything for it?"

Jake narrowed his eyes. "What's that supposed to mean?"

"It means there's a hell of a big difference between not stopping me and actually helping me," she said. "If we're going to make a life together, I'll need your support. It's hard enough to do what I'm about to do without having someone close by who doesn't want me to do it."

"All right." She could tell he was trying to calm down. Around them, diners got back to their meals, although people were keeping an eye on them. "Why don't you tell me about it? Tell me why you want to be a vet so bad. What all that school is going to look like."

"You really want to know?" She was suspicious of his intentions.

"I really want to know."

"I want to be a vet because I love working with animals. I've told you all I do at the clinic, giving shots and stitching up wounds and all kinds of things. I'm good at it; I've got steady hands and a strong stomach. I could do so much more, I know it, and Chance Creek could use another vet. We're desperately short handed; you know that as well as I do."

"All this school. How will you pay for it?"

Hannah looked down. Jake tugged her hand.

"Answer the question."

"I talked to Bella about it the other day," she said. "And she made me an offer."

"What kind of offer?" His tone went hard.

"She offered to fund my schooling, since I got her on the show that made her a millionaire. Billionaire," she corrected herself. "I didn't want any money—I certainly didn't expect it. She won it fair and square, you know? But she wants to even things out a bit, so she's going to pay for it. All of it. I'll keep working part-time with her through the next semester and during the summers, too, just to keep my hand in the business, but I can pick when to take my classes and I'll have so much more time for studying. And when I head to Colorado, I won't have to work at all. That will make it so much easier!"

"For you," he said. She could tell he wasn't happy with the idea.

"So, I'm going, Jake. There's nothing to discuss. If you can't support me in this, we don't belong together."

For a long moment she thought he'd agree with her. His grip on her wrist was tightening until her hand began to feel numb. When she tugged against him, he sighed and let go. "I'll support you. It's not easy; the truth is I don't want to be apart from you for a single day, let alone four years. And I want to start my family now, not some time in the future. But if you'll marry me, I will support you. I'll be there however you want me to be. I promise."

She eyed him warily. "What's the catch?"

He leaned forward. "You have to marry me now. Before Christmas."

Hannah blinked at him. Was he serious? He looked serious. Her heart was beating hard in her chest. She had just gotten a glimpse of the man she'd spend the rest of her life with and he was as formidable as he'd been irresistible to her before.

Still, he had given in to her. In their struggle to reach a mutual path, she'd been so afraid she'd be the one to lose. It hadn't turned out that way, though. It would have with Cody.

Jake was different. Jake could meet her halfway.

"Okay," she said.

For a long moment Jake didn't respond. Then he sat up. "Okay? As in—yes?"

"Yes." Hannah nodded. A smiled tugged at the corner of her mouth. "Yes. I'll marry you."

"It's about time!" some wag from across the restaurant yelled. Scattered applause let them know everyone present had watched the course of the conversation. Jake grinned, and the hard man—the one with eyes like ice—slipped away. Hannah was happy to see the Jake she knew. He opened the ring box again, pulled out the ring, slid it onto Hannah's finger, and the place erupted in cheers.

"Phew," Sarah-Jane said, finally delivering the dinner rolls safely to their table. "I thought that wasn't going to work out there for a minute."

"You and me both," Jake said. But he kept his gaze on Hannah and his fingers caressed hers.

Married. She was going to get married to Jake Matheson. Gladys would have a home. He would support her career. She was getting everything she ever hoped for.

Jake lifted her hand to his lips and kissed it. "Can't wait for our wedding night," he drawled and she had to laugh, wondering how on earth it could top the nights they'd already had. She felt giddy with relief—light-headed—but through it all remained a small thread of doubt.

Would Jake's change of heart last?

Chapter Fourteen

THEY ENDED UP getting their food to go, and by the time Jake opened the cabin door he couldn't wait to get Hannah into bed to celebrate their engagement in the best way possible. He took her hand and led her to the stairs. She followed willingly enough. He still couldn't believe she'd said yes. Couldn't believe the concessions he was willing to make to get her to do it. The thought of her traveling to Colorado for four consecutive years left him cold with dread, but he decided not to worry about that until the time came for her to go. That was three-quarters of a year away and by then all kinds of things could change.

By then they could have a child.

He knew that when Hannah confessed the deal she'd made with Holt, he should have done the same. He should have told her everything. The truth was he'd known he was seconds away from losing her—losing everything he wanted. When he'd tried to tell her, the words hadn't come. What difference did it make anyhow? He wasn't getting married because his father wanted him to. Not anymore. He would stand up in church and make his vows today if he could, even if his deal with his father had never happened.

Upstairs, he shut the guest bedroom door behind them and led her to the bed. But instead of pushing her down on top of it, he paused beside it and took her into his arms. He began with a simple kiss. Light and feathery at first, he quickly deepened it, showing her his need. She answered him hungrily and he wondered if she wanted it to be a night to remember, too. He'd do his best to make it so.

He undressed her as they kissed, fumbling with his fingers at her shirt buttons and at the clasp of her bra. She helped him without pulling back, entering into his unspoken game to get naked without breaking contact. Once their clothes were gone, he moved his lips to her chin, her neck and down to her breasts. He laved first one nipple then the other, spending time worshipping both before moving lower still.

Hannah gasped as he worked his way down to her navel, beneath it and farther down still. When he parted her folds and kissed her in a more intimate way, her breath quickened and she made a little sound. Jake backed her up until she leaned against the desk, and spread her legs to get better access to her. His ministrations soon had her moving against his mouth and he moaned against her, turned on by the way she responded to him.

Some minutes later, he rose up and she cried out in disappointment, but when he wrapped his arms around her and lifted her onto the desk she slid her arms around him in turn and drew him close.

He sheathed himself in a condom quickly, lifted her legs to open her wide and settled himself against her core. She was wet and hot and ready to take him, so he didn't hesitate. Instead, he pushed forward, burying himself in her. Hannah arched back, her hands fumbling for purchase on the top of the desk. Gripping its edges she pushed back toward him, sinking him deeper still.

Jake bit his lip, fighting for control. This position allowed such deep access into her, spread her so wide for him it was hard to hold back. He pulled out and pressed in, and nearly came undone.

Figuring he'd better get to it or lose himself altogether, he started to rock his hips, moving inside her. Hannah moved with him, riding him up and down with little cries of desire that urged him on. He increased his pace, holding nothing back until she bounced in his arms, her breasts bouncing, too. They mesmerized him.

Jake gripped her hips and pulled her toward him as he thrust against her. He couldn't stop himself now if wanted to, and he didn't want to. Hannah clutched the desk, arched her back and met him stroke for stroke. He could tell from her cries she was close… close…

With a final moan she threw back her head and shuddered against him, her release overtaking her. Jake went over the edge with her, his thrusts slow and deep. When they were done, he lifted her up, carried her to the bed and climbed on with her, still joined together. Lying side by side, Jake stroked her hair gently. "I'm glad you didn't give up on me, Hannah."

"Me, too." She snuggled in close.

"Don't think we're done here, either," he whispered into her ear. "Because we're just getting started."

She kissed him on the chin. "I'm counting on that."

WHEN HANNAH WOKE up the next morning, she found Jake propped up on one elbow, watching her.

"Morning," she said softly, all too aware of everything they'd gotten up to the night before. She sat up, and a delicious ache between her legs reminded her all too well of every position they'd tried out during the night. She'd never been in a relationship like this, where nothing was off the table. When Jake suggested something—usually with his body, not his words—her body couldn't wait to meet him halfway. She swung her legs over the side of the bed and stood up, knowing she was giving Jake an eyeful. Hoping she was. "Jake…"

"Do you have to get up already?"

"Don't you?"

"We have time for one more round. A quickie. Please?"

How could she resist a handsome man when he begged? A handsome, naked man who was climbing off the bed to come after her and take her in his arms? When he pulled her close for a kiss she couldn't resist kissing him back. When they parted she looked over his shoulder at the diamond winking on her finger. Engaged. She was engaged to Jake.

"Please?" He nuzzled her neck.

"Okay. One more round," she said against her better judgment. Soon Holt would turn up for their daily showdown. She didn't want Jake here to see that, so she'd have to make this quick.

But they weren't quick and by the time they were showered and dressed, Holt was overdue. Hannah dreaded Jake running into his father now that he knew what Holt had done. That confrontation was bound to get out of hand.

She followed Jake downstairs. "You better get going." She glanced toward the door nervously.

"I'm going." But he didn't go. He popped a couple of pieces of bread in the toaster and found a plate.

"But if you don't hurry you'll—" She bit off the end of her sentence.

"I'll what?" When she didn't answer, Jake came to stand close to her. He tipped her chin up, traced his thumb over her lips, and a shiver of desire rippled through her from stem to stern. "I'll what, sweetheart?" He dipped his head to kiss her and Hannah rose on her tip-toes to meet him. She figured sooner or later Jake's kisses would become old hat, but for now each one was special, a new exploration of his mouth, of him.

"Well, well. This is sweet." Holt opened the door without preamble.

Jake jerked back in surprise. "Dad? What are you doing here?"

"Running late?" Holt made a show of looking at his watch.

"Just seeing my girl off to work." Jake's voice had a

hard edge. He dropped a kiss on Hannah's forehead and steered her toward the door. Maybe he didn't want her present for their showdown, either. Hannah went to collect her purse and coat.

"Hold up there," Holt said when she tried to slip past him toward the door. "Don't you have something to tell me before you go?"

That ought to do it, she thought.

She was right.

Jake stepped before him, his hands on his hips. "I'll do the talking for her, Dad. Yes, we slept together last night. Made love three or four times, didn't we, Hannah?"

Hannah closed her eyes. Was she really supposed to answer that?

"I know all about your threats and the way you forced Hannah to be with me. You ought to be ashamed of yourself," Jake went on.

"You ought to be ashamed of yourself for the way you've dragged your feet this long instead of settling down. Not my fault you needed some prodding."

"It is definitely your fault," Jake said. "Maybe the reason I've dragged my feet so long is I'm afraid to bring a wife to live near my pain in the ass father!"

"You saying you want to leave? Because if you do there's more where you come from. Ned would be happy to manage the place."

"Well, maybe he should!" Jake exploded. "Maybe I'm sick and tired of you pushing me around! Maybe it's time for you to back the hell off!"

Hannah slipped between them and bolted out the door.

JAKE WATCHED HER go. So did his father.

"Maybe you better think hard about what you really want," Holt said when she was gone. "I'm not interested in threats or tantrums. You know the deadline. Get married or get out."

He strode from the house and slammed the door behind him. Jake swore and pulled on his outer gear. No matter how angry he was, there were still horses and cattle to feed and jobs to attend to and if he stuck around inside these four walls he'd explode. He found Ned in the barn some minutes later mucking out the horses' stalls. He wasn't Jake's first choice of people to talk to—not by a long shot—but he had to talk to someone, and Ned would have to do.

"You won't believe what Dad did."

"I bet I will." Ned flung a forkful of muck into a wheelbarrow.

Jake hesitated. Ned was right—they all knew Holt was capable of just about anything. "He forced Hannah to sleep with me."

Ned chuckled. "Did he now?"

"He did! The old man is a lunatic."

Ned stopped shoveling. "Know what I've seen every day this week?"

"What?"

"You and Hannah cuddling and kissing every minute you think you're alone."

Jake frowned. "You've been spying on us?"

"I didn't have to spy. You're out on your front porch smooching every damn morning."

"Well, still…"

"Still what? Maybe Dad pressured her into something, but it ain't sleeping with you."

Jake blew out a breath. "It still isn't right; the way he interferes with us."

"Kind of like the way you interfered with me? Forcing me to rent a room to Mia?"

Ned had him again. Damn, this wasn't going the way he wanted it to. "That's different."

"Really? How?" Ned leaned on the end of the pitchfork and waited for an answer.

"All right, maybe it isn't different. But what the hell am I supposed to do now?"

"About what?"

"About everything! Take Hannah, for instance. She's going to marry me and then leave me high and dry for four years." At Ned's puzzled expression Jake gave him a rundown of the situation. "So I get a wife and I get to stay in control of the ranch, but I end up alone for the next four years. What's the good of that?"

"Seriously? You're asking me? If you keep control of the ranch, I get shafted again."

"You've always known that's the way it would be." Jake didn't need one of Ned's sulks right now, even though his brother was right. Ned couldn't help being born second any more than Jake could help being first. It was pure luck. Good luck for him, bad for Ned.

Wouldn't he be as sour as Ned was if the tables were turned?

"Fine. You're right—I always have known I'd get the shaft in this family. So let's talk about you." Ned's voice was thick with sarcasm. "You know what your problem is? You've got to turn around your thinking. Stop looking at Hannah's four-year absence as an obstacle."

"How else can I look at it?"

"As an opportunity."

Jake found his temper fraying. "What kind of opportunity could it possibly be?" For once couldn't someone just answer his questions directly? Did everyone in his family have to play games?

"It's an opportunity for me to run the ranch if you go with her." Ned's quick grin didn't reach his eyes.

"Perfect. That's just perfect. Thanks for the help." Jake knew he should never have brought this subject up with Ned. It wasn't fair of him to complain in front of him, anyway.

"If staying here is your goal, I guess you're right; you're in a tough place." Ned resumed his work.

Jake's hands itched to grab his brother and shake him. Of course that was his goal. It had always been his goal. Instead, he grabbed the pitchfork from Ned, overcome with an anger that demanded immediate action. "Go on. Get out of here. I need to think."

"Sure thing." Ned disappeared swiftly.

Jake didn't notice the wooden handle of the pitchfork in his hands, or the smell of the old hay and horse dung he scooped out of the stalls. When he ran the wheelbarrow outside and dumped the manure to age in a pile, he didn't notice the cold air biting his cheeks. *If that was his goal. He could see Hannah going to Colorado as an opportunity.* Just like Ned had said—an opportunity for his brother to win.

Still, Ned's words stuck with him while he worked. Could he choose another goal? One served by moving to Colorado with Hannah?

Jake trudged forward with his wheelbarrow load. What the hell would that be?

Chapter Fifteen

ALL DAY THE glittery diamond on her ring caught Hannah's attention and each time it did, her stomach gave a little twist of hope and anticipation.

Mixed with fear.

What had happened between Holt and Jake after she left? Had they come to blows? Would Jake still want to marry her?

It was too good to be true, the way Jake had capitulated to her demands. Could he make good on those promises?

What if he didn't?

Jake finally texted her at noon to let her know he'd handled Holt and she didn't have to worry about him anymore. He sent her a picture of Gladys, too, which made her smile. Maybe Jake did understand what was important to her. Maybe this would all work out.

Maybe.

By the time she made it home she was all pins and needles. She couldn't wait to be with Jake again. Couldn't wait to talk to him more about their plans for the future.

Couldn't wait for a repeat of their previous night, either.

She knew the talking should come first. They needed to make sure they were really on the same page as far as plans went, but all thoughts of that went out the window when she walked in the door and found the table lit with candles. She'd planned an easy dinner, but Jake was there before her. She recognized the logo of a local Chinese restaurant on a bag on the counter. He'd placed the food in serving bowls and set the table for two.

"Wash up and have a seat." He met her at the door with a soul-searing kiss. Tingles of desire swept through her, but she did as she was told and met him at the table a few minutes later. They took their time eating, but kept their conversation light. Jake held her hand through most of the meal and she could barely taste her food when his blue-eyed gaze held hers. She knew the night ahead of them would be one to remember. How would they make love tonight? Where would they make love?

The possibilities were endless.

After they'd cleaned up the meal, Jake led her to the couch and pulled her down onto his lap. She met his kisses eagerly, relishing the slow pace he was setting tonight. For once there was no question about the outcome of their relationship. They would be married. They would spend their lives together.

Starting with tonight.

JAKE WAS ON fire. He hadn't thought he could want Hannah more than he already did, but tonight was different. Tonight he knew without a doubt he'd be sleeping with her, so he could anticipate it all day. After working outside all morning, he'd come to a single conclusion; there was no way around the years that Hannah would be gone. He'd have to suck it up like a man and endure them until they were over. Then he'd have Hannah beside him for good.

Once that was settled, he'd let his thoughts wander to happier subjects. He'd imagined countless ways they could be together as he accomplished his chores. Her body was his playground and he loved every curve of it. He meant to play hard tonight. All night. If Hannah's ardor was any indication, so did she.

As her fingers slipped to the buttons of his shirt Jake knew there were matters they should talk about, but he couldn't remember what they were. Soon she had tugged the shirt off of his shoulders and smoothed her hands over his chest.

"You are so… yummy," she said, trailing kisses over his chin, down his neck and across his shoulder. Jake decided two could play this game and found the hem of her shirt, tugging it up over her head. As she straddled his lap, her bra displayed her breasts to perfection and he bent forward to trace some kisses of his own down her creamy skin to the cleft between them. Hannah moaned and thrust them forward. Jake's groin jumped.

He swept his hands up to cup them, relishing the lacy fabric of her bra under his fingers. He kneaded them until he felt the points of her nipples pushing hard against the layer of cloth.

Hannah rocked her hips against him, grinding against

his hardness. There were too many layers between them still. Jake wanted them gone. He slipped his fingers under the band of the bra and snapped it with one jerk. When Hannah gasped, he cupped both breasts and sucked first one nipple then the other into his mouth. Laving them almost roughly with his tongue, he was rewarded when Hannah arched back and held onto him for dear life. He wanted to be inside her, now. Her bra was gone, but both their pants remained.

Jake surged to his feet with Hannah still wrapped around him. Reaching under her ass—pausing only to give it a good, two handed squeeze—he unbuckled his belt, unzipped his fly and dropped his jeans to the ground, kicking them away. He supported Hannah while she undid hers, then turned around, dumped her unceremoniously on the couch and pulled them off by their cuffs.

Hannah laughed, but didn't hesitate to shimmy her panties off and throw them across the living room. Bared to his view, she lay back and stretched. As her breasts lifted, Jake heard an animal sound come from deep within his throat but he was already reaching for her, pulling her back onto his lap as he sat down on the couch once more.

"Like this?" Hannah got up and straddled him again. When she pressed up against him she was hot and ready.

"Exactly like this." He pulled her close and wrapped his arms around her. He wanted to feel every inch of her against him. Her breasts against his chest set him on fire, the peaks of her nipples tantalizing. He slid his fingers under her ass and lifted her into place.

As she slid onto him, slick with need, he groaned, trying not to spill inside her like some untried schoolboy. She was so hot, so sexy. So everything that he'd ever wanted. He flexed into her and pulled back, loving the position but frustrated at not having more control. Hannah pushed up with her thighs then sank back onto him and he thought he'd go over the edge again. It took all his control to hold back as Hannah found her pace, lifting and falling, lifting and falling, her tempo increasing as her body responded to him. She ground down against him and then lifted again, ground down as if hungry for every inch of his hardness.

As she moved faster, harder, Jake gripped her with his hands, encouraged her, loved what she was doing. Her movements bounced her breasts against him, increasing his pleasure, his desire. No longer in control, he thrust into her, going deeper, using his hands to press her down on top of him.

They reached their peak together, both calling out. Hannah arched back, her silky hair feathering over his hands, which still gripped her ass. Jake bucked against her so hard he thought he'd hurt her, but her cries of pleasure didn't change to pain. He couldn't help himself anyway; his need for release was so great—so overpowering.

When they collapsed together they were both winded. Hannah giggled against his shoulder. "Do you think we'll ever get tired of doing this?"

He shifted to lay her down on the couch and cover

her with his body. "Why don't we find out?"

HANNAH SIGHED AS Jake began to nibble her earlobe and trace lazy kisses down her neck. She felt as languorous as a kitten in the warm cabin. Jake had laid a fire in the fireplace before she came home and it added to the ambience. She could stay here forever with Jake, making love and just being together.

As his hand slid up to circle her breast she wondered for a moment whether she could keep up the pace. Surely he couldn't be ready for another round so fast, but… yes, she thought maybe he was. Her own body responded to that idea with more desire than she expected. Normally she needed some recovery time, too, but now a pulse of want beat between her legs and she was warm and wet…

Hannah's eyes flew open. She sat straight up, pushing Jake aside. "Damn it!"

"What?"

"You didn't use protection! You…" A wash of cold swept over her, perking her nipples, but she didn't care about that. "Damn it, Jake! I trusted you!"

He froze in his position on the couch, only his gaze shifting from side to side as if he was replaying the last fifteen minutes in his mind. "Shit."

"Yeah—shit!"

"I forgot. You didn't say anything!" From his expression he was just as shocked as she was. What was it about Jake that made her lose her mind? What made her trust him so much when he obviously wasn't trustworthy?

She crawled off the couch, nearly losing her balance before she untangled herself from him. Standing up, she put her hands on her hips. "We've used it every single time. You thought something changed?"

"I didn't… think." Jake stood, too. "You didn't either, I guess." He tried to draw her into an embrace. "What does it matter? You already thought you could be pregnant. We're engaged now. Whatever happens, we'll be together."

She pushed him away. "No, we won't. I can't even trust you to keep me from getting pregnant when you know I don't want to be. You only care about yourself—what you want! You'd be happy if I couldn't go to school. You probably planned this!" She raked her hair back from her face with both hands. "You did, didn't you?"

"Of course not!" Jake said but she had already spun away. She headed for the stairs at a furious clip. "Where are you going?" he called after her.

"To sleep." She spun around halfway up the steps. "And I don't want company!"

Chapter Sixteen

WHEN JAKE WOKE the following morning Hannah had already gone. He'd spent the night in his own room, his bed strange and uncomfortable after all the nights he'd spent in Hannah's. He'd wracked his brain for something to say or do to fix the situation. He must have finally fallen asleep close to dawn. Now his head hurt, his mouth was dry and his eyes felt like they were on fire.

He stumbled through a hot shower, dressed and descended to the kitchen to find a pile of paperwork on the table pertaining to Hannah's college admittance. She must have woken up early, eager to plan for a future that didn't include him. She'd made notes on a piece of paper of all the courses she wished to take. According to the documents, she could go online to sign up for them.

Jake sat down heavily and read through all of the information, paging through the glossy pages that touted all that Montana State had to offer. He recalled doing the same thing back in high school in his guidance counselor's office. He knew he'd never go to school—Holt would never have countenanced it—but the brochures had fascinated him.

Mr. Helmsly, the counselor, couldn't understand why he didn't apply. He was a city transplant and didn't understand rural thinking yet. Jake had known what his occupation would be from the moment he was born. A rancher, just like his daddy. You learned ranching on a ranch, not behind a desk.

He understood perfectly why Hannah would want to go, however. He sure had wanted to.

Jake picked up a thicker booklet that listed all the college's majors. He traced a finger down the list, and stopped at one that caught his eye. *Natural Resources and Rangeland Ecology*. He read through the course offerings. *Natural Resources Conservation. Montana Range Plants lab. Livestock in Sustainable Systems.*

What would it be like to meet with other ranchers interested in taking the business to a whole new level? What would it be like to have the latest information at his fingertips—to know what sustainability meant, not just guess at it? No one else on the Double-Bar-K even seemed to be interested. Evan Mortimer was, but in a theoretical way, not as someone who'd grown up on a ranch.

Jake flipped through the rest of the information, found a website URL and brought his laptop down to the table. An hour later when Ned poked his head in to see why the hell he wasn't attending to his chores, Jake was almost done with his application. With their rolling admissions, he'd find out in a day or two if he'd get in.

Bursting with the secret, he joined his brothers outside preparing to ride out to check the herd.

"What's gotten into you today?" Ned asked suspiciously.

"Nothing." The truth was Jake had no idea what had gotten into him. He couldn't leave the ranch and attend college.

So why had he just sent in an online application to Montana State?

"HASN'T ANYONE EVER told you about birth control?" Claire said. Hannah, Claire, Autumn, Morgan, Rose and Bella had all gathered for a late afternoon emergency meeting at the pet clinic. Bella had already ushered the last client of the day out the front door and now the women sat on the plastic waiting room seats and discussed Hannah's predicament. Hannah had decided that her need for support outweighed the humiliation of admitting she screwed up her protection not once, but twice in a two-week span.

"Of course. I told you; the condom broke the first time. That's not anyone's fault. And last night—we just got carried away."

"You don't think Jake did it on purpose, do you?" Rose asked.

"I don't think so," Hannah said slowly. She had at first, but now that she'd cooled down, she doubted that was true. She was the one who'd straddled him. She was the one who set the pace. She'd forgotten all about the condom, too. The problem was that she was used to being on the Pill. This condom stuff was new to her. That was no excuse for her negligence though, or for Jake's.

"For someone who really wants to go to college you sure seem determined to get stuck right here," Claire said.

"Claire!" Morgan said. "That's not helpful."

Tears spilled from Hannah's eyes. "But she's right. What am I doing moving in with Jake, sleeping with him, becoming engaged to him, having sex with him—unprotected sex—if I really mean to leave?"

"Are you having second thoughts about becoming a vet?" Bella asked gently.

"No! Not at all!"

"Are you… scared?" Rose ventured.

Hannah's tears fell more thickly and she swiped at them brusquely with her sleeve. She was scared, but why? She knew she could handle the academics—she'd always been terrific at school. She knew she could handle the messier side of animal care, too. She helped out all the time in the clinic and shelter. Blood didn't faze her. She wasn't afraid of diseases or death. She had a steady hand and a steady personality.

Except when it came to Jake.

"I think we have our answer," Claire said caustically. "What on earth are you afraid of?"

"Losing Jake," Autumn said. It wasn't a question, but Hannah nodded. She mopped her eyes with the handkerchief Autumn passed her and raised her head.

"He doesn't want to wait to get married or start a

family. He's already thirty-three."

"Can't you do both?" Morgan asked.

"The problem is that she'll need to go somewhere like Colorado for vet school," Bella told her. "There aren't any local programs for that."

Hannah looked from one of them to the next. "So what do I do? If I forget about school I'll resent Jake, but if I go I might lose him."

"Are those really the only two options?" Claire asked.

"I don't know."

"You should copy us. We're making all of our plans work by helping each other," Morgan said, indicating Claire, Autumn and Rose. "By living so closely together and making the ranch a joint venture, we can pitch in when it's needed. Since Rob is still injured, Cab's been filling in for him. When we start having our babies, all the men will have to pick up the slack, but since we're due at different times, we'll be able to help each other, too. You don't have to go it alone if you don't want to. Jake's parents and brothers all live right there. Why can't you talk to them and see if you can work something out?"

"But how do you work out me being away from home for four years?" Hannah said. She didn't bring up the fact that she wasn't comfortable asking Jake's family for help—not after the way they'd treated her so far. And she couldn't ask her parents, either. They were barely keeping themselves afloat.

That seemed to stump everyone. "I'm not saying it

will be easy," Morgan said. "But it is possible. Why not start from there?"

JAKE WAS CURRY-COMBING Chester when Rob found him in the stables. The smooth motion of running the comb through the gelding's hair soothed him, as did the presence of the patient beast. He'd had Chester for years now and while he knew it was sentimental, he always felt the horse knew when he was particularly troubled and did his best to be extra patient and helpful that day.

"Hannah seems to be in a state today," Rob said.

"You've seen her?" Jake looked over his shoulder.

"No—but Morgan and the rest of the women have all gone to Bella's clinic for a powwow."

"Huh." He didn't like the sound of that one bit. He went back to stroking Chester with the brush but now his movements felt choppy, out of whack. "You came here to tell me that?"

"I don't want to see you screw up a good thing."

"How do you figure I'm doing that?"

"You just started seeing Hannah. Now the two of you are engaged? Don't you think you're moving a little fast?"

"Ain't that the pot calling the kettle black?" Jake said.

Rob had the grace to look away. He and Morgan had a whirlwind courtship. "Yeah, well. I had something to offer Morgan. The land she needed for her winery. And even if I did propose before we dated much, I poured on the romance after that, believe me. From what I hear you've got Hannah cooking your meals and cleaning your house like she's some kind of maid."

"It isn't quite like that." Should he tell Rob what their father had done?

"Really? Have you done anything romantic for her?"

Jake thought hard. "I bought her dinner last night. I bought her a ring, too."

"You think that's enough?"

Jake's temper flared. "I reckon I can court a woman without your help."

"Oh, yeah? Then why does your fiancée have her friends rallied round her like Custer's last stand?"

Jake couldn't quite find an answer to that. "Fine. Romance. More of it."

"You know she wants to go veterinary school?" Rob asked.

"Of course. I told her she could." Jake kept on working. Rob caught hold of his arm.

"Take that tone about it and you'll lose her. The most romantic thing you could do is support her."

"I'm not taking a tone." Jake tried to pull free. "I am trying to support her. In fact…"

"Look, cut the crap. Morgan texted me what the real problem is. You keep trying to get Hannah pregnant. You think that's going to solve your problems? Is that your grand plan?" Suddenly Rob was in his face, furious. "If you really want to marry that girl, if you're really in love with her, how about you stop thinking about what she can do for you and start thinking about what you can do for her."

"I'm not trying to get her pregnant." Jake shoved

him away. He wasn't. Really. After all, he'd just sent an application in to Montana State. He had no idea why—it wasn't like he'd be able to go, but at least he'd sent it in. That ought to count for something.

"But you screw up twice in two weeks? That sounds a whole lot like trying to me. Get behind your woman's dreams and help make them come true; that's what a real man would do."

Jake dropped his arms, suddenly tired of the whole conversation. "Make her dreams come true? When they're going to take her away from me? Away from this place?"

"Are you really that short-sighted? Jake, she's going to be a vet. You're a rancher. You ranch *animals*." Rob emphasized the last word. "She'll doctor up animals when she's done with school. What's the problem?"

"I'll tell you what the problem is." Jake advanced on him. "Four years of school in Colorado, that's the problem. By the time she's done I'll be an old man. What if she doesn't want me anymore? What if she meets someone else while she's out there? Four years is a hell of a long time to be apart."

"So don't be apart. Go with her."

"And leave the ranch? Lose my place? Because once Ned gets a hold of it, he won't let go."

"You know how this is going to turn out? I think I do. You'll alienate Hannah, drive her into another man's arms, split up and end up stuck here for the rest of your life hating this ranch that you think you love so much. All because you're too stubborn to see what's in front of your face."

"What? What's in front of my face?" The horses in the stalls around them moved nervously. Jake knew they should take this outside but they were too far gone in the argument to move.

"Opportunities. You've got one chance here to get the woman you love and the life you want."

Jake shook his head. "No—I've got one chance to choose between the woman I love and the life I want."

"God, you are blind. There's always another way, Jake. Always." Rob stomped out of the barn. Jake threw the curry comb down and kicked it across the floor.

Damn Rob and damn everyone else, too, with their possibilities. He could have the ranch or he could have Hannah. That was the choice before him. It was black and white, crisp and clear, as simple as…

Another possibility struck him, so bold it nearly blinded him. He stood stock-still, afraid if he moved the idea would vanish.

Could it work? Should he even try?

He pulled out his cell phone.

Chapter Seventeen

WHEN HANNAH WALKED into the cabin an hour later, Jake was waiting for her in the kitchen. He was bent over the toaster lifting two frozen waffles out. Breakfast sausages sizzled on the stove. A jar of applesauce sat in the middle of the table which he'd set for two. It wasn't as elegant as the take out dinner he'd arranged for them the night before, but the fact he'd done the cooking himself brought tears to her eyes.

She hated not trusting Jake. Hated that she could think for a minute he might botch their birth control in order to make her pregnant and keep her here. She knew he loved her. Knew, too, that he wanted to spend the rest of their lives together, but without solid trust, how could they make anything work?

"Dinner's ready," Jake said jauntily, but he wouldn't meet her gaze.

She took off her coat and dropped her purse on the couch. "I think we really need to talk."

"I think so, too." Jake pointed to a stack of papers by each plate. "I printed us out some lists."

"Lists?"

"Wash up first. Then I'll tell you what it's all about."

Hannah made her way to the bathroom wondering if Jake had found yet another way to distract her from her purpose. When she came back, the plates were loaded with food. Her stomach grumbled but she pursed her lips, ready to stick to her guns.

"Sounds like someone's hungry."

"I skipped lunch." She took her seat. He touched her hand on his way around the table and she bit her lip. She wouldn't let him sweet talk her again, but if she was honest with herself, she craved his closeness. All the talk this afternoon about heading out to Colorado and leaving Jake behind had made her sad. What she had with him was special; she didn't want to lose it.

"What's the paperwork about?"

"Chores," Jake said. "I listed every one I could think of around here. We both work full time, so it makes sense that we should divide them between us."

"Really?" Hannah blinked, surprised. "I didn't think you felt that way."

"It's not the way my folks do it. But it's been pointed out to me that there's more than one way to get things done. Why don't we start by marking the ones we don't mind doing. Then we'll compare lists and divide up what's left. We can shift things around until it's fair."

Hannah wasn't sure why tears pricked her eyes again. She'd cried plenty at the clinic and she hadn't thought she had any tears left. Blinking them back determinedly, she ran down the list and checked the chores that bothered her least. Vacuuming. Changing the sheets. Cooking. She loathed grocery shopping so she left that one blank. The same with scrubbing the toilets. But there were many things on the list that she really didn't mind doing—not if Jake was pitching in, too.

"Want some wine?" She hadn't notice him get up and grab the bottle.

"Better not," she said.

"Oh. Right."

"This looks good." She indicated the meal before them. She stabbed a forkful of sausage and brought it to her mouth.

He grinned. "Breakfast for dinner is my favorite meal. Mom always made it when Dad was out of town, which wasn't often. That made it even more special."

Hannah pictured the four blond Matheson boys around the table with their mother and smiled, misting over again. What were they like when they were little? Sweet? Mischievous? She'd never heard one of them bad-talk Lisa. She must have been one hell of a mother. Must still be.

"You all right?" Jake said.

"Yeah. I'm emotional today," Hannah said. "I was thinking about what you looked like when you were little."

He cast her a curious glance. "I've got a picture. Want to see it?"

Hannah nodded. Jake was only gone a minute. He pounded up the stairs to his bedroom then back down again a few moments later and handed her a photograph in a silver frame. The Matheson family. It was a professional photograph and they were grouped together in a typical arrangement. Holt and Lisa in the center, the boys around them. Jake looked to be six or seven, his hair several shades fairer than it was now. Ned and Luke were slightly shorter than him and Rob was only about four, a tow-headed boy with his finger in his mouth.

"You all are adorable," she said. "Your parents must have been so proud." And indeed, they did look proud—and happy. Holt stood ramrod straight but he was smiling and his arm was around Lisa. His other hand rested on Jake's shoulder. She imagined Jake felt the weight of Holt's expectations every day of his life.

"Don't be fooled," Jake drawled. "If I recall correctly, Ned and Luke had a fistfight just moments before this was taken."

"Still, you look sweet."

He took the photograph back. "Family is everything, you know."

"I guess." She sounded dubious, even to herself. She cared for her parents and they cared for her, but they'd been wrapped up in their own troubles for so many years she didn't spend much time with them. Maybe she should change that.

When they finished eating, they swapped their lists and haggled over the remainder of the chores. To her surprise, Jake didn't balk at all at taking on the grocery shopping as long as she planned her lists ahead of time. "I'm not running back to the store because you forgot milk." And she acquiesced to mopping the floors. "But you better start taking your shoes off when you come in the house."

They decided to take turns with the toilets, and the rest of the chores sorted out easily. Jake hung the lists on the refrigerator door and decreed that the penalty for non-compliance was a kiss.

"None of the chores will get done," Hannah protested.

Jake thought again. "Sex?"

"Whoever doesn't do their chores gets a chore assigned to them by the other one," Hannah countered.

"That's not half as fun."

"So now we know how we'll get through the next semester." Hannah became serious. "What about when I go to Colorado?"

"Don't you worry about Colorado. We'll figure that out when we get to it."

LONG AFTER HANNAH fell asleep that night, Jake lay awake. These past few days had been the best of his life. He woke to a beautiful, naked woman in his bed, talked and cuddled with her, ate a quick breakfast and left to get to his work, then came back after ten to twelve hours to find a delicious dinner on the table and a fiancée who was even more delicious when they climbed back into the sack.

He could tell Hannah appreciated the way he'd set up a system to split the chores, and he was thankful he'd thought to do it before his father's harebrained plan to turn her into a clone of his mother had done too much damage. In fact, he was damn lucky she'd stuck around this long after the way Holt and Ned had treated her. He meant to show her he could change—that he could grow right along with her as she went to school and pursued a new career. He'd set up a meeting with the Mortimers for Friday night. Evan had already expressed interest in a joint venture. Jake hoped he could interest him in something long-term. When Jake had asked him on the phone how the house-hunting was going, he was secretly pleased when Evan sighed.

"It's not. We haven't found anything that works for us yet."

Jake heard the frustration in his voice. He understood it. When a man made plans he liked to get right to them, but no one could ranch without ranchland.

"Talk to you Friday," Jake said. He couldn't wait.

Meanwhile he did his best to get his ducks in a row. He blew through his chores as fast as possible, stealing hours at his laptop while Hannah was at work to solidify his research. His plan was a tricky one. His position wasn't nearly as strong as he'd like it to be, but he knew Evan shared his interests and he already came to Jake for practical advice.

Would Evan be interested in a long-term plan that brought their two capabilities together?

Or was he gambling everything on wishful thinking?

Chapter Eighteen

THE FOLLOWING MORNING Hannah's jeans didn't fit. At least, they were harder than usual to zip up and the waistband constricted her when she finally buttoned it. Either she'd eaten far more of Jake's waffles and sausages than was good for her or she was…

Pregnant.

She put a hand on her belly and tested it. She knew it was silly—even if she was pregnant she wouldn't show for months. But her breasts were tender and heavy when she pulled on her bra and she felt… different.

Knowing she would be late for work, she nevertheless sat down on her bed and tried to contemplate what it would truly mean if she was pregnant. Did she really think she could tackle coursework on top of everything else? She counted out the months. She'd be due sometime in the middle of the summer, so it was possible she'd be ready to return to classes in the fall. But could she move to a whole new state and attend a brand new school with an infant less than six weeks old?

No.

It was as simple as that. She couldn't. Not alone. Not without a lot of help. Still, she could take one semester off and start again the following January. She wouldn't be the only woman to try for a higher education at the same time she raised a child.

Jake had said they'd figure it out when the time came. She wished she could trust that was true. Trying to put the conundrum out of her mind, she stood up and hurried downstairs, but thoughts about the possible pregnancy, her child, and her future plagued her throughout the day. The problem was she didn't trust Jake, not after everything he'd pulled. Holt had undermined her confidence in the whole family, and like Autumn said yesterday, Jake's family were the ones she needed to rely on if she was going to pursue her education and career while raising a child. Bella sent her sympathetic looks now and then but didn't press her to talk and Hannah appreciated that. She doubted she could speak her heart without breaking down again.

By the end of the day her nerves were on edge and she wanted to get home and take a long, hot soak, but just as she pulled on her jacket to leave, lights flashed across the windows of the clinic and a moment later a desperate hammering came at the door.

Bella rushed past her to unlock it and staggered back when a hysterical woman launched herself inside, a Doberman in her arms.

The Doberman whimpered and barked in pain. A long gash sliced its side. The woman—Harriet Lynch—was covered in her pet's blood and beside herself. "I was sorting tools in the shed and she got in and cut herself on a saw blade before I could stop her," she cried. "Can you help her?"

"Of course." Bella immediately jumped into action. Hannah dropped her coat and purse and followed the other two women into the examining room, moving automatically to prepare a sedative. She and Bella worked together for the next hour, cleaning the wound, stitching it and giving Stella—the Doberman—an antibiotic shot. "She'll need to stay here for several days," Bella told Harriet, "but she'll be okay. You got her here in plenty of time."

When Harriet broke down in tears of relief, Hannah couldn't help but tear up, too. This damned emotionalism. Usually she could keep a professional distance, but not today. Feeling her shoulders slump with resignation, she decided it was time to face the facts. She had to be pregnant. Nothing else would make her act like this.

Once Stella was settled in for the night and Harriet had gone home, Hannah said good-bye to Bella and drove the roads out to the Double-Bar-K slowly. She was due to get her period on Friday. If it didn't show up, she'd buy a pregnancy test Saturday morning and learn her fate. She already knew what it was, though.

While this morning she'd almost convinced herself she was ready for a family, the events of the afternoon gave her conviction that she was meant to be a vet. The thought of taking both on at once felt overwhelming. Who would help her when times got tough—when she was hundreds of miles away from everyone she knew attending school? How could she keep a baby away from its father for months at a time? She drove up to Jake's cabin more confused than ever.

When she let herself in there was no dinner on the table, even though she was late. Apparently tonight Jake meant for them to stick to their appointed chores. Resentment spiked through her. Couldn't he give an inch—just this once?

He sat at the table, staring into his laptop. When he didn't even greet her or ask about her day, she dropped her purse in irritation and stripped off her coat. Kicking off her boots, she paced to the kitchen, pulled out the boneless chicken she'd defrosted for the meal and banged it on the counter. The sound jolted Jake out of his reverie.

"Oh. Hey."

"Hey yourself," she said. She shoved the chicken aside, slapped a cutting board on the counter and began to slice onions.

"I got some interesting news," he said slowly, still bent over his laptop.

"Oh, yeah?" She threw the onions in a pan with a slab of butter and turned it on. Rinsing two green peppers, she set to work chopping them as well.

"Yeah. It's kind of a funny story," he began.

"Don't you care about my day?" She cut him off. "A dog—a Doberman—someone's pet—nearly died in my arms this afternoon. It would have died if Bella and I hadn't been there to save it."

Jake looked up and blinked. "That's… great. Good

job."

She slapped the knife down on the cutting board. "You know what? It is a good job. It's a great job. Veterinarians help people and animals. We save lives. We make lives better. It's not some stupid, silly pastime!"

"I never said it was," Jake said. "But today—"

"You never said it wasn't, either. All you talk about is your precious ranch. Your family. Your herd. What about me? You never say anything about me!"

"That's not true. Hannah—" He started to rise.

"I'm sick of it! I'm sick of coming last!"

He reached his feet. "Hannah, I applied to Montana State, too. And I got in!"

Her jaw dropped open. "You what?"

"I'm going to college! Isn't that great?"

A red haze spread before her eyes. "You're… going to college? *You* are? When you knew it was my dream and you didn't want me to go? You wouldn't support me, but now you expect me to turn around and support you? What the hell do you expect me to do, stay here and run the ranch while you go to classes?" Her voice had risen to an uncomfortable octave. White hot anger pierced her. Could he be so self-centered?

"No, of course not!"

"What did you think? Did you even think at all?"

Jake's expression turned hard. "I thought we would go together! I guess I thought wrong!"

"We can't go together. Someone has to work and support the baby."

"And you thought that would be me. How convenient for you." Jake stood up and faced her, a muscle tensing in his jaw.

"Convenient? There's nothing convenient about it. It's not convenient for me to have a husband when I'm trying to go to school. It's not convenient for me to live on this ranch and have all the extra chores I have around here, and it sure as hell isn't convenient to have a baby which I wouldn't be having if it wasn't for you!"

"If I'm so damn inconvenient then why don't you just leave!" Jake kicked the chair away. "It's what you've tried to do since the moment you got here!"

"Fine. I will!" She grabbed her purse and her coat and headed for the door, tears already stinging her eyes. Just as she reached it, something twisted low in her abdomen and she grabbed for the handle to support herself. A hard cramp gripped her, and a familiar warm, stickiness pooled between her legs.

Her period had arrived right on time, and it was going to be a doozy.

"Well, go on. I thought you were leaving," Jake's hard voice sliced coldly through her.

Hannah opened her mouth in a silent cry of pain as tears slipped down her cheeks, but she didn't turn around. He was right. It was time for her to go. There was no baby.

She was free.

Loss and loneliness overwhelmed her, but she kept her back to Jake, her tears blinding her until she had to feel her way out of the door and down the porch steps. In her truck she wiped them roughly away with her coat sleeve and backed out of her parking spot as fast as she could. Bumping and bucking down the dirt lane to the road, she vowed she would never come back to the Double-Bar-K. Jake was the most self-centered man she'd ever met. She couldn't wait to leave for Colorado.

WHEN A KNOCK sounded on the door twenty minutes later, Jake leapt to his feet, hoping against hope it was Hannah. As angry as he'd been when she left, he'd long since simmered down and realized he'd presented his information all wrong. Hannah had obviously had a long day. While the e-mail acceptance letter had surprised and excited him when it arrived today, he should have been paying more attention when she got home. If only he'd let her know that he didn't plan to ditch the ranch—or her—they could have discussed all the possibilities. Now she thought he placed his own education and advancement above hers. That wasn't the case. He had no idea how they'd balance things when both of them started taking classes, but he liked the idea that they could go on this adventure together.

Too bad he'd blown it.

He opened the front door to find his mother on the porch.

"Can I come in?" She hugged her jacket tightly closed against the wind.

"Of course." He stepped back and she came inside, her gaze taking in the bags of groceries still on the counter, the laptop on the table, the half-prepared dinner on the stove and, he supposed, Hannah's absence.

"I saw Hannah drive out of here a little while ago like she was being chased by the devil. I thought you'd go after her but I didn't see your truck leave. Did something happen?"

Jake indicated that she should sit down. She chose the sofa and he sat in an easy chair. "We had a fight."

"Over what? If you don't mind my asking."

Jake found it hard to look his mother in the eye. "I blurted out some news. Didn't prepare her for it. She took it the wrong way."

"What news?"

"I got into Montana State."

Lisa cocked her head. A little smile played at the corners of her mouth. "Montana State? You applied to college?"

"Yes, ma'am."

"It's about time." Lisa leaned forward and swatted him on the knee. "I always thought you were smart enough to get something out of it."

"Dad won't like it much."

"Nope. He won't. But it isn't his life." She considered him. "What made Hannah so mad?"

"She's starting classes in February and everyone's been telling her she can't go if she's pregnant. When I blurted out that I got in, I guess she figured I was saying that she oughta stay home and I should go instead."

"But that's not what you meant."

"No." He shook his head. "But I don't know what I do mean. I don't know how the two of us can go, and I don't know how we can be a family when she's going to need to spend all that time in Colorado. And I don't know what we'll do about kids, now or later."

"You can figure all of that out," Lisa said.

"You think so?"

"Do you love her?" Jake nodded. Lisa raised her eyebrows. "Then it's simple. You give a little, she gives a little and everyone around you helps out all they can. That's life, Jake."

"I don't even know where she is. She just took off. I don't even know if she loves me."

Lisa held her gaze steady on him. "This is a small town, Jake. Find her."

Chapter Nineteen

"ROOM TWENTY-TWO." The desk clerk at the Big Sky Motel handed Hannah a plastic key card and she exited the office and climbed the concrete steps to the second floor. She let herself into the plain, drab room and shut the door behind her, exhausted and numb. She had her answer. Jake didn't care about her at all. He couldn't have come up with a better way to demonstrate that than doing what he did tonight.

Jake was going to Montana State. Just like that. Forget the ranch. Forget her dreams. Forget her.

More importantly, there was no baby and she couldn't believe how bitterly disappointed she was. She was cramping painfully and her head had begun to pound, too. Why hadn't she recognized all the signs that her period was arriving? She felt worse today than she usually did when it came, but that was the stress piled on top of everything else. Otherwise, all was normal. Bloating, crankiness, being way too emotional? Check, check and check. She should have known she wasn't pregnant. She shouldn't have let herself get attached to the idea.

And why had she let herself get attached to Jake, the one man guaranteed to leave her heartbroken? She couldn't blame anyone else for her predicament. Not even Holt, damn him. He'd started the whole thing off, but he'd told her clearly her job was to prime the pump to get Jake interested in the idea of settling down. Even he had known she wasn't the right woman for him to settle down with.

Hannah perched on the motel room bed, her arms wrapped around her stomach. Still in her winter jacket, she was cold down to her bones. Maybe a hot soak would help calm her down. Good thing she wasn't hungry since she hadn't eaten dinner and she'd have to go out if she wanted food now. She didn't think she could face the world tonight, not when all her dreams were crashing down around her head. A bath and bed. That was the best plan. She would try again tomorrow.

She turned the television on to mask the emptiness of the room, hoping it would mask the emptiness inside her, too. As she walked toward the bathroom she passed the room's long, low bureau topped with a large mirror. She'd aged ten years in the last hour. Her face was taut with sorrow. Her hair limp. Her body hidden by the thick winter coat. She looked like the kind of woman who lived alone and existed on the margins. The kind who ran to a motel room instead of home to a family when times got tough. She hadn't had anyone to depend on for a long, long time. This was normal for her. Nothing had changed.

But something had changed. For one moment she'd let herself imagine a life that contained a husband who loved her. A child. In-laws. A home. All the things she'd never let herself picture before because she couldn't stand the disappointment if it didn't work out. She'd set herself up for heartbreak and heartbreak had arrived, right on schedule. The pain of it doubled her over until she wept into her hands.

When the knock sounded on her door ten minutes later, Hannah didn't want to answer it, but if the insistent pounding drew her neighbors' ire she'd have even more fuss to deal with. She dragged herself up off the bed, scrubbed at her face with the arm of her jacket and approached the door cautiously. A glance through the peep hole showed Holt standing outside.

She rested her forehead against its smooth surface in defeat. "Go away, Holt."

"I'm not leaving until you let me in."

She knew him well enough now to know he'd make good on his threat. Taking a deep breath, she opened it. Shrugging out of her jacket finally, she tossed it on the bed and faced him.

"What do you want?"

"I think the real question is, what do you want?" He kept his coat on and stood near the door, his tall, broad frame taking up all too much space in the room.

"I don't have the energy for games tonight." She felt raw and tired—too tired for this conversation.

Holt peered at her and she knew he was taking in her reddened eyelids and splotchy face. "There's no baby, is there?"

A sob rose in her throat again. She forced it down and shook her head.

"Jake doesn't know." It wasn't a question.

She shook her head again. "No."

"Shouldn't he?"

"He won't care. He doesn't care about anyone besides himself."

"My son cares about you, that's for damn sure. Why else would he chase all over creation to help you round up that bison and cart it over to our ranch even though he knows I wouldn't cotton to it? Why else would he spend all his time for the past two weeks either with you or mooning over you? You think we told him to do any of that? Hell, no!"

"Holt, just leave me alone, would you? It's all over—"

"It's not over." Holt approached her. "You're crying yourself silly over here. And I bet my son's pacing like a wild animal back at home. I saw you race out of there like a bat outta hell. Don't worry; I sent Lisa to talk to Jake. I figured I'd better come talk some sense into you. The two of you love each other; you're just being a pack of fools!"

"We're not foolish. We're realists. We can't make this work."

"Can't or won't?"

"What's the difference?"

"There's a world of difference. Sit down." He pointed to the bed. When she didn't budge he folded his arms across his chest. "Do an old man a kindness by listening to me for a minute. Maybe you'll learn something."

"I want to be alone."

"I'll leave as soon as I've said my piece."

"Fine!" Hannah plunked herself down on the bed, too exhausted to fight anymore.

"I nearly lost Lisa once out of stubbornness." He began to pace as he talked. "It was over a dress, believe it or not. This was back in the days when we were getting started and struggling a bit. I'd just increased the herd far faster than my father ever would have done. I made a bet and used credit. He would have been furious. That bet paid off in spades, though."

She could tell Holt had traveled back to those days in his mind. He was seeing something other than the motel room in front of him.

"Truth was I nearly over-extended myself and I was hell-bent on paying back that loan as fast as possible. We pinched every penny we could for several years and some pennies we didn't have, too. One day Lisa asked for some money to buy a new dress. She was hosting a fundraiser for some cause or another. Something church-related." Holt waved a vague hand. "She'd been wearing the same dress for three years to all of these functions and she was bound and determined to have a new one. She wanted fifty dollars." He rubbed a hand across his jaw. "Fifty dollars." He turned bright eyes toward Hannah. "I said no. She could keep wearing that dress another year. I was still wearing the same old suit I always wore when I dressed up, wasn't I? I didn't understand it was different for her. That her friends were talking—saying I didn't value her. I didn't care. She knew the truth but it killed her to think that everyone else didn't. She wanted that dress to show them that her husband…" His voice got a little unsteady. "…wasn't a cheapskate who neglected his wife. I refused."

Holt sighed and for a minute Hannah thought that was the end of the story, but he continued slowly. "We bickered over it for a few days and then Lisa stopped talking to me. I figured she was sulking and I wasn't going to put up with that so I stopped talking, too. We went three days like that. Worst days of my life."

Hannah pressed her lips together to keep tears from sliding down her cheeks again. She'd cried enough today. She didn't need to do it again. "What happened?" she asked when Holt hesitated.

"She gave me an ultimatum finally. Fifty dollars or she was leaving. I was furious. Oh, we had a row. Then she said something that's stuck with me to this day. She said, 'Am I not worth fifty dollars to you?'" Holt stopped speaking and watched her expectantly. When she didn't say anything he shrugged and turned to leave. "I suppose I've done all I can. I'll say good-night now."

"Wait. I don't understand." Hannah rose to her feet. "What does that have to do with me?"

Holt paused by the door. "I guess it's time to ask yourself. What is Jake worth to you?"

And he was gone.

JAKE HAD EXHAUSTED all of Hannah's contacts and he still hadn't found her. She wasn't at Morgan's place, or at the Cruz ranch with Autumn, Claire or Rose, and she wasn't with Bella, either. After his mother returned to her house he decided he wouldn't stop looking for her until he found her and explained everything. Who knew how long that would take? Before he set out to scour the town he decided to stop by his brothers' cabins and ask them to take on his evening and morning chores.

Ned met him at the door of his cabin and seemed reluctant to let him in. When he finally did, Jake understood why. Gone was Mia's pink décor. The cabin was back to normal. But the meal Fila was cooking in the kitchen was anything but. The whole place smelled of foreign, exotic spices that made Jake's mouth water.

"What are you making?" he asked Fila, then realized Ned had been elbow-deep in food preparation, too.

Ned? Cooking?

He suppressed a smile, amazed that he could still do so.

"What do you want?" Ned asked gruffly, obviously steeling himself against ridicule.

"Just to see if you could help take on some of my chores tonight." He explained about the fight and Hannah running off.

"Sorry to hear you're having troubles," Ned said. Behind him Fila nodded.

"Thanks." Jake quickly turned back to the door, unnerved by his brother's compassion. "I'll go pass the news to Luke."

It wasn't until he was out the door that he realized Ned should have been jumping for joy. After all, if he didn't marry Hannah, Ned would get control of the ranch. Maybe he'd only waited for Jake to close the door before he started celebrating, but when Jake looked back he could see Ned and Fila through the front window of the cabin. Ned wasn't jumping. He was bent back over his work.

At Luke's cabin, things were as he expected. Pink ruled the day and Mia was singing a pop song in the kitchen while waiting for the microwave to cook a frozen meal. Luke was already scooping forkfuls of macaroni and cheese from another cardboard container.

When Jake explained what he needed, Luke made a face. "Why don't you just let her go?" he said.

Jake bristled. "Why would I do that?"

"You're obviously not on the same page. You want to stay here, she wants to go to Colorado. And this whole pregnancy thing—what's that about?"

"It's about the condom breaking." Jake clenched his fists.

"Are you sure? Or is she just using it as an excuse to make you do what she wants you to do?"

Behind him, Mia's eyebrows shot up.

"She'd never do that."

"Sure she would. Let her go," Luke said. "No pregnancy, no problem. Am I right?"

Mia spoke up angrily. "A baby isn't a problem."

"It is when it's not wanted," Luke said.

Jake grabbed him by his collar before he finished the sentence and yanked him to his feet. "Surprise or no surprise, you better believe that baby is wanted. Grow the hell up, Luke." He slammed him back in the chair. "Sorry for the disturbance, Mia."

"That's okay," she said automatically, but he could tell it wasn't. He'd never seen the young woman upset before. Her face had turned an odd shade of white and her lips were compressed in a thin line. As he let himself out the front door he hoped for Luke's sake he had a good defense ready for what he'd just said.

He was going to need it.

Chapter Twenty

WHAT WAS JAKE worth to her?

Hannah curled up under the covers in her shirt and panties and tried to answer that question. Was she willing to compromise to be with Jake?

How much?

Becoming a vet was non-negotiable. The work called to her like nothing else did. And having a veterinarian on a ranch would be a helpful thing, not a hindrance.

She'd assumed that after her years of school she'd join Bella in the pet clinic, but she didn't have to. In fact, after her time with Gladys she'd found herself growing interested in livestock. That was Bella's brothers' specialty. Craig's clinic handled cattle, horses and other farm animals. Bella took care of pets almost exclusively. Hannah had no doubt there was room in Chance Creek for an additional vet of either kind. Both Bella and Craig had been overworked for years.

Could she open her own clinic on the Double-Bar-K?

What about Jake wanting to attend school? She

pulled out her phone and logged onto the motel's Internet access. Checking out Montana State's agricultural programs, she found several that she could see would interest him and felt ashamed she hadn't even stopped to ask which one he'd applied to. He was so fascinated by the idea of sustainability. That's why Gladys had caught his interest in the first place. Evan Mortimer was interested in sustainability too, and he had money to invest. Could their interests meet in the middle somewhere?

One of the reasons ranchers in this part of the state didn't ranch bison was a lack of infrastructure. What if she concentrated her veterinary practice on unusual and exotic farm animals? Could she help open up the area to more experimentation in livestock? Could she, Jake and Evan work together?

She sat up straight, feeling hope for the first time but almost as quickly she slumped again. What about Holt? What about the Double-Bar-K?

Could Ned and Luke step up to fill the gaps temporarily while Jake went to school? Would Holt allow a bison herd on the ranch? What would happen when Jake finished school and wanted to get back to work on the Double-Bar-K? Would it be too hard to partner with Ned? Would Holt even allow it?

So many questions and ifs—but for the first time she considered the people around them and how their dreams and plans might dovetail into hers. She and Jake had a whole community of friends and family who might support their journey.

But she'd have to trust Jake. And he'd have to trust

her, too. They'd have to learn to make sure both were being served by their actions instead of basing all their plans only on themselves.

Could they do it? Would Jake want to?

She picked up her phone.

THANK GOD HANNAH had finally called. She hadn't said much—just asked him to come to the motel in town. Jake had just opened the door to his truck when he spotted his father's Chevy rumbling down the dirt track. Holt pulled in next to him and rolled down the window. "Going somewhere?"

"I'm going after Hannah."

"That's good, but I've got news for you first. I've just been to see her."

"How did you know where to find her?" Jake demanded. It burned him to know that Holt could guess her whereabouts when he hadn't been able to.

"How many places are there to go in this town? She's at the Big Sky Motel."

"I know—she just called."

"Well, she's waiting for you, but there's something you need to know first." Holt looked grim and Jake's heart sunk.

"What's that?" He braced himself for some new blow. His father seemed to love to provide them.

Holt hesitated. He looked old tonight. Almost… sad. "I'm sorry, son. There's no baby this time."

"No…" Jake trailed off and looked away. "Hell," he said quietly.

"There'll be other chances in the future. Hannah needs you to be with her, though. Go talk to her."

"I will."

"And son?"

Jake hesitated, his hand on the door. "Yeah?"

"Don't let her use this as an excuse to postpone the wedding. The two of you need to get hitched more than ever. Come to dinner on Saturday night. We'll hammer out the details."

Jake nodded. He couldn't even think that far ahead. He climbed in his truck and started the engine. He wanted to ask what Holt had said to her, but didn't want to waste any more time. His father waved, turned his truck around and headed back toward the main house. As Jake drove down the long lane and toward town, he had to swallow hard a couple of times. No baby. He felt its loss as if he'd already held it in his arms.

When he reached the Big Sky Motel, he took the stairs two at a time to the second floor and banged on her door. "Hannah? Open up."

After several agonizing moments, Hannah opened the door. Her hair fluffed in its usual halo around her head. Her face was white and strained, her eyes lined with red. She was dressed only in her shirt and panties and he could tell by the disheveled covers she'd been curled up in bed.

"Are you okay?" He pushed his way into the room and gathered her into his arms.

"I… got my period."

"I know," he said softly. He pulled back and

searched her face, expecting relief or at least acceptance. What he saw instead mirrored his own reaction. Bitter disappointment.

Tears brimmed her eyes. “Oh, Jake.”

She didn’t need to say anything more and neither did he. He pulled her in close, wrapped his arms around her and let her cry.

WHILE SHE SHOWERED, Jake ordered a pizza and when she got out of the bathroom he tucked her into bed, heaping the covers around her. When the pizza arrived he made sure to block any view of her the delivery boy might get. She appreciated his concern for her privacy. She felt too raw, too vulnerable to come in contact with anyone.

Anyone except Jake.

They ate in silence, Jake sprawled out next to her on the bed. He kept close to her, pressing his leg against hers as if he knew she needed some contact to keep her grounded. She hadn’t expected such an ache inside her chest at the loss of the idea of being pregnant. She had no idea she’d become attached at all to that idea, much less would mourn its absence.

“I would never go to school and leave you behind,” Jake said at one point.

“I know.” She did, too, now that she thought about it. Jake would never steal her dream but he might get caught up in it. She leaned against him. Why had she jumped to such awful conclusions?

“Are we going to be all right?” he asked.

"I don't know. But I had an idea. A start of one," she amended when he turned to face her. She filled him in on her interest in treating bison and other alternative livestock. She spoke about Evan's interest in bison as well and the fact he and Bella were looking for land to build on. "Maybe there's some way we could work together."

Jake nodded slowly. "I've actually been thinking the same thing. I scheduled a meeting with Evan and Bella for tomorrow night."

"Really? What will you say to them?"

"That we should join together the way Ethan, Jamie, Rob and Cab have done on the Cruz ranch with their families."

"What about your Dad? Will he go for it?"

"I don't care anymore. He's promised to let me head up the Double-Bar-K soon. Sooner than you think," he added. "When I'm in charge I'll share most of the management duties with Ned and Luke. I'll give them more of a say than they've ever had before. They'll like that. In exchange, I'll carve off a corner of the ranch for a bison herd. I'll ask Evan to help fund it. I know he's interested. And if I give Ned and Luke what they want, they'll be on our side, too. That's how we'll get through the next few years, by asking our friends and family for help. By the time you've gone through vet school and I've gotten my degree, we'll be sitting pretty. There are all kinds of things we can do."

She could only stare at him. "You really think Holt will let you do that?"

"I know he will. You just get busy planning that wedding. I'll take care of everything else." He bent down and kissed her nose. "I love you, you know. We'll make this work."

"But how do I pull a wedding together in two weeks?"

"Simple." He kissed her again. "You ask for help."

Chapter Twenty-One

WHEN JAKE DROVE Hannah home early the next morning, flakes of snow were drifting down. This far into December it was high time for a real snowstorm. It suited his mood, too. Quiet. Cold. Drifting. He bundled Hannah into the house and back into bed although she protested that it was far from necessary. Since Ned and Luke were already covering his morning chores, he cleaned up the previous night's clutter and made both himself and Hannah a large breakfast which they ate in bed. Afterward, they leaned against the headboard with their laptops and alternately talked and researched all the choices ahead of them.

After lunch Hannah insisted on getting up, taking a shower and getting dressed in preparation for their dinner meeting with Evan and Bella. Once in a while he saw a sad look cross her face and he knew she was thinking of the baby they wouldn't have just now, but she was bouncing back already, buoyed up by their impending wedding and the idea of partnering with Bella and Evan. They prepped the house and meal together, moving easily around the kitchen as if they were an old married couple. Jake was nervous about Evan and Bella's reaction to his proposal, but he decided that even if they said no, he and Hannah had other options. The important thing was that they were together.

Evan and Bella arrived at six, rosy-cheeked from the cold. Jake had worried the meeting would be awkward but he forgot all about that within a few minutes. Bella and Hannah moved into the kitchen as Bella updated her about the state of the clinic and Evan joined him in the living room after Jake fetched him a cold beer.

"I hope you brought me here to take me up on that joint venture," Evan said right away.

"Actually, that's exactly why we invited you," Jake said. "I think I'll be able to clear the way for a herd on the ranch in a month or so."

Evan nodded. "That's great. I'd hoped we'd have our own place by now. I planned to offer some of our land for the project if you'd help oversee the herd in exchange, but we still haven't found a place that has everything we need."

"Don't worry about it. I'll happily provide the land if you'll foot the bill for the herd." Here was where it got sticky. "I wish I had the cash, but…"

"That's just fine. That's what my trust is for—investing in new ideas. Ranching bison definitely qualifies. Just let me know when you're ready to get started."

"Right after the wedding." Jake reached out to take Hannah's hand as she and Bella joined them. "Two short weeks."

"Where will you go on your honeymoon?" Bella asked Hannah.

"We're not taking one. Instead, both of us are starting classes in February."

"No kidding!" Evan said. "What are you studying, Jake?"

"Natural resources and rangeland ecology."

Evan whistled. "Between your ideas and mine we'll keep ourselves busy for years with trials and projects."

"I look forward to it."

WHILE DINNER WITH Bella and Evan had gone far better than Hannah could imagine, the upcoming meal with Jake's parents and brothers to discuss wedding plans left her weak with dread. She was relieved that Lisa was hosting the meal, but as Hannah prepared to walk the short distance to the main house with Jake, her stomach was in knots. Things never went smoothly in the presence of Jake's family. Holt probably would try to dictate the style of her wedding dress or come up with some new set of rules she had to adhere to. She'd spent the day at the Cruz ranch going over details with all her friends. They'd brainstormed a guest list and made lists of all the necessary preparations, too. They'd divided these tasks among all of them. With so many helpers it no longer seemed impossible to pull the ceremony and reception off in such a short period of time. The activity had helped keep her mind off the baby that never was. As Jake had said, they'd have other chances. For now they'd concentrate on the wedding and preparing for school.

Autumn put in a call to Ellie's Bridals and cajoled Ellie to stay open late Monday night so they could all go together to help her pick out a dress after work that day. Morgan had fiddled with her hair, coming up with possible style ideas while Claire tallied the number of tables and chairs they'd need for the dinner. She'd had a great time with her friends, but now that she was alone with Jake she began to worry again. Even though Autumn had offered the Cruz Big House for a backup wedding location, Hannah knew that it was crucial for Jake to be married at the Double-Bar-K. She prayed Holt wouldn't throw a monkey wrench in the works just for spite.

When they arrived, Ned and Luke were already seated at the dining room table, along with Fila and Mia. Rob and Morgan were there, too. Lisa took the pan of brownies they'd brought and shooed them in to take their places. Hannah greeted the other women happily. She hadn't expected Mia and Fila to come. Although Mia greeted her warmly, she sat primly next to Luke without once looking his way. Luke looked at her plenty and his desperation was almost palpable. Jake had filled her in on his faux pas about the baby and she knew better than Jake why Luke deserved Mia's cold shoulder. She suspected from Luke's continued interest Mia hadn't told him about her own pregnancy yet. What would happen when she did?

Where would Mia go?

Mia was probably asking herself that same question.

Most likely she would get through the rest of December here with Luke and then skedaddle back to the Cruz ranch the moment their guests left. Hannah needed to speak to her and urge her to tell Autumn that she was pregnant. She knew Autumn—there would be a room for Mia at the ranch as long as she needed one. As broke as she was with a baby coming, she would need one for a long time to come.

Fila remained as silent and pale as she always was. Ned directed a word at her once in a while and she answered him, but Hannah could tell she was still having a hard time. She berated herself for how absorbed she'd been in her own problems. Neither Mia nor Fila should have left the Cruz ranch. She could only hope the time would pass quickly for them until they could return to it.

Morgan, by contrast to the other two, was blooming with good health and the early stages of her pregnancy. For all the time she'd spent at the Double-Bar-K, it amused Hannah to think she still saw Morgan more often at the Cruz ranch than she did here. They'd have to work to change that.

When Holt came into the room and took his seat, all conversation around the table fell away. He didn't seem to notice this. Instead he waited impatiently until Lisa began to bring in the meal.

"Can I help?" Hannah jumped to her feet.

"Not this time. This time you're the guest of honor." Lisa beamed at her.

Mia and Morgan took the hint and followed her back to the kitchen. In a few more moments they'd filled the table with food.

For a short time the room was filled with noise while everyone passed the dishes around and helped themselves to the meal. As soon as the clatter died down, Holt spoke up.

"I'm glad to see the two of you have finally come to your senses. High time you got married."

Lisa turned to Hannah. "On the twenty-first? Will you let me host the wedding here?"

"Oh, I hoped you would ask," Hannah said. "I know it would mean the world to Jake."

"It would mean the world to me, too," Lisa said. "Let's put our heads together about the menu tomorrow and all the other plans."

"I've got guest lists and everything else," Hannah said with a wink at Morgan. That load lifted off her chest, she attacked her ham with gusto.

"What about all that college business?" Ned spoke up.

"We've figured that out," Jake said quickly. "Hannah will go to Colorado. I'm going to Montana State."

Lisa's smile widened, but Holt frowned and Hannah swallowed. *Uh oh.* Here's where the trouble would start.

She was right. Holt set down his knife and fork and wiped his hands on his cloth napkin. "What do you mean you're going to Montana State?"

JAKE FACED HOLT with confidence. He was marrying Hannah, after all. Holt had gotten what he wanted. Now he was going to have to compromise a little—just like the rest of them.

"I'm getting my degree."

"Who's going to run the ranch?"

"Me. And Ned. And Luke."

"How's that going to work?" Ned said.

"The three of us can figure it out."

"What about children?" Lisa asked unexpectedly.

"We'll work that out, too. Look around this table." Jake gestured at each of them in turn. "We've got five men and five women here on the ranch. We ought to be able to help each other. If Ned, Luke and Rob will pitch in to cover my chores when I'm at school, I'll pitch in and help them when I'm home. Hannah and I have decided to go ahead with children as soon as we're married. We hope you all will help with them, too."

"Why should we?" Ned exploded.

Lisa thumped her hand on the table. "That's enough. Don't you disrupt this meal."

"I'll say what's got to be said," Ned persisted. "If you leave the ranch then I'll become manager. It's as simple as that."

"We'll share it." Jake kicked him under the table. If Ned balked then Holt would balk too and he hadn't even told them about the bison herd yet.

"Don't kick me. And don't try to get one over one me, either. If you leave, you don't stay head of the ranch."

"I'm marrying Hannah, and I will stay head of the ranch." Jake glared at him.

"That's not the deal. That's not what Dad said and

you know it!" Ned stood up and threw his napkin on the table. "You don't just have to marry her, you have to stay here!"

"THAT'S ENOUGH!" Lisa stood up too. "If you two can't behave then leave the table!"

Hannah couldn't seem to breathe. This had all turned out much worse than she thought. Her mother-in-law was furious. Holt looked like he'd swallowed a bug. Ned was ready to leap across the table and strangle Jake, and Jake…

Was looking at her. Guilt, horror, panic crossed his face in quick succession.

Ned's words caught up to her. *You don't just have to marry her, you have to stay here.*

What did he mean by that?

Jake had to marry… her? Or what? What would he lose?

The answer hit her like a slap to the face.

He would lose the ranch.

"Hannah." Jake reached for her but she stared at him, dumbfounded. "Hannah—it's not like that."

"Sure it is," Ned sneered. "Dad forced your hand just like he forced hers. The two of you let him play with you like a couple of dolls. Well, I'm not getting played. Time for you to stand by your word, Dad." He faced Holt. "If Jake can't do his duty, then I'm the one in charge. You said so yourself."

Jake turned to Holt and she realized it was true. Holt must have blackmailed Jake the same way he'd done with her. And as much as it killed her, she couldn't even blame Jake for falling for it. Look at her; she'd slept with a man to get a home for her bison. How paltry an excuse compared to Jake losing the livelihood he'd worked for all his life.

No wonder he'd insisted on marrying right away. No wonder he'd capitulated to her demands when the deadline drew near. She covered her mouth with her hand when she thought of how happy she'd been just a few short moments ago. In love with Jake. Their future mapped out. So sure it could work.

A tear splashed down her cheek as the whole house of cards came tumbling down.

Did Jake even love her?

Was any of this real?

Morgan leaped to help her as she stumbled to her feet. "I'm sorry," she said to Lisa, whose face was white with shock. "I have to go."

"No." Jake blocked her way. "Not yet. Dad? We're waiting for your answer. All of us are."

Holt looked around the table. He seemed almost bewildered by the hubbub and once again Hannah saw a flash of the old man he'd become. The last thing she wanted was to feel sorry for him—not now—but she knew Holt didn't have a clue how to fix this.

"Ned's right," he said finally. "That was the deal. If you can't do the job, it's his."

Jake nodded. "Fine. That's just fine. I've given everything to this place. Everything." A muscle pulsed in his jaw. "But that's obviously not enough. If none of you plan to be here for me when I need you, then to hell with it. I won't be there for you, either. Come on, Hannah."

She shook her head, meaning they weren't a pair. She wasn't going with him anywhere. She couldn't find her voice, though, and she let Jake hustle her from the room.

"Wait!" Lisa called after them. "Where are you going?"

Hannah closed her eyes at the pain in her voice. Lisa would pay the biggest price in this argument that was splitting her family apart.

No. She was the one who'd pay an even bigger price when she left Jake for good.

"Don't worry. We won't bother you anymore," Jake hollered back. "We're leaving the Double-Bar-K."

Chapter Twenty-Two

JAKE LEFT HANNAH in the cabin's guest room packing and retired to his own room to make a phone call. His hands shook so hard he could barely work his phone but at last he got Cab Johnson on the line.

"Cab? It's Jake. Got a minute?"

"Sure thing," the sheriff said. "You got trouble?"

"Of a kind. Nothing for you to worry about, though. I just wondered who was staying at Carl's house now that you've moved in with Rose."

"I'm still watching over it," Cab said. "We stay there two or three nights a week so Carl can keep his insurance policy on it. That house is becoming a millstone around my neck."

"Could Hannah and I stay there for the time being?"

"Sure thing." Cab sounded surprised. "Any particular reason you're leaving the Double-Bar-K?"

"Two particular reasons. My Dad and Ned."

Cab chuckled. "Family, huh? They'll get you every time. Why don't I come over right now and drop off a key."

"We'll be ready for you."

"Say, you wouldn't want to buy Carl's place, would you?"

"I thought it wasn't for sale."

"It is now. Carl just asked me to list it."

Jake whistled. "Wish I had the cash. I'd buy it in a heartbeat."

"Oh, well—I thought maybe I could save myself some hassle."

Jake gripped the phone. "I might know of a buyer, though. Let me give them a call and I'll tell you when you get here."

"Sure thing."

Jake hung up and placed another call.

HANNAH WAS PACKED when a knock sounded at the front door. Since she didn't have much to begin with it didn't take long to gather it all back together. She heard Jake open it and Cab's booming voice filled the house. A moment later there was another knock. She frowned—was Jake having a party down there?

She crossed the room to the door and moved to the balcony. From here she could see the entrance and living room. Cab, Evan and Bella stood near the door, their coats still on. Jake was there, too. He glanced up, saw her and waved her down.

Hannah heaved a sigh. In all the fuss Jake didn't seem to realize she'd had enough of this. All the lies, secrets and games that surrounded their relationship deprived it of any value it might have had for her. How could she ever trust him again, knowing he would use his marriage to her to secure the ranch? How could she trust herself when she'd played Holt's stupid games, too?

She took the stairs slowly, worn out to the point of giving up. She tried to put on a brave face for their guests but assumed from their startled glances that she'd failed. Bella frowned but before she could speak Jake said, "Hannah and I are moving to Carl's house for the time being. We thought you might want to come along and take a tour of the place since it's just gone up for sale. Cab has the key. He'll open it up for us."

"Really?" Bella exclaimed. She turned to Evan with shining eyes. "It's going to be the one. I know it."

"Don't get too excited before you see it," Evan cautioned. "We've been here too many times before," he told Jake and Hannah.

"Jake, can I have a word with you?" Hannah asked.

"Why don't we start loading your things," Evan said. He and Cab got to it while Hannah led the way back upstairs. Once in the guest room, she shut the door and faced Jake.

"I'm not going to Carl's."

"Hannah." He took her hand. "I know how it looks. Believe me, I know exactly how it looks, but while my Dad might have influenced my wedding date, he did not influence the woman I chose to marry. Not one bit."

"He influenced the decisions you made," she pointed out. "You never would have agreed to my going to school if you hadn't had to. You knew you couldn't find someone else in the time you had left, so you gave in to me."

"I gave in to you because it was the right thing to do," Jake said. "I'll admit, when you were the only one going to school, I hated the idea. I was selfish. I didn't want to be apart from you. Once I started thinking about going myself, that changed. Four years isn't long at all. Four years is a tiny part of our lives. Do I wish I could spend every night with you? Hell, yes. Will I probably spend a mint flying back and forth to see you in Colorado? Double hell yes. I love you. I. Love. You. I'm a jealous, possessive, horny man who wants his wife by his side, but I'll do whatever it takes to make you happy. Don't you know that yet? I'm sorry it took me this long to figure it all out. I should have seen it clearly sooner. I didn't and you ended up getting hurt." He touched her face. "Can you forgive me?"

"How can you give up the Double-Bar-K?"

"The Double-Bar-K means nothing to me. Not compared to being with you." He leaned down and kissed her and after a moment she gave up fighting him. Her anger was for Holt, not for Jake. She knew Jake loved her. Every touch of his hand and mouth told her so. Jake pulled back and looked at her, love shining in his eyes. "Now, we could stand up here kissing until they've got all our stuff loaded," he said softly, "but that's not fair to our guests. Let's get down there and go see Carl's house."

"Too bad we can't just buy it. That would solve everything," Hannah said.

Jake just smiled.

A HALF-HOUR LATER, Jake helped Hannah unload their belongings while Cab took Bella and Evan on a tour of Carl's house and property.

"Pretty swank," Jake said as they carried their suitcases into the suite Cab had pointed them to. He'd never been farther into the Carl's house than the large foyer. The house was different than he'd expected. Western in terms of structure and furnishings, but more like a museum when it came to decorative elements. There were statues and vases and works of art on the wall that obviously cost Carl a bundle. He'd never seen anything like this in Chance Creek.

"This room is bigger than your cabin," Hannah agreed.

"Not quite. But pretty damn close." With a bedroom, combination kitchen and living room and its own full bathroom, the suite was self-contained with its own separate entrance. He looked out the window and saw Cab showing the other couple the remains of the garden his brother Rob had built just months ago. Poor Carl; at that point he'd still thought he'd bring a bride home to the house soon. Jake wondered how the man was faring in California.

Pretty well, he supposed, if he was ready to get rid of his ranch. Would Bella and Evan take the bait? Would they allow Hannah and him to keep renting this part of the mansion? He sure hoped they would. He also hoped that sooner or later he and Hannah could buy into the ranch on a partnership basis, but that was down the road.

When they met up a half-hour later in Carl's enormous living room, he could tell the deal had already been struck.

"We're taking it," Bella confirmed. "It's perfect. There's plenty of room for us to live and Evan to run his business. We'll build a clinic twice the size of the one I have in town and a bigger animal shelter, too. When you're a veterinarian you can join my practice." She beamed at Hannah. "And…" She looked to Evan.

"And we hope the two of you will consider this your home, too. I know it's not the same as having your own place, but while you're away at school we can keep an eye on the place, and when you're home maybe sometimes we can take off on a vacation or two." Evan squeezed Bella. "With the rest of my family and business headquartered back in California, I should travel there frequently. Having someone else on site, even part of the time, would be a huge relief."

Jake felt a smile spread across his face. Exactly what he'd hoped for. "It's a deal." He shook hands with Evan. Bella squealed and hugged Hannah. "We'll be like sisters! I've never had a sister!"

"Neither have I." To Jake's relief, Hannah smiled.

He'd lost one family tonight but it looked like he'd gained another one. It didn't matter if they weren't related by blood. Friendship would have to do.

He had a feeling it would do just fine.

Chapter Twenty-Three

"I GUESS WE CAN change our wedding date now," Hannah said when Bella, Evan and Cab went home. Since they hadn't managed to eat at his parents' place, they planned to drive into town and hit the Burger Shack. Hannah thought of Lisa's enormous dinner sadly. She hoped someone managed to enjoy it.

She hoped Lisa was all right, as well. It must be tough to be the matriarch of a family that was comprised of five strong-willed men. She knew that Lisa must want them all to get along, but surely she knew by now that wouldn't always happen.

Hannah assumed that one day she and Jake would patch things up with his folks. For a while things would be uncomfortable but time would pass and hurt feelings would smooth over.

She wasn't sure about the wedding, though. Without Jake's family there it would be a sad affair.

"I don't want to change our wedding date. Do you?" Jake led the way out to his truck and opened the door for her.

"I don't want to, but I also don't want a lot of empty seats at the ceremony. Besides, it's supposed to be at your parents' house."

"We can do it at the Cruz ranch." But his voice told her he wasn't happy with that, either.

"Maybe we should put it off until spring. By then they'll come around, don't you think?"

He waited until they'd both climbed in to answer. "I don't want them just to come around. I want them to accept me how I am and to accept you, too. I don't want to play these games. I do want to get married from home, but the Double-Bar-K isn't my home anymore. You think Evan and Bella would mind if we used the mansion?"

"We could always ask. You'll still invite your family though, won't you?"

Jake frowned. "I'll invite them."

"Even Ned?"

He laughed humorlessly. "Especially Ned."

She turned to him in surprise. "Why especially?"

"For all I've been a prisoner of Dad's games, it's been worse for Ned. Always second in line. Always hoping for a chance at first. Now that I'm out of there and have something else to look forward to—something even better," he reached over and squeezed her hand, "I say let him have his chance. He deserves it."

"Really?"

"Really." He glanced her way. "I should have gotten out of there a lot sooner. None of this would have happened. My Dad wouldn't have had the chance to hurt you."

"And you and I might never have gotten together. No, as much as I despise his methods, I can't complain about the results of your father's evil plan."

Jake laughed. "Glad to hear it. My home is with you now, you know. They can't touch us anymore."

"No. They definitely can't touch us now. I know we'll make a good life together."

"I know that, too."

JAKE REMEMBERED HIS bold words when they ran into Ned at the Burger Shack fifteen minutes later.

"How'd you track me down?" Ned said when he caught sight of them in line behind him.

"I was about to ask you the same thing." Jake sensed Hannah's discomfort. "Why don't you grab us a table, honey," he told her. "I'll grab the grub."

"Okay." She left quickly enough that he knew his instincts were right.

"I won't change my mind," Ned said. "It's only fair I get a chance to manage the ranch."

"I agree. I'm not coming back."

Ned searched his face, suspicious. "Where will you go?"

"Carl's place. The Mortimers are buying it. We'll rent from them for now. Evan and I have plans."

"Huh." Ned shoved his hands in his pockets. He didn't look like a man who was celebrating a victory. Was Ned disappointed?

"The Double-Bar-K is all yours."

"Yeah. Well, good," Ned said grudgingly.

"Want to join us?" Jake gestured to the table across the room where Hannah sat gazing back at them worriedly.

"Nah. I'll head back home." Ned hesitated before turning back to the counter where his turn had come to order. "Thanks. For backing off."

"No problem."

Ned hurried away as soon as he got his order and Jake brought his tray of food to the table Hannah had secured.

"That looked like it went okay," she said.

"Better than I expected. I told him the Double-Bar-K was his. He said thank you."

"Almost civilized."

"Almost," Jake agreed. "You think my Dad will leave it at that?"

"Are you kidding? He's got two more sons to marry off. Batten down the hatches and hide your women."

Chapter Twenty-Four

THE NEXT WEEK passed in a blur for Hannah. She spent Sunday revising her wedding plans to take into account the new location. Morgan came over and together they devised ways to use the house's present décor to stand in for wedding decorations. With the ceremony slated for four in the afternoon, with a sit down dinner to follow, the biggest problem would be to find enough tables and chairs for all the guests. Party rental companies were overbooked, so she spent the next few nights calling everyone she knew to beg and borrow as many of them as possible. Table cloths and place settings were easier to locate and the celebration quickly took shape. Autumn had volunteered to handle the catering, with the help of several other women. Hannah accepted the offer with pleasure and knew the food would be great.

She rushed out invitations on Monday morning, and spent a hilarious evening at Ellie's Bridals with Mia, Fila, Autumn, Rose, Morgan, Bella and Claire. The elderly proprietress regaled them with stories of wedding disasters while Hannah tried on dress after dress until Ellie pulled out *just the thing.*

Just the thing turned out to be an off-the-shoulder gown with a slim fitted bodice and a flowing skirt. Delicate stitchery on the bodice turned the plain dress into something spectacular, and Hannah felt like a princess in the gown. A collective sigh from her friends told her this was indeed the one, and the transaction was wrapped up quickly. It required a minimum of alteration and she received it several days before the twenty-first rolled around.

More snow fell in the meantime, making the view out the windows of Carl's home sparkle in the lowering sun. The ceremony would be held in its enormous living room at the back of the house, where large windows would let in the last of the light. Afterward they'd set up tables and shift the rows of chairs to circle them. An awkward arrangement, but one Hannah knew wouldn't put out her country guests one bit.

They hired a local band to play after the supper and she suspected the party would last longer than most, since she and Jake had no honeymoon to leave for. That was all right. Any night in bed with Jake was a honeymoon, she mused.

If only Jake would patch things up with his father, everything would be all right.

THE NIGHT BEFORE the wedding, all of Jake's regrets overwhelmed him. Hannah was putting up a brave front and he knew she was genuinely happy to marry him, but the rift between him and his parents was leaching all the joy out of the occasion. No matter how many times he assured her he was fine, and no matter that his parents had duly sent their reply card with the number of guests filled in with a *two*, she couldn't get past the idea that she had broken up his family and he knew it would forever mar her memory of her special day.

He didn't know what to do about it, though. He knew from past experience that one didn't reason with Holt. You either agreed with him or you didn't. If you didn't, he treated you like you didn't exist, until he had need of you again. Then he'd pick right up where he left off as if nothing had ever been wrong. If Hannah could be patient it would happen sooner or later.

He wished it would happen sooner.

When Ned called, he and Hannah were going over their lists one last time before they called it a night. Hannah was pale with tension. She was worried over all the final details. Jake had begun to wish they had put the wedding off, both so she'd have more time to arrange things and so his Dad would have more time to come around.

Why did he care so much what the old man thought, he wondered as he pulled his phone out of his pocket. All Holt did was cause trouble.

"It's Chester," Ned said without preamble. "He's hurt. Thought you'd want to know. We've got a call in to Craig Chatham, but he's out at another ranch and he'll be a while. You'd better get over here."

"Be right there." He relayed the message to Hannah.

"I'll be back as soon as I can. Don't wait up."

"I'm coming with you. Maybe I can help."

One look at her face told him not to argue. He wanted to, though. If he had to put Chester down, he didn't want her anywhere near.

He didn't want to put Chester down, either. The horse had been with him through thick and thin. As they shut the door behind them and clattered down the porch steps to his truck, Jake kicked himself for not asking Ned what happened. He drove the short distance down the road to the Double-Bar-K as fast as he could. They bumped down the dirt lane, parked in front of the main house and got out of the truck.

"In the barn." Ned intercepted them. He'd obviously been waiting for their arrival.

"How bad is he hurt?"

"Hard to tell. He has a pretty good gash. Looks like a nail worked loose on the wall of his stall. He must have scraped against it. He's lost a lot of blood and needs stitches, I can tell you that much. We got him into another stall, but that's about it."

Jake blanched. "How soon will Craig be here?"

Luke shrugged. "As soon as he can." He looked at Hannah. "Think we should call Bella?"

"Yes. I'll call her."

By the time they reached the barn, she'd phoned Bella and told her what had happened. Bella said she was on her way, but it would be fifteen minutes at least until she arrived. Inside they found Holt and Ned both doing their best to soothe Chester. The horse was sidestepping in its stall, whinnying in pain. Blood ran down its flank from an angry wound. Jake's heart sank as the horse reared up and kicked the side of the stall. Chester was getting frantic from the pain.

"Do you have any medical supplies?" Hannah asked.

"Yes. In the storage shed." It was Ned who spoke up. Jake had gone to Chester, murmuring to him. The horse whinnied again.

"Show me."

Jake was dimly aware that they'd left the barn, but he was too busy trying to calm Chester to pay them much attention. "There, boy. Come on, settle down. That's a good boy." He kept up a stream of easy words and motioned for Holt to step back. His father did so, leaving him alone with the horse. After some long moments, Chester quieted a little. He still shuffled in his stall and whinnied now and then, but Jake kept murmuring to him, kept soothing him as best he could.

Soon Hannah was back. "I have what I need to stitch him up if you trust me. Otherwise you can wait for Bella."

Jake glanced at Chester's flank again. Too much blood was draining away. Chester couldn't take much more of that.

"Do you trust me, Jake?"

"Yes." He nodded. "Tell me what to do."

"If you can keep him calm, I can give Chester a local anesthetic. When it kicks in I can clean the wound and stitch him up. If you think he'll fight us, we'd better wait for Bella to sedate him."

"I can keep him calm." He wasn't sure Chester could wait that long.

They worked in tandem, Jake keeping Chester as calm as possible while Hannah cleaned a patch of his hide and administered the sedative. Her movements were easy and careful, and Chester tolerated her presence well, as long as Jake kept up his monologue. Jake knew his long relationship with the animal was paying off. Chester trusted him, and Jake trusted Hannah.

Soon her lithe fingers had cleaned the wound with antiseptic from the first aid kid, threaded a needle and were suturing the gash. She worked methodically but quickly and in less time than Jake would have imagined, the work was done.

"Thank you." His voice was gruff and he cleared his throat.

She came to touch his arm. "Of course. I know he means the world to you. I would do anything to help him."

In that moment, Jake understood thoroughly why Hannah needed to be a vet. Caring for animals, healing them in order to heal their owners' hearts was as much a part of her as this ranch was for him.

As this ranch had been for him. He swallowed against the raw burn in his throat, knowing that it wasn't his ranch anymore. He had turned his back on it. He and Hannah had thrown in their lot with the Mortimers and there was no going back now.

"That's some first-rate stitching."

Jake was surprised to find Holt standing beside them

inspecting Hannah's work.

"Thank you." She stepped back.

"A veterinarian would come in handy here on the ranch."

She gave Holt a funny look. With a last glance at Chester, she gathered her medical supplies. "I'm going to put these away. Keep him as still as you can. When Bella gets here she'll look over the wound and then cover it up."

Jake nodded. To his surprise Holt stayed by his side. He leaned against the doorframe to the stall. "Are you really going through with this—moving to Carl's house?"

"It's Evan and Bella's house now. Besides, that's what you wanted, right? For me to leave."

"You know damn well that's not true." He shook his head. "If someone had told me that every time I got one of you boys sorted out another one would go off half-cocked, I might not have been so quick to have four of you. You're like cockroaches when the light turns on, scurrying every which way, no sense at all. Everywhere I look, there are giant boots about to step on your heads and squash the daylights out of you." He blew out a breath. "Not a single one of you ever thinks to look up."

"Thanks a lot. It's a flattering analogy."

"Maybe it ain't flattering, but it's true."

"Did you ever think we have enough brains to plot our own course?" Jake struggled to keep his voice down. He didn't want to rile Chester. "Maybe what looks to you like blind flight is actually a carefully crafted plan."

"I doubt it."

Why did he even try? Holt couldn't be reasoned with. "Why don't you go on to bed. I can handle this from here."

"Why? So you can scurry away again as soon as my back is turned?" Holt looked him in the eye. "Are you ever coming home?"

"No."

Holt sagged against the door frame. "Then what's the use?" His voice thickened with emotion.

Jake felt intensely uncomfortable. "The use of what?"

"Everything. All of this. I did it for you. It was all supposed to be for you. The ranch, the herd…"

"For my brothers and me."

"For you especially." Holt braced his hands on his thighs as if he'd run a long race and couldn't catch his breath. "You're my heir. You're supposed to take my place. Now you've left…" He shook his head. "I told that girl of yours you'd jump the fence."

"You pretty much forced me to. You all right?" He had to ask the question even though he didn't want to. Holt looked mighty gray.

"I'll live," Holt said, brushing his concern away. "All I wanted was my family here. My sons and their wives and their children."

"I know," Jake said with a sigh. The trouble was, he did know. Holt was a nightmare at inter-personal relations, but when you clawed through all his baloney there was often a good intention buried there somewhere. "But you can't force people to do your will, Dad.

You have to give them options."

Holt looked up at him, his breathing still shallow. Jake was just about ready to call for an ambulance when he spoke. "How about this option? I give you two hundred acres, just like Rob got. You move back onto the ranch. That wife of yours can either start her own clinic when she's done her schooling, or work with her friend up the road."

Jake scowled. His father wanted to negotiate? Now? "Ned won't like that."

"Ned will still run the show. I'm just offering you a place to stay. A bit of land to do your *experiments* on."

"Like Rob?"

"Exactly."

"And you wouldn't interfere?" Was he really having this conversation? Everything had already been settled. He'd left the Double-Bar-K, gotten out from under his father's scheming ways.

"No, sir. I've learned my lesson. You can't teach a cockroach anything."

Jake rubbed a hand over his face and thought it over. Two hundred acres wasn't enough to do all the things he wanted to do, but it was enough land for them to build a home of their own on. Definitely enough to build a clinic for Hannah. "I'll have to ask Hannah. We've made plans with Bella and Evan."

"They're just down the road."

"That's true. We could still work together and take care of their place when they go away." They could keep the bison herd at their place, too—it was a large spread.

He felt wary, though. There'd been too many tricks—too many twists he hadn't seen coming. He wavered, not knowing what to say. On the one hand he'd always thought the Double-Bar-K would be his home forever. On the other hand, he'd begun to get used to the idea of truly being his own man.

"Consider it a wedding gift." Holt straightened up slowly and came to shake Jake's hand. "I'd like to have you back. It's not the same without you."

A rush of feeling washed over Jake. His father cared whether he stayed or went. He realized now he'd never been truly sure about that. And the Double-Bar-K still meant as much to him as it ever had. It would be strange not to be in charge of the cattle herd here, but it would be a relief, too, in some ways. He wanted to concentrate on other things. He wanted to go to school. Maybe he'd even transfer to Colorado with Hannah when she went. Anything to make her journey to becoming a vet easier. If they were together, they could think about starting a family along the way. Having their own acreage on the ranch would give them so many options. "I'd like to come back. Thanks, Dad." He clapped his father on the shoulder, the nearest any of the Matheson men came to a hug.

"I hope you'll still help out with the main work we do here." It was a testament to how far they'd come that Holt was asking rather than demanding.

"Of course."

Holt nodded and turned to the door. "Ned, did you hear all that?"

Ned straightened from where he'd been leaning against the far wall of the barn, hidden in the shadows. "I sure did. Jake, don't you think you and Hannah better get home? You've got a wedding tomorrow. I'll sit up with Chester and wait for Bella. I can sleep in here tonight if need be."

"I don't want to leave him." Jake hesitated. It was the night before his wedding, though. His bride needed some sleep.

"You're leaving him in capable hands. Just like you're leaving the ranch."

Jake sized his brother up. Maybe Ned did deserve this chance to prove himself. "All right. I'm counting on you, though."

"I won't screw it up." Ned's voice was caustic.

As he left the barn to find Hannah, Ned called out, "You better stop in to see Mom; she's got something to say to you."

Jake just bet she did. He retrieved Hannah and led her inside the main house, pausing on the front porch to fill her in on his father's offer. To his surprise, she launched herself into his arms with tears of joy. "That's so much better. I knew it would kill you to move away from here for good. This is your home. Our home, now. Did your dad really say he'd build me a clinic?"

"You bet. I think he likes you."

"I don't know whether to be glad or scared." She kissed him on the mouth. "I'm so happy. It's all going to work out!"

"I know." And he did. With things patched up between him and his father, he could really move forward into his new life. He led the way inside, where the smell of his mother's roast beef overwhelmed him the moment he stepped through the door. "What's cooking?" he asked as he entered the kitchen.

"Your wedding supper, I hope," Lisa said. Jake gazed around him in surprise at the large aluminum tins filled with every country delicacy imaginable. "I'm nearly done," she huffed, lifting an enormous roast out of the oven. "I just need to slice this up to store in the refrigerator overnight."

"But, Mom… you realize we've got food coming to Carl's place. Autumn's handling it."

"The hell you do." Lisa stood up and put her hand on her hips. "I nearly died when I read the location of your wedding on your invitation. Which I should have been the one to send, thank you very much!"

"We did the best we could, considering the circumstances. Dad didn't leave us much choice."

"Circumstances have changed, haven't they? And as for your father," Lisa shook her head. "Let's just say I gave him a piece of my mind after you left the other day. I can't believe the shenanigans he gets up to. Not that he wasn't provoked." She gave him a hard look.

"I take responsibility for my part in it." Jake knew he should never have made fun of his father or his brother. "Still, he went a little overboard, don't you think?"

Lisa chuckled. "I think your father likes matchmaking."

"Is that what he calls it?" Hannah's eyes were wide with disbelief.

"You're getting married tomorrow, aren't you? I called every last person I could think of to tell them about the change of venue. You're getting married in my house. Not Carl's house. Mine."

Jake rolled his eyes at her tone. "What about Hannah?" He nudged her. "She's worked all week to get ready. What about Autumn? She's making all the food."

"You know what? I'm happy about the change of venue," Hannah said. "Your mother can kidnap my wedding any time. I'd much rather have it here."

"That's good to hear, because I'm not giving it back," Lisa said. She hurried across the room to give Hannah a hug. "But Autumn's still helping me. You should see all that she's got cooking at her place. Please don't be mad."

"Are you kidding? I'm overjoyed! We tried decorating Carl's living room—I mean, Evan and Bella's living room—with all those Ming vases and the place ended up looking like a museum. This is so much better." Hannah gestured to Lisa's Christmas decorations which filled the house with red and green. "Did you tell Bella and Evan that the wedding has changed venues? They were so nice about letting us use their new place to host it."

"They were the first people I called. Don't you worry about a thing—it's all under control. Go get some sleep," Lisa told them. "Be back at noon tomorrow. Bring your things. You'll get dressed upstairs."

"Yes, ma'am," Hannah said with a grin.

"Now you're beginning to understand what it is to be a Matheson," Jake said.

"I'm also beginning to understand who's really in charge around here." Hannah nodded at Lisa. "It sets the perfect precedent for my own family." She gave Lisa a peck on the cheek, then sidled over to Jake and gave him a squeeze.

"We'll see about that." He bent down to kiss her, knowing that right now he'd do whatever it took to make his wife happy.

ON THE DAY of her wedding, Hannah loved the feeling of being almost outdoors in the snowy landscape while she said her vows. The ceremony was held in Lisa's glassed-in solarium, with temporary heaters working overtime to warm the usually chilly room. Mia and Fila acted as her bridesmaids, with Bella as her Matron of Honor. Jake stood straight and strong beside her and her heart tripped in excitement when he said, "I do."

They'd kissed so many times in the last few weeks, but when the Joe Halpern, the minister, gave Jake permission to kiss his bride, Hannah could barely stand for the rush of desire that shot through her again. When he drew her to him, his hand warm on the small of her back she was grateful the congregation couldn't know what was running through her mind.

Tonight they'd sleep together as husband and wife. All worry forgotten. All questions answered. They'd given their word; whatever they had to face from now on they'd face together. They'd reach their dreams together, side by side, backed by a family that supported them too.

Jake slipped his free hand under the nape of her neck and lifted her to meet his mouth, starting the kiss gently, but soon deepening it, letting her know he, too, was overcome with desire for their new life together.

The assembled crowd began to clap, then whoop as the kiss went on and on. When they finally broke apart,

Hannah was blushing and she hid her face in the crook of Jake's arm. He led her gently back up the aisle and tugged her into his father's office for a moment alone before facing the crowd again.

"You okay?" he asked, sitting on the edge of his father's desk and pulling her between his legs.

"More than okay."

"Think we did the right thing?"

"I know we did."

He smiled and kissed her again. "Think we can tell all these people to go home so we can get to bed?"

She laughed. "I think we'd start a riot. Everyone knows your mother and Autumn have been cooking all night. We'll have to feed them if we want to get rid of them."

"All right. But don't plan on leaving our bedroom for days."

"That's all right by me," she said. She kissed his cheek. "I love you."

"I love you, too."

The door swung open, and Jake and Hannah jerked apart when Holt walked in.

"I thought I'd find you two in here. No time for your dillydallying; get out there and attend to your guests."

"Yes, sir," Jake said, giving him a mock salute.

Holt waited for them to cross the room. "It sure took a passel of hard work to get you two together. How are we going to get your brothers hitched?"

The **Cowboys of Chance Creek** series continues with **The Cowboy Rescues a Bride**.

Be the first to know about Cora Seton's new releases! Sign up for her newsletter here!

Other books in the Cowboys of Chance Creek Series:

The Cowboy Inherits a Bride (Volume 0)
The Cowboy's E-Mail Order Bride (Volume 1)
The Cowboy Wins a Bride (Volume 2)
The Cowboy Imports a Bride (Volume 3)
The Cowgirl Ropes a Billionaire (Volume 4)
The Sheriff Catches a Bride (Volume 5)
The Cowboy Rescues a Bride (Volume 7)
The Cowboy Earns a Bride (Volume 8)
The Cowboy's Christmas Bride (Volume 9)

Sign up for my newsletter HERE.

www.coraseton.com/sign-up-for-my-newsletter

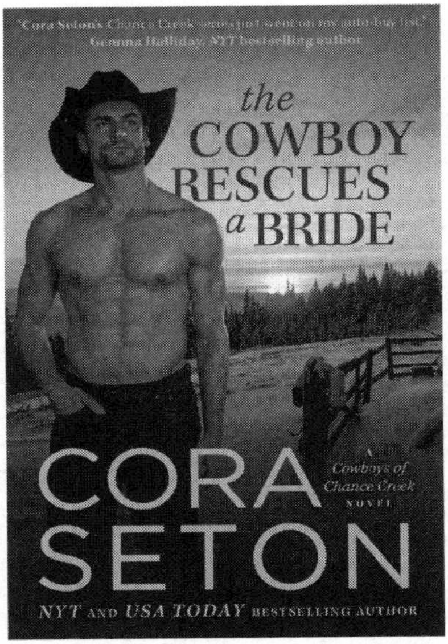

Read on for an excerpt of
The Cowboy Rescues a Bride.

NED MATHESON SHOVED his hands in the pockets of his thick, tan shearling work coat and hunched his shoulders against a strong wind sweeping east across the snow-covered pastures of the Double-Bar-K. The sun wasn't up yet on this January morning, and Montana winters were known for their brutality, but that wouldn't stop the animals that inhabited the ranch from waiting for him to tend to them.

He knew what it felt like to wait for something—and how good it felt to finally get it. After thirty-two long years of waiting, he was finally coming into his own.

Finally taking charge of his family's cattle herd, after years of playing second fiddle to his older brother, Jake. He'd always known he was capable of running the family business—he was as good a judge of the stock as anyone, as cunning in negotiations, and he was the only one of his brothers who could repair all the equipment they used on the ranch as well as do all the other chores around the place. He should have been put in charge a long time ago. Instead, it took Jake coming to loggerheads with his father and moving onto his own acreage to clear the way for him.

None of that was on his mind, though, as his footsteps crunched over the frozen snow on his way to the barn. He wasn't paying attention to the cattle grouped over by the brush to the south in the home pasture, out of the wind, nor was it on the task ahead of him—hauling hay to a sheltered feed spot and making sure all the cattle were in good shape. Instead, he was thinking of a certain slim young woman with a dark, thick, waist-length braid, brown eyes that searched him out when she thought he wasn't paying attention, a low, musical voice that hooked his heart every time she spoke, and a sweet, curving mouth that hardly ever smiled, except when they were alone in his cabin.

He'd just left her there, in fact. Which sounded far more salacious than it was. Fila Sahar shared his cabin, but she hadn't shared his bed and he figured it would be a while before she did.

If ever.

He shook his head ruefully. That was frustration talking. They'd get there eventually. Fila just wasn't your run-of-the-mill young woman. You couldn't pick her up at a bar, take her out a few times and talk her into coming home for a little fun. Her circumstances made her different. When they were together it would be because he'd persuaded her to be together for good.

And he would persuade her of that.

Eventually.

"You're taking your time this morning."

His father's buzz-saw voice cut through his pleasant reverie and snapped his head up. Holt was leaning in the doorway of the trim red and white barn. Ned wondered how long he'd been there at the mercy of the cold, bitter wind. Why the hell was the man waiting out here?

"I talked to Ethan last night."

Ned knew he meant Ethan Cruz—their next door neighbor. The Cruzes had owned their ranch just about as long as the Mathesons had worked the Double-Bar-K. Two of the oldest ranching families in the county, the older generation had been something of rivals, but the younger generation got along just fine. Ned's youngest brother, Rob, was one of Ethan's best friends and a part-owner of the Cruz ranch, and Ned, Jake and Luke all went to the Cruz's Thursday night poker and pool games each week.

"What did he have to say?"

"His guests have all gone back home. The Big House is empty. They want Fila and Mia back."

Ned shouldered his way past his father into the barn and flicked on the lights. No need to have this conversation out in the dark and cold. Not that it was warm in here. Holt followed him inside. "Did you hear me?"

"I heard you. I don't think either of them wants to go back."

"I wasn't asking you. I was telling you."

Ned turned to face him. "You're telling me who can and can't live in my cabin?"

"I built that cabin for you."

Ned bit back a sharp retort. It was the least his father could do for all the work he'd done on this place. Knowing they'd each inherit a share of the ranch someday, he and his brothers had been content for years to work the spread in exchange for room, board and a small allowance. Lately, though, they'd come to realize the true cost of such an arrangement. Holt had always ruled their lives with an iron fist, but it wasn't until the last few months that he'd begun to interfere in their love lives. Jake and Rob were both married because of his interference, but both had managed to convince him to carve off a chunk of the spread for their very own. He'd figured he'd be the next one Holt tried to marry off.

So why kick out Fila? Ned was pretty sure he knew.

His father leaned closer. "She's not the one for you."

Ned stilled. "I say she is."

Holt's expression hardened. "I say she ain't. And you don't want to push me."

So this was how it was going to go. If he was truthful, Ned had expected it might, but he'd hoped against hope his father would surprise him. Holt Matheson was a man of contradictions. Since most folks in Chance

Creek had known him all their lives, they knew that underneath his aggravating bluster lay a man who loved his family, his town and all of America. Those who didn't know him generally counted him a jackass. Ned understood his father's shades of gray. Holt counted on things staying within a strict framework that he understood. Whatever was native to Chance Creek was good. Whatever was foreign to it was bad. The more foreign it got, the worse it was to his way of thinking.

Which left Fila shit out of luck.

Despite Holt's classification system, Fila wasn't actually foreign. Born in Connecticut of Afghan parents, raised as American as apple pie for her first twelve years, she'd traveled to the country of her parents' birth to attend the funeral of her grandmother and there disaster had struck. The funeral procession was attacked by Taliban warriors, Fila's parents were killed in front of her, and she was taken captive. Raised in a remote Afghan mountain village for the next ten years, Fila did what she had to in order to survive. When her chance to escape came, she took it and made her way here—to the home of the woman whose organization, Aria's House, helped her return to the United States. Aria Cruz had already passed away, but her son, Ethan, and his wife, Autumn, took Fila in, gave her a home and a place to get back on her feet.

That made Fila as American as any of them.

But Holt couldn't see it. Especially when the Taliban men that had followed her to Chance Creek to retrieve her ended up shooting Rob in the shoulder before they were captured. Rob was fine—nearly fully recovered—but Holt couldn't forgive Fila her part in the incident. Ned was afraid he never would.

That didn't mean he was going to change his mind.

"You're the one who shouldn't push things." He met his father's steely gaze with one of his own. "She's the one I mean to marry. Best get used to it right now."

Holt's face changed color, but his tone remained steely. "You marry that girl and I'll cut you right out of my will. You will be dead to me!"

"Better start making funeral arrangements then." Ned turned on his heel and headed back toward the door, anger simmering throughout his bloodstream. "Make my casket walnut. I've always been partial to a walnut casket."

"Goddamn it!"

Ned slowed to a stop despite himself. That break in Holt's voice wasn't something he was accustomed to. He waited for more. He wasn't disappointed.

"I could accept a first-generation American. It's not what I want for my son but I could accept it. I could accept a woman who for all intents and purposes practices a different religion—"

"Fila's not all that religious—"

"That's why I said for all intents and purposes," Holt snapped. "I could even accept you falling for a girl that nearly got your brother killed, seeing as I doubt she meant for that to happen."

"No, I doubt she did."

Holt ignored his sarcasm. "But I cannot stand here

and watch you hitch yourself to a damaged woman."

Ned stiffened. "What the hell do you mean by that?"

Holt must have caught his tone. Realized he'd gone too far. For once he explained himself. "I mean that girl can't hardly meet a man's eyes. She can't hardly walk out her door. She has no skills. She's frightened of her own shadow. What kind of partner is she going to be for you? You're going to be her nursemaid, not her husband. You think you can heal her? You can't."

Of all the things his father could have said, this was the one that cut him to the quick—because it was true. He did want to heal Fila. He thought he could. Holt's words highlighted his darkest fear.

Maybe Fila was beyond saving. Maybe she'd never confront her demons and win.

"Watching you marry that girl will be like watching you commit suicide. You can't ask that of me."

How the hell could he answer that?

Ned decided he couldn't. He walked out the door.

FILA HUMMED ALONG with the pop song playing on the iPod Ned had stationed in a dock on the kitchen counter this morning for her. She'd been able to find an online radio station that played hit music from the last decade—all the songs she'd missed while she'd been away. She was determined to learn them, to recapture her lost years. Pop music was one of the things she'd missed the most during her time in captivity.

She moved around the pleasant room quickly, gathering the ingredients she needed to make *bolani*—potato and green onion-filled flatbreads—one of Ned's favorite Afghan dishes. She loved this now-familiar space with its hardwood floors and trim, and the wide windows that looked out over the pastures to the south. At first she'd been terrified to move in with the silent cowboy who owned the house when Ethan and Autumn needed her bedroom for an influx of paying guests, but she'd soon found that Ned's brusqueness hid a tenderness she would never have credited in the man, especially since she'd heard the way everyone else talked about him. If she listened to gossip she'd think Ned was a fighter, but she'd never seen such a thing. Bringing her the iPod was just the latest in a long line of considerate gestures he'd made toward her.

As the song's chorus sounded, Fila tried to sing along, but the sound of her own voice ringing out in the otherwise quiet house brought her up short and had her glancing over her shoulder to see if anyone had heard. She dropped the measuring cup she'd begun to dip into the bag of flour and gripped the counter to keep herself on her feet as waves of fear and nausea spun over her frame. She gripped the inch-thick wood with both hands, fighting against the urge to run upstairs and hide in her bed, to wrap herself up in her quilts and huddle there until her breathing slowed again.

There was nothing here to fear. She was alone. She was safe.

The Taliban were thousands of miles away.

Probably.

No, definitely.

Fila straightened again. This was America. This was Chance Creek—not the hills of Afghanistan, where singing a pop song got you beaten—or your food withheld for two days. This was Chance Creek, where country music spilled from every radio, and listening to pop music—while not exactly approved of—was definitely tolerated. She made herself focus on the song again, already familiar with the words although it had come out during the time she was away. She waited for the chorus to come around again, then once more joined in, singing an entire phrase before her body reacted and shut her down. Her pulse increased, her breaths came short and quick as she gripped the counter harder. She braced herself for a slap or a pinch or a harsh volley of words, none of which came, of course.

She was safe. No one wanted to hurt her here.

Fila took deep breaths like Autumn had taught her—in through her nose and out through her mouth. Still the fear rolled over her, her stomach pitching and tossing like a ship on the waves. When she couldn't stand it anymore, she sunk to the floor to crouch on her knees, her fingers sliding from their handholds until she was balled up on the hard wood, her arms wrapped around her chest, her shoulder pressed against the cabinets that supported the butcher block island where she'd begun to work.

She fought back the tears that threatened to fall and swallowed past the burning lump in her throat. She couldn't even sing. The Taliban had taken that from her just like they'd taken everything else.

She couldn't sing, she couldn't laugh, she couldn't venture out past her front door without feeling like she'd pitch up the contents of her stomach at any moment.

Fear was her constant companion, just as it had ever been in the little village in Afghanistan. She'd thought she'd outrun it. She'd thought she'd conquered it during her flight home.

But it had followed her here and refused to give up its grip on her life.

She couldn't let it beat her. She couldn't let them win—those wiry men with piercing eyes and furious tempers, with their diatribes against everything and everyone and their need to hem her in, cut her down, dictate her every move, steal her words, steal her parents, steal her home—

Fila lurched to her feet again, damned if she would let them control her now. She leaned on the counter, not caring that the flour had tipped over, not caring that her clothes were dusted in white. She lifted her voice again, softly but at least out loud—at least audible, if only to her. She raised her voice again, catching the chorus as it came around a third time, pairing her words to the singer's, her tones to the melody coming out of the iPod dock.

As her hands shook, her stomach cramped and tears ran down her cheeks, she sang along until the song ran out. Then she dashed for the bathroom and heaved until her stomach was as empty as it ever was on a snowy day in the middle of the Hindu Kush mountains of north-eastern Afghanistan.

End of Excerpt

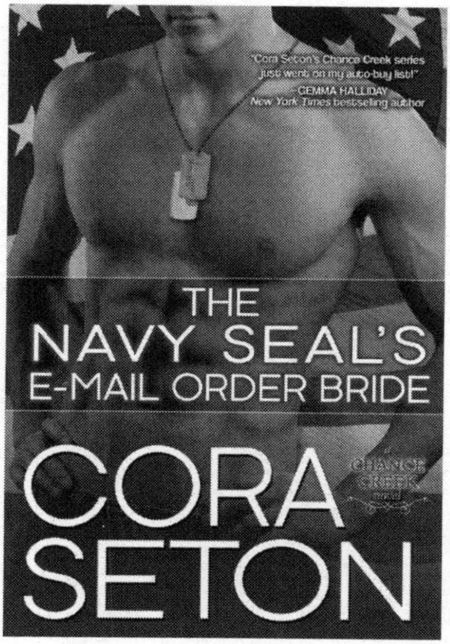

Read on for an excerpt of Volume 1 of
The Heroes of Chance Creek series –
The Navy SEAL's E-Mail Order Bride.

"BOYS," LIEUTENANT COMMANDER Mason Hall said, "we're going home."

He sat back in his folding chair and waited for a reaction from his brothers. The recreation hall at Bagram Airfield was as busy as always with men hunched over laptops, watching the widescreen television, or lounging in groups of three or four shooting the breeze. His brothers—three tall, broad shouldered men in uniform—stared back at him from his computer screen, the feeds from their four-way video conversation all relaying a similar reaction to his words.

Utter confusion.

"Home?" Austin was the first to speak. A Special Forces officer just a year younger than Mason, he was currently in Kabul.

"Home," Mason confirmed. "I got a letter from Great Aunt Heloise. Uncle Zeke passed away over the weekend without designating an heir. That means the ranch reverts back to her. She thinks we'll do a better job running it than Darren will." Darren, their first cousin, wasn't known for his responsible behavior and he hated ranching. Mason, on the other hand, loved it. He had missed the ranch, the cattle, the Montana sky and his family's home ever since they'd left it twelve years ago.

"She's giving Crescent Hall to us?" That was Zane, Austin's twin, a Marine currently in Kandahar. The excitement in his tone told Mason all he needed to know—Zane stilled loved the old place as much as he did. When Mason had gotten Heloise's letter, he'd had to read it more than once before he believed it. The Hall would belong to them once more—when he'd thought they'd lost it for good. Suddenly he'd felt like he could breathe fully again after so many years of holding in his anger and frustration over his uncle's behavior. The timing was perfect, too. He was due to ship stateside any day now. By April he'd be a civilian again.

Except it wasn't as easy as all that. Mason took a deep breath. "There are a few conditions."

Colt, his youngest brother, snorted. "Of course—we're talking about Heloise, aren't we? What's she up to this time?" He was an Air Force combat controller who had served both in Afghanistan and as part of the relief effort a few years back after the massive earthquake which devastated Haiti. He was currently back on United States soil in Florida, training with his unit.

Mason knew what he meant. Calling Heloise eccentric would be an understatement. In her eighties, she had definite opinions and brooked no opposition to her plans and schemes. She meant well, but as his father had always said, she was capable of leaving a swath of destruction in family affairs that rivaled Sherman's march to Atlanta.

"The first condition is that we have to stock the ranch with one hundred pair of cattle within twelve months of taking possession."

"We should be able to do that," Austin said.

"It's going to take some doing to get that ranch up and running again," Zane countered. "Zeke was already letting the place go years ago."

"You have something better to do than fix the place up when you get out?" Mason asked him. He hoped Zane understood the real question: was he in or out?

"I'm in; I'm just saying," Zane said.

Mason suppressed a smile. Zane always knew what he was thinking.

"Good luck with all that," Colt said.

"Thanks," Mason told him. He'd anticipated that inheriting the Hall wouldn't change Colt's mind about staying in the Air Force. He focused on the other two who were both already in the process of winding down their military careers. "If we're going to do this, it'll take a commitment. We're going to have to pool our funds and put our shoulders to the wheel for as long as it takes. Are you up for that?"

"I'll join you there as soon as I'm able to in June," Austin said. "It'll just be like another year in the service. I can handle that."

"I already said I'm in," Zane said. "I'll have boots on the ground in September."

Here's where it got tricky. "There's just one other thing," Mason said. "Aunt Heloise has one more requirement of each of us."

"What's that?" Austin asked when he didn't go on.

"She's worried about the lack of heirs on our side of the family. Darren has children. We don't."

"Plenty of time for that," Zane said. "We're still young, right?"

"Not according to Heloise." Mason decided to get it over and done with. "She's decided that in order for us to inherit the Hall free and clear, we each have to be married within the year. One of us has to have a child."

Stunned silence met this announcement until Colt started to laugh. "Staying in the Air Force doesn't look so bad now, does it?"

"That means you, too," Mason said.

"What? Hold up, now." Colt was startled into soberness. "I won't even live on the ranch. Why do I have to get hitched?"

"Because Heloise says it's time to stop screwing around. And she controls the land. And you know

Heloise."

"How are we going to get around that?" Austin asked.

"We're not." Mason got right to the point. "We're going to find ourselves some women and we're going to marry them."

"In Afghanistan?" Zane's tone made it clear what he thought about that idea.

Tension tightened Mason's jaw. He'd known this was going to be a messy conversation. "Online. I created an online personal ad for all of us. Each of us has a photo, a description and a reply address. A woman can get in touch with whichever of us she chooses and start a conversation. Just weed through your replies until you find the one you want."

"Are you out of your mind?" Zane peered at him through the video screen.

"I don't see what you're upset about. I'm the one who has to have a child. None of you will be out of the service in time."

"Wait a minute—I thought you just got the letter from Heloise." As usual, Austin zeroed in on the inconsistency.

"The letter came about a week ago. I didn't want to get anyone's hopes up until I checked a few things out." Mason shifted in his seat. "Heloise said the place is in rougher shape than we thought. Sounds like Zeke sold off the last of his cattle last year. We're going to have to start from scratch, and we're going to have to move fast to meet her deadline—on both counts. I did all the leg work on the online ad. All you need to do is read some e-mails, look at some photos and pick one. How hard can that be?"

"I'm beginning to think there's a reason you've been single all these years, Straightshot," Austin said. Mason winced at the use of his nickname. The men in his unit had christened him with it during his early days in the service, but as Colt said when his brothers had first heard about it, it made perfect sense. The name had little to do with his accuracy with a rifle, and everything to do with his tendency to find the shortest route from here to done on any mission he was tasked with. Regardless of what obstacles stood in his way.

Colt snickered. "Told you two it was safer to stay in the military. Mason's Matchmaking Service. It has a ring to it. I guess you've found yourself a new career, Mase."

"Stow it." Mason tapped a finger on the table. "Just because I've put the ad up doesn't mean that any of you have to make contact with the women who write you. If it doesn't work, it doesn't work. But you need to marry within the year. If you don't find a wife for yourself, I'll find one for you."

"He would, too," Austin said to the others. "You know he would."

"When does the ad go live?" Zane asked.

"It went live five days ago. You've each got several hundred responses so far. I'll forward them to you as soon as we break the call."

Austin must have leaned toward his webcam because suddenly he filled the screen. "Several hundred?"

"That's right."

Colt's laughter rang out over the line.

"Don't know what you're finding so funny, Colton," Mason said in his best imitation of their late father's voice. "You've got several hundred responses, too."

"What? I told you I was staying…"

"Read through them and answer all the likely ones. I'll be in touch in a few days to check your progress." Mason cut the call.

★ ★ ★

REGAN ANDERSON WANTED a baby. Right now. Not five years from now. Not even next year.

Right now.

And since she'd just quit her stuffy loan officer job, moved out of her overpriced one bedroom New York City apartment, and completed all her preliminary appointments, she was going to get one via the modern technology of artificial insemination.

As she raced up the three flights of steps to her tiny new studio, she took the pins out of her severe updo and let her thick, auburn hair swirl around her shoulders. By the time she reached the door, she was breathing hard. Inside, she shut and locked it behind her, tossed her briefcase and blazer on the bed which took up the lion's share of the living space, and kicked off her high heels. Her blouse and pencil skirt came next, and thirty seconds later she was down to her skivvies.

Thank God.

She was done with Town and Country Bank. Done

with originating loans for people who would scrape and slave away for the next thirty years just to cling to a lousy flat near a subway stop. She was done, done, done being a cog in the wheel of a financial system she couldn't stand to be a part of anymore.

She was starting a new business. Starting a new life.

And she was starting a family, too.

Alone.

After years of looking for Mr. Right, she'd decided he simply didn't exist in New York City. So after several medical exams and consultations, she had scheduled her first round of artificial insemination for the end of April. She couldn't wait.

Meanwhile, she'd throw herself into the task of building her consulting business. She would make it her job to help non-profits assist regular people start new stores and services, buy homes that made sense, and manage their money so that they could get ahead. It might not be as lucrative as being a loan officer, but at least she'd be able to sleep at night.

She wasn't going to think about any of that right now, though. She'd survived her last day at work, survived her exit interview, survived her boss, Jack Richey, pretending to care that she was leaving. Now she was giving herself the weekend off. No work, no nothing—just forty-eight hours of rest and relaxation.

Having grabbed takeout from her favorite Thai restaurant on the way home, Regan spooned it out onto a plate and carried it to her bed. Lined with pillows, it doubled as her couch during waking hours. She sat cross-legged on top of the duvet and savored her food and her freedom. She had bought herself a nice bottle of wine to drink this weekend, figuring it might be her last for an awfully long time. She was all too aware her Chardonnay-sipping days were coming to an end. As soon as her weekend break from reality was over, she planned to spend the next ten months starting her business, while scrimping and saving every penny she could. She would have to move to a bigger apartment right before the baby was born, but given the cost of renting in the city, the temporary downgrade was worth it. She pushed all thoughts of business and the future out of her mind. Rest and relax—that was her job for now.

Two hours and two glasses of wine later, however, rest and relaxation was beginning to feel a lot like loneliness and boredom. In truth, she'd been fighting loneliness for months. She'd broken up with her last boyfriend before Christmas. Here it was March and she was still single. Two of her closest friends had gotten married and moved away in the past twelve months, Laurel to New Hampshire and Rita to New Jersey. They rarely saw each other now and when she'd jokingly mentioned the idea of going ahead and having a child without a husband the last time they'd gotten together, both women had scoffed.

"No way could I have gotten through this pregnancy without Ryan." Laurel ran a hand over her large belly. "I've felt awful the whole time."

"No way I'm going back to work." Rita's baby was six weeks old. "Thank God Alan brings in enough cash to see us through."

Regan decided not to tell them about her plans until the pregnancy was a done deal. She knew what she was getting into—she didn't need them to tell her how hard it might be. If there'd been any way for her to have a baby normally—with a man she loved—she'd have chosen that path in a heartbeat. But there didn't seem to be a man for her to love in New York. Unfortunately, keeping her secret meant it was hard to call either Rita or Laurel just to chat, and she needed someone to chat with tonight. As dusk descended on the city, Regan felt fear for the first time since making her decision to go ahead with having a child.

What if she'd made a mistake? What if her consultancy business failed? What if she became a welfare mother? What if she had to move back home?

When the thoughts and worries circling her mind grew overwhelming, she topped up her wine, opened up her laptop and clicked on a YouTube video of a cat stuck headfirst in a cereal box. Thank goodness she'd hooked up wi-fi the minute she secured the studio. Simultaneously scanning her Facebook feed, she read an update from an acquaintance named Susan who was exhibiting her art in one of the local galleries. She'd have to stop by this weekend.

She watched a couple more videos—the latest installment in a travel series she loved, and one about over-the-top weddings that made her sad. Determined to cheer up, she hopped onto Pinterest and added more images to her nursery pinboard. Sipping her wine, she checked the news, posted a question on the single parents' forum she frequented, checked her e-mail again, and then tapped a finger on the keys, wondering what to do next. The evening stretched out before her, vacant even of the work she normally took home to do over the weekend. She hadn't felt at such loose ends in years.

Pacing her tiny apartment didn't help. Nor did an attempt at unpacking more of her things. She had finished moving in just last night and boxes still lined one wall. She opened one to reveal books, took a look at her limited shelf space and packed them up again. A second box revealed her collection of vintage fans. No room for them here, either.

She stuck her iTouch into a docking station and turned up some tunes, then drained her glass, poured herself another, and flopped onto her bed. The wine was beginning to take effect—giving her a nice, soft, fuzzy feeling. It hadn't done away with her loneliness, but when she turned back to Facebook on her laptop, the images and YouTube links seemed funnier this time.

Heartened, she scrolled further down her feed until she spotted another post one of her friends had shared. It was an image of a handsome man standing ramrod straight in combat fatigues. *Hello*. He was cute. In fact, he looked like exactly the kind of man she'd always hoped she'd meet. He wasn't thin and arrogant like the up-and-coming Wall Street crowd, or paunchy and cynical like the upper-management men who hung around the bars near work. Instead he looked healthy, muscle-bound, clear-sighted, and vital. What was the post about? She clicked the link underneath it. Maybe there'd be more fantasy-fodder like this man wherever it took her.

There *was* more fantasy fodder. Regan wriggled happily. She had landed on a page that showcased four men. Brothers, she saw, looking more closely—two of them identical twins. Each one seemed to represent a different branch of the United States military. Were they models? Was this some kind of recruitment ploy?

Practical Wives Wanted read the heading at the top. Regan nearly spit out a sip of her wine. Wives Wanted? Practical ones? She considered the men again, then read more.

Looking for a change? the text went on. *Ready for a real challenge? Join four hardworking, clean living men and help bring our family's ranch back to life.*

Skills required—any or all of the following: Riding, roping, construction, animal care, roofing, farming, market gardening, cooking, cleaning, metalworking, small motor repair…

The list went on and on. Regan bit back at a laugh which quickly dissolved into giggles. Small engine repair? How very romantic. Was this supposed to be satire or was it real? It was certainly one of the most intriguing things she'd seen online in a long, long time.

Must be willing to commit to a man and the project. No weekends/no holidays/no sick days. Weaklings need not apply.

Regan snorted. It was beginning to sound like an employment ad. Good luck finding a woman to fill those conditions. She'd tried to find a suitable man for years and came up with Erik—the perennial mooch who'd finally admitted just before Christmas that he liked her old Village apartment more than he liked her. That's why she planned to get pregnant all by herself. There wasn't anyone worth marrying in the whole city. Probably the whole state. And if the men were all worthless, the women probably were, too. She reached for her wine without turning from the screen, missed, and nearly knocked over her glass. She tried again, secured the wine, drained the glass a third time and set it down again.

What she would give to find a real partner. Someone strong, both physically and emotionally. An equal in intelligence and heart. A real man.

But those didn't exist.

If you're sick of wasting your time in a dead-end job, tired of tearing things down instead of building something up, or just ready to get your hands dirty with clean, honest work, write and tell us why you'd make a worthy wife for a man who has spent the last decade in uniform.

There wasn't much to laugh at in this paragraph. Regan read it again, then got up and wandered to the kitchen to top up her glass. She'd never seen a singles ad like this one. She could see why it was going viral. If it was real, these men were something special. Who wanted to do clean, honest work these days? What kind of man was selfless enough to serve in the military instead of sponging off their girlfriends? If she'd known there were guys like this in the world, she might not have been so quick to schedule the artificial insemination appointment.

She wouldn't cancel it, though, because these guys couldn't be for real, and she wasn't waiting another minute to start her family. She had dreamed of having children ever since she was a child herself and organized pretend schools in her backyard for the neighborhood little ones. Babies loved her. Toddlers thought she was the next best thing to teddy bears. Her co-workers at the bank had never appreciated her as much as the average five-year-old did.

Further down the page there were photographs of the ranch the brothers meant to bring back to life. The land was beautiful, if overgrown, but its toppled fences and sagging buildings were a testament to its neglect. The photograph of the main house caught her eye and kept her riveted, though. A large gothic structure, it could be beautiful with the proper care. She could see why these men would dedicate themselves to returning it to its former glory. She tried to imagine what it would be like to live on the ranch with one of them, and immediately her body craved an open sunny sky—the kind you were hard pressed to see in the city. She sunk into the daydream, picturing herself sitting on a back porch sipping lemonade while her cowboy worked and the baby napped. Her husband would have his shirt off while he chopped wood, or mended a fence or whatever it was ranchers did. At the end of the day they'd fall into bed and make love until morning.

Regan sighed. It was a wonderful daydream, but it had no bearing on her life. Disgruntled, she switched over to Netflix and set up a foreign film. She fetched the bottle of wine back to bed with her and leaned against her many pillows. She'd managed to hang her small flatscreen on the opposite wall. In an apartment this tiny, every piece of furniture needed to serve double-duty.

As the movie started, Regan found herself composing messages to the military men in the Wife Wanted ad, in which she described herself as trim and petite, or lithe and strong, or horny and good-enough-looking to do the trick.

An hour later, when the film failed to hold her attention, she grabbed her laptop again. She pulled up the Wife Wanted page and reread it, keeping an eye on the foreign couple on the television screen who alternately argued and kissed.

Crazy what some people did. What was wrong with these men that they needed to advertise for wives instead of going out and meeting them like normal people?

She thought of the online dating sites she'd tried in the past. She'd had some awkward experiences, some horrible first dates, and finally one relationship that lasted for a couple of months before the man was transferred to Tucson and it fizzled out. It hadn't worked for her, but she supposed lots of people found love online these days. They might not advertise directly for spouses, but that was their ultimate intention, right? So maybe this ad wasn't all that unusual.

Most men who posted singles ads weren't as hot as these men were, though. Definitely not the ones she'd met. She poured herself another glass. A small twinge of her conscience told her she'd already had far too much wine for a single night.

To hell with that, Regan thought. As soon as she got

pregnant she'd have to stay sober and sane for the next eighteen years. She wouldn't have a husband to trade off with—she'd always be the designated driver, the adult in charge, the sober, wise mother who made sure nothing bad ever happened to her child. Just this one last time she was allowed to blow off steam.

But even as she thought it, a twinge of fear wormed through her belly.

What if she wasn't good enough?

She stood up, strode the two steps to the kitchenette and made herself a bowl of popcorn. She drowned it in butter and salt, returned to the bed in time for the ending credits of the movie, and lined up *Pride and Prejudice* with Colin Firth. Time for comfort food and a comfort movie. *Pride and Prejudice* always did the trick when she felt blue. She checked the Wife Wanted page again on her laptop. If she was going to pick one of the men—which she wasn't—who would she choose?

Mason, the oldest, due to leave the Navy in a matter of weeks, drew her eye first. With his dark crew cut, hard jaw and uncompromising blue eyes he looked like the epitome of a military man. He stated his interests as ranching—of course—history, natural sciences and tactical operations, whatever the hell that was. That left her little more informed than before she'd read it, and she wondered what the man was really like. Did he read the newspaper in bed on Sunday mornings? Did he prefer lasagna or spaghetti? Would he listen to country music in his truck or talk radio? She stared at his photo, willing him to answer.

The next two brothers, Austin and Zane, were less fierce, but looked no less intelligent and determined. Still, they didn't draw her eye the way the way Mason did. Colt, the youngest, was blond with a grin she bet drew women like flies. That one was trouble, and she didn't need trouble.

She read Mason's description again and decided he was the leader of this endeavor. If she was going to pick one, it would be him.

But she wasn't going to pick one. She had given up all that. She'd made a promise to her imaginary child that she would not allow any chaos into its life. No dating until her baby wore a graduation gown, at the very least. She felt another twinge. Was she ready to give up men for nearly two decades? That was a long time.

It's worth it, she told herself. She had no doubt about her desire to be a mother. She had no doubt she'd be a great mom. She was smart, capable and had a good head on her shoulders. She was funny, silly and patient, too. She loved children.

She was just lousy with men.

But that didn't matter anymore. She pushed the laptop aside and returned her attention to *Pride and Prejudice*, quickly falling into an old drinking game she and Laurel had devised one night that required taking a swig of wine each time one of the actresses lifted her eyebrows in polite surprise. When she finished the bottle, she headed to the tiny kitchenette to track down another one, trilling, "Jane! Elizabeth!" at the top of her voice along with Mrs. Bennett in the film. There was no more wine, so she switched to tequila.

By the time Elizabeth Bennett discovered the miracle of Mr. Darcy's palace-sized mansion, and decided she'd been too hasty in turning down his offer of marriage, Regan had decided she too needed to cast off her prejudices and find herself a man. A hot hunk of a military man. She grabbed the laptop, fumbled with the link that would let her leave Mason Hall a message and drafted a brilliant missive worthy of Jane Austen herself.

Dear Lt. Cmdr. Hall,

In her mind she pronounced lieutenant with an "f" like the Brits in the movie onscreen.

It is a truth universally acknowledged, that a single man in possession of a good ranch, must be in want of a wife. Furthermore, it must be self-evident that the wife in question should possess certain qualities numbering amongst them riding, roping, construction, roofing, farming, market gardening, cooking, cleaning, metalworking, animal care, and—most importantly, by Heaven—small motor repair.

Seeing as I am in possession of all these qualities, not to mention many others you can only have left out through unavoidable oversight or sheer obtuseness—such as glassblowing, cheesemaking, towel origami, heraldry, hovercraft piloting, and an uncanny sense of what cats are thinking—I feel almost forced to catapult myself into your purview.

You will see from my photograph that I am most eminently and majestically suitable for your wife.

She inserted a digital photo of her foot.

In fact, one might wonder why such a paragon of virtue such as I should deign to answer such a peculiar advertisement. The truth is, sir, that I long for adventure. To get my hands dirty with clean, hard work. To build something up instead of tearing it down.

In short, you are really hot. I'd like to lick you.

Yours,
Regan Anderson

On screen, Elizabeth Bennett lifted an eyebrow. Regan knocked back another shot of Jose Cuervo and passed out.

End of Excerpt

The Cowboys of Chance Creek Series:

The Cowboy Inherits a Bride (Volume 0)
The Cowboy's E-Mail Order Bride (Volume 1)
The Cowboy Wins a Bride (Volume 2)
The Cowboy Imports a Bride (Volume 3)
The Cowgirl Ropes a Billionaire (Volume 4)
The Sheriff Catches a Bride (Volume 5)
The Cowboy Lassos a Bride (Volume 6)
The Cowboy Rescues a Bride (Volume 7)
The Cowboy Earns a Bride (Volume 8)
The Cowboy's Christmas Bride (Volume 9)

The Heroes of Chance Creek Series:

The Navy SEAL's E-Mail Order Bride (Volume 1)
The Soldier's E-Mail Order Bride (Volume 2)
The Marine's E-Mail Order Bride (Volume 3)
The Navy SEAL's Christmas Bride (Volume 4)
The Airman's E-Mail Order Bride (Volume 5)

The SEALs of Chance Creek Series:

A SEAL's Oath
A SEAL's Vow
A SEAL's Pledge
A SEAL's Consent

About the Author

Cora Seton loves cowboys, country life, gardening, bike-riding, and lazing around with a good book. Mother of four, wife to a computer programmer/ eco-farmer, she ditched her California lifestyle nine years ago and moved to a remote logging town in northwestern British Columbia. Like the characters in her novels, Cora enjoys old-fashioned pursuits and modern technology, spending mornings transforming an ordinary one-acre lot into a paradise of orchards, berry bushes and market gardens, and afternoons writing the latest Chance Creek romance novel on her iPad mini. Visit www.coraseton.com to read about new releases and learn about contests and other events!

Blog:

www.coraseton.com

Facebook:

www.facebook.com/coraseton

Twitter:

www.twitter.com/coraseton

Newsletter:

www.coraseton.com/sign-up-for-my-newsletter

46168869R00182

Made in the USA
Middletown, DE
25 July 2017